MW00716874

YELLOWFIN

Also by Mark Brown

Game Face

YELLOWFIN

A BEN McMILLEN HAWAIIAN MYSTERY

MARK BROWN

OX BOW PRESS • WOODBRIDGE, CONNECTICUT

Mahalo to—

Kahea Beckley
Eileen D'Araujo
Jean Greenwell
Alyson Hagy
Gloria Llacuna
Auntie Eleanor Mikida
Lucille Morowitz
Keali'i Reichel
Auntie Maile Richard
Jim Rizzuto
Andy Roy
Dr. Deen Wong

Maui Historical Society
Kona Historical Society . . .

for making this book possible

Original cover design and illustration by Ben Brown—with the exception of the *'ahi* which was re-drawn with the permission of Chuck Johnston of the *Hawai'i Fishing News*; original *'ahi* illustration by Les Hata

Published by
OX BOW PRESS
P.O. Box 4045
Woodbridge, Connecticut 06525

Copyright © 1992 by Ox Bow Press
All rights reserved.

Printed in the United States of America

Library of Congress Cataloging-in-Publication Data

Brown, Mark, 1947–
    Yellowfin / Mark Brown.
        p.   cm.
    ISBN 0-918024-93-5
    (acid-free paper)
    I. Title.   II. Title: Yellowfin.
PS3552.R6942Y45   1991
813'.54—dc20   91-36801
                                                        CIP

The paper in this book meets the guidelines for permanence and durability of the Committee on Production Guidelines for Book Longevity of the Council on Library Resources.

for my *hulu mākua*—Frances and Morris Brown,
who met for the first time on December 7, 1941

the land and the sea

the land
the rich red earth
nourishing coffee trees
and farther south
fresh lava flows of black ribbon
forming new land

scatter half my ashes there
for there I shall start anew . . .

a single drop of water
traveling the oceans and the seas
carrying life
carrying death
returning in eight million years
and then starting the journey again

cast my remaining ashes into the sea
for I wish to travel the earth forever . . .

—Ahi Ishizu

Yellowfin

Ahi swallowed. His eyes moved slowly around the room until they fixed on one of his paintings. Then he closed his eyes and tried to control his breathing. He thought first about his granddaughter. Home in Sapporo, teaching English to seven and eight year olds in a small school in the foothills. She was coming to visit in a few months. He doubted he'd ever see her again. He was thankful she wasn't here now. Abruptly, his mind shifted to the Second World War. The thought of it disgusted him. Many times he wished it had taken some other course. He hadn't prayed for a Japanese victory. No, Ahi was one who felt his country was wrong. That familiar guilt seeped into his stomach. In his position, knowing what he did, he could have done something more. He could have told somebody. He could have gotten word to the Americans. But instead he had fled to the Big Island, Hawai'i, a few days before the attack on Pearl Harbor and hid among the Japanese coffee farmers who knew nothing of the approaching warships and attack planes. They only knew that a stranger had shown up and offered to help with the crop. They gave him food and clothing, and later, a small parcel of land. Others, members of the Japanese Secret Service, thought he had returned to Japan, to hide in the hills of the remote Ryukyu Islands, to wait out the war. A coward, a thief, but most significantly, a traitor.

Now, as he sat bound, a prisoner, he wondered how long they had looked for him. A small pained sigh came from deep inside. Fifty years. He'd covered his tracks well. Until now. Until this man found him.

He thought about the farmhouse, built by a single pair of hands—his. He remembered clearing the land, planting the coffee trees from seedlings: Three acres—neat rows, carefully trimmed and cultivated. He thought of the veil of white blooms that covered the Kona hillsides in early spring. The smell of gardenias—the coffee plant's relative.

Ahi made a meager living growing Kona coffee on his farm, isolated in the hills of South Kona near Ka'ū. No help. No other workers. Just him. Five in the morning until dusk, six days a week. He had a few friends, but none too close. Only three things mattered to Ahi. His coffee trees, his granddaughter's weekly letters, and his favorite pastime—painting scenes of the Japanese countryside from memory.

He opened his eyes when he felt the man's breath. The man's eyes were dark gray pools, unblinking, penetrating. Suddenly, the blade of the knife flashed in front of Ahi's face. Ahi didn't move. The knife was extremely thin. It looked razor sharp.

The man raised his eyebrows and his nostrils flared grotesquely. "Well, old man?"

Ahi offered no response. Not even the recognition that the man had spoken.

The man lowered the switchblade. "Your fingernails seem a trite long, old man. May I trim them for you?" He didn't wait for an answer.

Ahi closed his eyes once more and envisioned a peaceful scene. A slow wide stream. A stately white heron feeding on goldfish. Deep green reeds all about. Some with cattails. Smooth, shining rocks at the water's edge. The surreal calm was broken as the blade sliced through his thumbnail and the tip of his thumb. Ahi tried to pull away, but the man had a powerful grip. As Ahi felt the blood flow from his thumb, his mouth filled with a metallic taste.

"How about a little wager, old man? Huh? . . . whaddaya say? I say you'll tell me before I get to . . . let's say . . . your seventh finger. Is it a bet, Ishizu?" He laughed and slashed through another fingernail.

A few minutes later, when the seventh finger was split and bleeding, the man stepped back. "You're tougher than I thought, Ishizu. From the old school, huh? You should have been a kamikaze pilot." He laughed, took out a tattered handkerchief, and wiped Ahi's blood from the blade. He put the bloodied rag away, but not the knife.

Ahi's hands were numb now. It didn't matter if the man cut the remaining three fingers. Ahi could feel no real pain, only the throbbing, tingling feeling in the joints of his fingers.

Suddenly a chill came over him reminding him that he was naked. How did the man know? How did he find him after all the years? Ahi's heart raced and his breathing kept pace.

He tried to remove himself from the scene. He thought of his paintings. He thought of the one that answered the man's question. With his eyes closed Ahi retraced the brush strokes in his mind. He wondered if the man would figure everything out after he was dead. Ahi Ishizu smiled to himself. Even if the man discovered where, he'd never be able to retrieve it. Never. On the other hand, maybe he should tell him. Let him feel the frustration.

The knife blade slit his eyelid. Ahi recoiled in excruciating pain. The chair he was bound to fell backward, crashing to the floor. Blood covered his face.

The man stepped closer. "Old man. I'm losing my patience. Where did you hide it? It's here on the Big Island, isn't it? Your backyard? Somewhere near the coffee trees? Under the house? Speak up, old man. Don't kid yourself. I *will* kill you. And I'll find it eventually . . . with or without your help."

Ahi remained silent, trying to take his mind off the bile rising in his stomach. His thoughts drifted up the mountainside where his *'aumakua* lived. Although he wasn't Hawaiian, he had adopted the owl—*pueo*—as his guardian protector. Every Hawaiian family embraced an *'aumakua*—a fish or a bird, an animal or lizard, even gods and goddesses, something or someone who was benevolent and brought good luck to the members of the family. When Ahi first reached the Big Island, he quickly understood how important this concept was, realizing it was much like the myths of Japan. He picked the *pueo* because it lived close to his farmhouse in the foothills, and because of what had happened to him during his first year there.

One day, while picking coffee berries, he had found a dead owl at the base of a coffee tree. He buried it there and said a prayer. The tree flourished. Instead of reaching its productive peak in its fifth year, this tree produced handsomely for ten years. Over that time, Ahi embraced the short-eared mountain owl as his protector.

Now, through blood-clogged eyes, he looked out of the tiny window above his kitchen sink. He needed his *'aumakua* now. Needed it to come crashing through the small window, powerful legs braced for attack, talons poised. Needed it to tear out the eyes of his attacker.

The man kicked him in the stomach. Ahi heaved and retched. The spasms didn't let up until the man pulled the chair upright. Then he pushed Ahi into one corner of the living room, so that the chair was wedged against the walls.

Ahi braced, expecting that his other eye was next, but what he felt was the man's hand on his testicles. The man squeezed hard. Ahi couldn't breathe. His brain felt heavy, yet at the same time, it floated. Nausea consumed him as if he were seasick. But he held on to his secret.

He opened his right eye, shaking his head and mumbling with much difficulty, "You . . . you are . . ." He was wheezing now. Blood dripped onto his cheek. "You are . . . mistaken," he gasped.

The blade sliced through his scrotum.

Ahi passed out.

The man was disgusted. He turned and looked out toward the sea. He was thinking—What do I do now?

2

A HALF MOON GREETED the beginning of August, although immense rain clouds had covered it, obscuring most of its glow. No stars were visible—the sky above the Hawaiian Islands was in turmoil. The leading edge of a tropical storm was one hundred and twenty miles to the southwest of the Big Island, and with each passing hour, a huge high-pressure system, right on its heels, propelled the storm more to the north, placing it on a collision course with the Kona coast. Gusty winds crossed the open Pacific at fifty knots, making the sea surge with twelve- to sixteen-foot swells. Fishing boats had been forced to cancel afternoon charters. On the beaches, palms were bent over, their fronds sweeping back and forth. Their trunks creaked and moaned. Some leaves had broken and were wedged into the sand.

In downtown Kailua, along Ali'i Drive, storefront awnings shredded in the wind. Most of the shops had closed early. Those with ocean exposure had boarded windows and doors. The Kailua shopping strip resembled the scene during the World War II blackout ordered after the attack on Pearl Harbor.

It was just past midnight. Under the sea the surface feeders packed tightly together, forming a silverish ribbon along the leeward coast of the Big Island. There were some *ono, aku,* and *mahimahi,* but mostly the band consisted of huge schools of yellowfin tuna, *'ahi,* swimming at ten miles an hour, striking at forty-five when baby squid and smaller fish crossed their path. The rough sea made the small fish nervous and easy prey for the hungry tuna, who are driven by voracious appetites no matter what the weather. Although the major feeding times are dawn and late evening, tuna are opportunistic feeders, always in the hunt.

Yellowfin can grow to a length of eight feet and weigh as much as several hundred pounds, but most are four or five feet long and weigh around a hundred. They have a more elongated body and smaller head than others in the tuna family. And as the yellowfin approach maturity their hindmost fins—the second dorsal on top and the anal on the bottom—reach extraordinary length, sometimes extending past the tail fin. The body is blackish-blue above, yellow along the sides, and mostly silver and pale yellow on the belly. The fins are yellow, as are the tuna's eyes.

————————

A little more than fifty years before, a man who was born and raised in Tokyo had been sent by his government to Honolulu. The Japanese Ambassador to the United States introduced this man to the American business community as a world-class economist, an expert in Far Eastern trade—a man who could open many lucrative channels of commerce. The man *did* have a degree in political science and another in economics, but he was neither a politician nor an economist. He was a spy. Though only twenty-five, he was a central figure in a plan of historical proportions. He was sent to gather intelligence on the deployment and movement of the U.S. fleet stationed at Pearl Harbor.

Early each morning he drove his beat-up car across the rocky terrain of Waipio Point to a concealed spot where he photographed the busy harbor and nearby Hickam Field. He spent the remainder of the morning in his office scanning local newspapers, clipping anything relating to

American naval and military matters. No item was too small. Everything was noted and then detailed in his reports.

Noontime usually found him lunching among the upper-echelon civil service employees at Brackey's, a favorite midday hangout. Never alone. Always engaged in interesting conversation, subtly siphoning information. Although the individual pieces of data seemed harmless, the entire picture, when pieced together, helped to create a devastating plan of attack.

Each day, promptly at four-thirty, the phony trade emissary showed up at one of the beachfront bars. More talk. More information. And over time, he became a fixture at the nightclubs that fronted Waikiki Beach and were filled with middle-ranking naval personnel. Military communications flowed as freely as the beer. The American servicemen figured the diminutive Japanese for a polite alcoholic, out for a good time, rubbing elbows with the Americans, feeling like a big shot. They treated him just above the level of a servant. He provided amusement for them.

He would smile back at them, raising his glass. With their heads back and their eyes closed they all downed beer after beer. They never noticed that *he* poured most of his in the sand.

This went on for more than two years. The young spy was extremely effective. He had no trouble predicting the entire fleet's upcoming maneuvers. His superiors were impressed. Especially when he told them how Sundays were basically treated as holidays. Those who made it back to ship slept in. Those who didn't, slept on the beaches—usually not alone. Skeletal staffs manned the ships—hung over, thankful it was Sunday.

But there was one thing he didn't know. He didn't know *why* he was spying. He was told that the Emperor was worried about an American attack by sea—that what he was doing was strictly a precaution. A great service to his country. He believed it. He lived by it.

Later, too late, he found out the truth.

Now he was an old man. But he'd get no older. Face down he floated across the path of the hungry tuna, looking defenseless, but still too large for them to hazard a chance. A few sharks had already taken his left arm and right hand, and his legs ended hideously below his knees. Torn flesh and shattered bone followed in his wake, attached to the trails of tissue and ganglion that dangled from his stumpy appendages. Bits of flesh broke loose as he tumbled into the troughs of the huge swells, free-falling every five seconds as the rolling waves crested and propelled his mangled body toward the reef a mile away.

A pair of inquisitive spinner dolphins ventured close and after a few passes they nudged the old man as if they were trying to revive him. They circled a few times, looping around his torso. Sad, uncanny, almost humanlike comprehension was evident in their eyes. After a few more nudges, they gave up and left him alone, bleating a melancholy song as they swam away.

The wind picked up another ten knots. Soon the heavy surf and the high tide drove the old man's body through a deep fissure in the coral bed. At the same time it began to get lighter, signaling the school of tuna to head farther out to sea in search of baby squid. They disappeared in seconds.

A rocky beach awaited his arrival. The old man was returning home— home to Kealakekua Bay, where he had come ashore fifty years before.

3

B EN MCMILLEN WAS PREOCCUPIED with memories of Melanie and
Harry Dagdag, and those thoughts were the cause of his grim expression and sour mood. Melanie's murder spilled out in a bold specter
of red in his mind—her face expressing terror and shock. Ben bit his lip.
Although he hadn't been there and had refused to look at the police
photos, he could visualize it easily. Three others had died the same
way—by strangulation—and then they had been ritualistically raped.
Ben had prevented there being a fifth victim. It was all hard to believe.

As he picked at the salmon filet, Ben caught Lisa's staring in his peripheral vision, but he kept his head lowered, cheek and chin resting in
the cup of his palm. He could feel her eyes trying to penetrate the shell
that surrounded him, and he could hear her feet nervously scraping
against the bare plank floor. Finally, he looked up from his plate, and
gave Lisa a smile. It was forced. He was down, but it wasn't entirely
because of the murders.

"Something wrong with your food?"
He shook his head. "No." He sighed. "I'm just tired."

Lisa's eyebrows narrowed. Her feet came to rest. "It's something else, isn't it? Something about us."

Ben's lips parted. He started to explain, but he didn't know where to begin. He took a deep breath and decided to keep what was really bothering him to himself. "I was thinking about Harry and Melanie. It's been getting to me more and more. People say time heals, but I'm not so sure . . . some things just don't go away." He paused and looked down at his plate, pinching the bridge of his nose. "I can't help but think that I could have prevented it." He looked up but not at her. "Maybe if I hadn't left the force . . . Shit! We were partners . . . and I left him."

Pursed lips. "It's not your fault, Ben. I know it's hard to get over . . . but you can't blame yourself." Lisa leaned forward. "These last few months all you've done is mope around. You hardly pay attention to what anyone says. Ben, it's . . . it's ruining our relationship. You're pushing everyone out of your life, especially me." Her eyes glazed. Now she looked down to hide her tears.

Ben reached out and held her hand. "You're right. Just give me more time. I'll be fine." He could tell she didn't believe him.

Lisa raised her chin a few inches. "Finish your fish." She made no attempt to hide the exasperation in her voice.

Ben smiled weakly and picked up his fork.

They were dining at the Bay Club in the Kapalua Resort on Maui's extreme northwest coast. The restaurant was one of the best on the Island. The food was always superbly prepared and the service impeccable, but what made the Bay Club memorable was the setting. Away from the rest of the resort, perched on a cliff, with a protected cove on one side and the pounding surf on the other, it was a plantation-style building with a rough stucco exterior and a wide veranda on the seaward sides. Two rows of Cook pines bordered the driveway. A flaming torch near the entrance illuminated palm trees that cast large wavering shadows across the front of the building.

Inside it was dimly lighted. The rattan chairs were wide and cushioned. The tables were generously spaced for privacy. And it was open air along the veranda. Ben had requested a table there. He and Lisa had been seated at the prime table, in the corner where the protected cove met the pounding surf and the sweet scent of the plumeria was strongest.

Ben McMillen was thirty, although recently he'd been feeling much older. He owned a small surf shop at the north end of Front Street in Lahaina, seven miles south of the Kapalua Resort. He called it *Swift Benny's*, a name bestowed upon him by his mother when he was a teenager, on the go, gobbling meals, wiping his mouth on his shirt sleeve, rushing off to play ball long past dark—or until they lost the ball. Swift Benny— five minutes to run home, five more to eat, and five back to the ball field. His Hawaiian grandmother, who had lived with his family in Pasadena for a few years before returning to Maui, fondly thought of him in another way. 'He keu 'oe a ke keiki ho'oniku 'a'ahu,' she used to say—'never was a child like you for getting clothes dirty and smelly.'

He had opened *Swift Benny's* two and half years before, after resigning from the Kona police force. Until then, he'd been a detective and Harry Dagdag had been his partner and best friend. Previously, they had been college roommates at USC and teammates on the Trojan football team. When Ben resigned it had nothing to do with Harry. It had to do with prejudice. Ben could accept most human flaws, but not racial discrimination. So when his mentor, Tobi Otaki, of Japanese-Hawaiian descent, was passed over for Captain, a position everyone knew he richly deserved, Ben followed Tobi's lead and resigned.

Two years passed. Then, Louis Serrao, who had been installed as Major of the Kona police force a few months after Ben and Tobi had resigned, asked Ben to come back and help on a case. Harry Dagdag's wife had been raped and murdered. The Kona police were consumed with the Ironman Triathlon, which meant extra shifts for security and crowd control. There weren't enough men to investigate every lead. And obviously, Harry couldn't be assigned to investigate his own wife's homicide. Without hesitation, Ben agreed to assist. His best friend needed help. But it had ended tragically, changing Ben's life forever.

The waiter interrupted Ben's sortie into the past, politely asking about dessert. Ben ordered coffee. Lisa asked for coffee and macadamia nut ice cream and two spoons. The waiter bowed slightly and left. Ben watched him for a few moments, then squared himself in his chair and gazed into Lisa Scott's eyes. She seemed uncomfortable, as if she was with someone she had just met, and not with her companion of the last ten months. The man who had saved her life.

As Ben watched her, he could see that she had trouble keeping her eyes on him. As if she would cry if she did. He pushed back the sleeves on his cotton sports jacket and rested his elbows on the table. Forming a tent with his fingertips, he studied her carefully.

She had brown eyes and black hair, and tonight she'd dressed her trim figure in a flowered sarong with a simple strand of cultured pearls about her neck. Ben watched her as she used the tips of her two middle fingers to wipe away tears in the corners of her eyes. He felt uncomfortable, like he was spying, so he shifted slightly to stare out over the water, focusing on the reflection of the moon. An 'Ole *Kū Lua* night on the old lunar calendar, seven nights past full.

They'd met almost a year before. Ben was walking along Front Street after having a couple of beers at Longhi's bar. He spotted her walking alone and followed her into Kimo's on the other side of the street. She sat at the end of the bar. The stool next to her was vacant. He smiled almost painfully as he remembered his opening line. 'I followed you all the way from the mainland.' She couldn't help but laugh as she said, 'You must be pretty patient, I've been here two years.'

Lisa worked for Hyatt Hotels and was currently assigned to the Hyatt Regency Maui in Kā'anapali, as Manager of Corporate Sales. Although no one really had to sell a company on the idea of holding its meetings at the Hyatt. The lobby was vaulted, with an open-air atrium filled with exotic plants and stone walkways. Valuable Oriental and Hawaiian art and artifacts were everywhere. There were pleasurable restaurants and a long stretch of quiet sandy beach. It all made the Hyatt a top-notch resort.

As sales manager, Lisa simply planned the business meetings as well as activities for the spouses. She added the fine touches, making it all paradise.

Ben knew the signs when she was content. Lisa would press her palms together, place them in front of her face with her thumbs resting against her chin and her fingers resting against her upper lip. The corners of her mouth turned up. Her eyes sparkled. But when something was bothering her—when she was sad—she sat upright, hands folded in her lap, the gleam gone from her eyes.

Her hands were in her lap now and her eyes looked empty.

He decided to bring it up—what was bothering him—and cleared his throat. He had barely opened his mouth when she interjected.

"You're thinking maybe we shouldn't see as much of each other, aren't you?" Her tone was accusing.

Ben felt naked. His expression exposed the truth.

"Well, I've been thinking the same thing," she added. "I still love you, but I think . . . well . . . things have gotten somewhat stale. Maybe it's a bit like island fever. There's never much separating us. Maybe we take each other for granted. Maybe we need a break."

Ben was surprised. Sure, Melanie's murder was on his mind. And Harry. But mainly his thoughts centered around Lisa. For the past few weeks he had been thinking about their relationship. He felt he needed some diversion from their daily routine. He wanted to be able say no if what she suggested wasn't to his liking. He needed some time to sort things out. But it sounded much different when someone said it to you. He suddenly felt scared. Defensive.

"Look, I still want you. I think it will work out in the long run. But, maybe . . . maybe you're right." He felt warm and wondered if his face was red. "Maybe we do need a break from each other." He exhaled deeply and cleared his throat. *Jesus, is this what I want? I thought she'd be hurt. It's me that hurts. She's taking this too well.*

"All I want is for both of us to have time to think *what it is* we really want. For the longest time I just wanted to marry you. Now I'm not sure.

Every time we even come close to the subject you back away. It's made me re-think. Although I feel you're the guy I want to be with, I think we both need some time to figure out what we want out of this relationship. Where's it going? You've had a lot of girlfriends. I know that. Is that what you want? You should think about it. You know what? I think you want to be a detective again."

Ben's mouth was dry. *Be a detective again. How did she know?* When he had walked away from it, he'd have bet anything that he would never return. Now he wasn't so sure. He certainly wasn't setting the retail world on fire, and it wasn't very challenging. He liked things you had to work hard for. Like the Triathlon. Like solving a crime. He used to live for the next challenge. Now he felt complacent. *'Wāhi ka niu'*—his grandmother would say to him when she wanted him to try something that was difficult. 'Break open the coconut.' It required commitment. He thought about that. When he'd been a detective, he was committed.

Coffee and dessert put the rest of the conversation on hold. They went about finishing dinner quietly, like two strangers. The pounding surf seemed to have Lisa's attention, if anything did. And as Ben sipped the dark blend, he sat stiffly, a little stunned. How was it that Lisa read him so easily? He *had* been searching for something these past few weeks. Was it his old job? Kona cop?

As they got up to leave, he wondered if Lisa had told him everything. He wondered if she had met another man. Lisa gave him a weak smile. It was hardly comforting.

———

As he drove south toward Lahaina, he wondered what Lisa was feeling. He'd left her at the door of her apartment with a simple kiss. Was she sorry they had broached the subject of separating? Or was she relieved that it was now out in the open? Was there someone else? He didn't think so. Lisa had always told him the truth. If there *was* someone, she'd have said so.

He shook his head, released his pressure grip on the steering wheel, blew out a long stream of air, and turned off Honoapiʻilani Highway onto Front Street. First he passed the Chart House restaurant, then a few small homes and apartments. Subconsciously, he slowed and then stopped. A stream of red brake lights faded into the night in front of him. Traffic was backed up. Ben checked his watch, holding it up toward one of the streetlights. It was a quarter to eleven. The tourists should be leaving Lahaina, not arriving. Then he leaned forward in his seat and saw rotating red and white strobe lights illuminating the palm trees that lined the road. Soon he could smell the smoke.

Ben edged over, parked on someone's front lawn, and got out. He wondered if a trash fire—someone burning dry palm fronds in violation of the Lahaina town ordinance—had gotten out of control.

As he got closer, he could see ashes and darker smoke streaming overhead, carried away by the wind. A sharp, unpleasant odor filled his nostrils—burning plastic. His eyes widened and his pace quickened until at last he was running.

He quickly approached the first of three fire trucks. A plastic yellow ribbon hung between two of the fire engines. Scores of people lined up behind the flimsy barrier. A Lahaina cop stood close by, making sure no one ventured closer.

Ben pushed though the crowd and ducked under the yellow ribbon. The cop tried to intercept him. "It's my place!" Ben shouted as he ran by.

Flames reached the top of the palms. Sparks and yellow fingers lighted the sky. Firemen uselessly aimed hoses at the blackening structure. *Swift Benny's* was about to collapse.

Ben stepped closer. He stood, unblinking, hardly believing this was happening. He could feel the heat. The smell of burning Styrofoam and plastic resin scorched his nostrils. He put his hand over his nose and mouth and retreated, transfixed by the enormous flames and billowing smoke.

The cop approached him and gently held his shoulder, guiding him toward the rear of a pumper truck. Someone handed him a cup of water. He gulped it at first. It was refilled, then he sipped.

"No one was inside, were they?" he asked through a hacking cough.

The cop shook his head. "Don't know. It was a huge fireball when we got here. All that plastic stuff, wooden frame building . . . it must've just exploded when it reached the kindling point. No one works this late, do they?"

Ben closed his eyes and thought for a moment. "We close at ten. I've got two girls working nights. They're usually out by ten-fifteen."

The cop nodded. "Give me their names. I'll have somebody check."

Ben gave him the names.

"What about upstairs?"

"I live there. It's a small apartment."

"You're lucky you were out. Like I said, this thing probably just went right up. You wouldn't have had any time."

Visions of a burning boat filled his head. He shook them free. "What about the workshop in the back?"

"Dunno."

"Hey, Ben!"

Ben turned and saw Annie, one of the girls who worked in his shop. They ran toward each other and hugged.

"You all right?"

She nodded. She was breathing hard. "Sharon and I closed up early . . . about a quarter to. It was slow. Too windy for the tourists."

"The workshop?"

"Locked up. Hogie left at five."

"Good."

"Oh, Ben." Annie was crying. "What are you going to do?"

He shook his head. "Just as long as everyone's okay. That's all that matters." They leaned against the fire truck, watching the blaze, completely hypnotized. A few minutes later Ben felt a hand on his shoulder. He turned. It was Lisa.

"Longhi called me. Is everyone okay?"

Annie smiled meekly.

Ben nodded and Lisa put her arms around him.

He looked over Lisa's shoulder and saw the building shift to one side. The framework creaked and moaned. Suddenly, it teetered and came apart, sending sparks and ashes everywhere. Instinctively, the crowd stepped back as they gasped.

Lisa moved next to him, one arm still around his waist.

Ben stood mesmerized, wondering if the heap of flaming timber symbolized the end of much more than his business. He turned his head and met Lisa's stare. It seemed as if she had been thinking the same thing.

4

B EN SAT ON THE EDGE of the bulkhead, his legs dangling over the
side. The 'Au'au Channel spread out before him. The Island of Lāna'i
was nine miles away—due west. He stared at its contour, not focusing
on anything in particular, his thoughts, like the clouds covering Lāna'i's
old mountains, were much too hazy.

Sleep had come sparingly since the fire. Lisa's bed, usually a source
of much pleasure, had simply been a place to lie down. After a quick
good-night kiss, they each would quietly turn their backs on one another,
retreating with their thoughts and fears like shellfish under attack. It was
armor—not *amour*.

Each night Ben ended up staring at the ceiling, watching the animated
shapes made by the headlights of the passing traffic. The lights reminded
him of the ghostly flames that had consumed his business.

Into the early morning hours, long after Lisa had fallen asleep, he
would lie there, restless, troubled, trying to sort out his options and to
make sense of his feelings. For long periods he watched her sleep, observing the lines that formed a frown around her mouth. He stroked her

hair lightly, careful not to wake her, needing to touch, but dreading conversation.

It was ebb tide. Five feet of beach was exposed. A speedboat passed and small waves unfolded onto the sand. Ben watched, arms resting on his stomach, as tiny translucent sand crabs scurried into their holes. Between waves hundreds of them approached the water's edge looking for plankton, then sprinted home just before the next wave. It reminded Ben of a cartoon.

The sun warmed his back and he stretched his shoulder muscles in response. A few thoughts circled about in his head. Rebuild? Find another location? Dump the whole thing and find a job? Several store owners had talked with him, offering jobs, most were for more money than he had paid himself. But they meant working on someone else's schedule. He didn't like that. He needed to be outdoors, at least for a portion of the day, not managing a bar or a restaurant, not grinning at tourists. The surf shop had been patronized mainly by Island people, surfing enthusiasts. Locals. People who were athletes. People like him. He thought about the triathlon. Wherever he worked, it had to allow him to maintain *his* training schedule. He knew that much. Ben glanced at his watch. Ten minutes more.

The ocean breeze refreshed him. The smell of salt was strong. He unfolded his arms and leaned backwards, arms outstretched, bracing himself against the ground. Next to him stood all that was left—the workshop where Hogie, his boardman, crafted the boogie and surf boards and made repairs. Behind him was a black heap of rubble—wood and synthetic fabric, soaked, blackened, smelling like a huge mound of smoldering cigarette filters. The surrounding palm trees were void of fronds. Others, a few yards farther away, tried to maintain their majestic carriage but with scorched trunks and burned leaves they looked more like monuments to the Brazilian rainforest.

His clothes were gone. And his furniture—although it had been sparse to begin with. The shop's entire inventory had been destroyed.

Shorts, tank tops, swim suits, Revo sunglasses, underwater plastic watches—all melted or incinerated. In the workshop there were a few surf boards still intact: three Styrofoam shells, unpainted, and finless, two others ready for the final coat of polymer. And in one corner, untouched, was his racing bike and four spare tires—the only personal possession that remained. But if you asked him to choose the one thing worth saving, that would be it—his bike. He reflected on what that said about his life. The most important thing was something that could easily be replaced.

Ben pushed himself up and faced the rubble. The scene was quiet, desolate. He gazed at the pile of burned wood, melted metal clothing racks—looking like lazy sculptures—charred remnants of fabric, mostly black, but with bits of color here and there. Someone clearing their throat cut through the silence.

"Ummm . . . *Aloha, Ben.*"

Ben looked up and gave his insurance agent a feeble grin. "Hey, Charlie." Charlie Pua extended his hand. Ben shook it firmly, twice, and let go.

"Tough luck, Ben. But . . . at least I was able to expedite this." He removed a brown envelope from the vinyl writing pad that had been tucked under his left arm. "It's for your personal property. Your inventory check will be a few more days."

"Thanks. Any idea what the total settlement will be?"

Charlie pursed his lips and held the flesh under his chin. "Probably in the neighborhood of seventy thousand. How much do you owe?"

"Don't know. 'Bout fifty, I guess. Maybe fifty-five."

Charlie nodded and gave him a grim look. "Sorry. Doesn't leave you much, does it?"

"What about the owner of the building?" asked Ben.

"He's covered. I assume he'll come see you about rebuilding when he figures out the finances. Hey, cheer up . . . it'll give you an opportunity to design it the way you want."

Ben's shoulders slumped.

Charlie Pua put his hand on Ben's back. "You're thinking of giving it up, aren't you?"

Ben looked at his insurance man with an empty face. "I don't really know. It's hard to think about starting over. It'll be months before the building's up. All the buying to do. Hiring new people . . . my people can't afford to wait around without pay until I'm ready to reopen. I don't know."

Charlie shook his head. "Hey. That's the natural reaction. Believe me, I know. Sit on it for a few days. It'll all work out. Look, I gotta go. I'll bring over the other check by the end of the week. Where can I leave you a message?"

"Over there." He pointed to the T-shirt shop across the street.

"Okay. Take care, Swift Benny."

Swift Benny. Somehow it's lost its ring.

He inhaled and exhaled a bit deeper than usual.

———————

Longhi's boasted over eighty brands of beer, a half dozen on tap. The restaurant and bar on Front Street was relatively quiet at eleven-thirty in the morning, most of the late breakfasters had finished a half hour before, and the lunch crowd didn't peak until one. But a few scattered groups remained. Long a favorite eatery of tourists and local people, Longhi's had recently opened for breakfast, big and heavy—meals that lasted until dinner. Three-egg omelettes filled with Portuguese sausage and shrimp, cinnamon French toast, macadamia nut pancakes, and Belgian waffles smothered with strawberries, kiwi, or papaya. Hash browns heaped high, rich Kona coffee, and thick, hand-sliced toast that you could stand on end.

The decor was black and white. Solid some places, checked in others. The upstairs was open air on two sides overlooking the activity on one of Front Street's busier corners. Longhi's trademark was a verbally recited menu with no mention of prices, but hardly a patron complained when presented with the bill because the food was great.

Ben hadn't sat at a bar before noon in a long time. He was on his third Beck's. A year before two beers wouldn't have been much of an anesthetic, but now his brain felt a bit numb. He rubbed his eyes with his palms and looked down the length of the bar. He was alone except for a waitress perched on the end stool, folding napkins. She stopped for a second, lifted her head, and gave him a smile. She was new and her skin was burned. He assumed her decision to stay was recent. The permanent tan would come in a few weeks. Ben smiled back and then returned his vacant gaze to his beer. He took another long draw and then licked his lips as he stared at his reflection in the mirror behind the bar.

Even though his face was partially hidden by amber bottles and stacks of sparkling glasses, his weary look was hard to hide. Frustration was clearly evident. The fight was gone from his dark eyes. Deeply wrinkled lines were etched across his forehead and today's shadow gave him a mean, sarcastic look. Ben thought about the smile he'd just received and realized after looking at himself that it was probably more pity than anything else. He became aware of his breathing as he watched his shoulders rise and sink with a chain ganglike rhythm.

The bartender sauntered over as only bartenders can, looking like a wiseman, but bearing no gifts. He asked Ben if he wanted anything to eat. Ben realized he had skipped breakfast, something he rarely did, so he ordered an omelette and toast. "And another Beck's."

"How 'bout some coffee instead?"

"Later."

After a few minutes, while he waited for his food and watched the people walking along Front Street, Ben became aware of someone standing behind him. He looked over his shoulder and his face lighted up immediately. He slipped off the bar stool, beaming from ear to ear. "Damn! Tobi. How are you? What are you doing here?" It was the only face in the world that could have brought him out of his depression.

Tobi bowed ceremoniously and then extended his hand, which Ben grabbed firmly and held.

"You look a little haggard," Tobi said.

"You know about my place." A soft-spoken statement.

"It is why I have come. To say how sorry I am. To see if you need help . . ." He grinned. "To offer you a job."

Ben's eyes narrowed and he cocked his head. "A job?"

Tobi took a quick glance around. He pointed. "Over here, at a table. After sitting on the floor most of my life, bar stools make me dizzy."

Ben laughed and followed, but his thoughts were on Tobi's mention of a job. "What job?"

"We have plenty of time to talk about that. First, how is Lisa? Well, I trust?"

Ben raised his eyebrows and a stupid smile filled his face. "Let's sit down."

Tobi Otaki had been Ben's mentor, the Lieutenant of Detectives during Ben's stint as a member of the Kona police force. When the Captain's post opened up, Tobi had been the logical choice. Actually, the only choice. But he hadn't gotten the job. A *haole* had—a white man. No matter how friendly the Islands seemed, no matter how much harmony seemed to flow from the tropical setting, prejudice still existed. Hawaiians did not hold many high offices in government or civil service. It had been Ben's first exposure to discrimination in the Islands—at least the first time he had to deal with it directly. It upset him. When he thought about it, he realized that all but a few of the top officers were *haole*. And then Tobi quit, something Ben knew a person of Japanese-Hawaiian descent, a traditionalist, an honorable man, would never do. But the pain and contempt had been too great. So Tobi left the force and soon after became employed as a gardener at an isolated Big Island resort. Ashamed. A failure, not as a policeman, but as a person who had been raised with traditional beliefs. You simply didn't quit. You never gave up. You turned the other cheek and worked that much harder.

Ben's personal protest against the treatment of his friend, the man who had taken special interest in a young, part-*haole* detective, was to quit as well. Now, he realized he'd been sorry ever since. Not that he hadn't done the honorable thing, but he missed being a detective.

They had never spoken to each other about it. Not directly. But it was always in their minds. They took comfort in knowing that they had, in a sense, stuck together.

Ben looked at Tobi, a compact man, no more than five-seven, with a white mustache and small white chin whiskers. He had tufts of silverish hair on the sides, longer gray in back, hardly any on top. Actually, less on top than the last time they'd seen each other, nine months before, when Ben had gone back to work on Melanie Dagdag's murder. When Ben had consulted with Tobi. And after the case was over, Major Serrao had transferred the Captain no one could tolerate and offered Tobi the position at Kona. The job he should have been given before.

Ben liked what he saw. Tobi's inner strength. His discerning confident manner. Still humble but no longer ashamed. A man who knew himself and what he wanted. *That* was something they didn't have in common. At least, not yet.

Ben dropped his head.

"Your expression makes me sad. I assume there are problems between you and Lisa."

Ben had that familiar feeling that Tobi was reading his mind. "I guess . . ."

Tobi gave Ben a wry look. "It would be hard for you to do much better than Lisa."

"I know." His mouth hung open, frowning. Ben was lost for words.

"I will be honest with you. The one thing I dislike is your fight to hold onto the part of your life that is past. The time when you spent too much time in single's bars and your relationships with women only lasted from Friday to Friday. After all you went through on the Dagdag case . . . well, it seemed sober you up. I thought you had a better grasp on what was important in your life." He inhaled slowly, concentrating on Ben's face. "But this is not a lecture. Either you feel strongly about something or you do not. I was never one who believed in in between. And no one can really explain it to you either. You have to feel it for yourself. Especially when we are talking about love. There is an old Hawaiian proverb . . . *pū'olo waimaka a ke aloha.* It means tears are bundles of love. You, my son, have yet to cry."

Longhi's experienced one of those noticeable silent moments that made everyone feel self-conscious.

Everyone except Tobi. "One day you will learn that crying is the most masculine thing a man can do."

Ben gave Tobi a slight smile. "I thought you said no one could explain it to me."

"If I had said I could explain it to you, you would not have listened as well."

Ben pinched the bridge of his nose, something he did when he felt a headache coming on. Then nodding his head slightly, he thanked Tobi.

Tobi clasped his hands and bowed his head.

"I'm not interrupting a prayer meeting, am I boys?" The waitress was holding Ben's omelette and toast. She placed them in front of him as he leaned back, making room for the meal. Then she took Tobi's order for a small piece of grilled *ono*, with lemon only, and headed for the kitchen.

When she was gone, Ben leaned forward in his chair. "Okay. Enough of that. What's this about a job?"

Tobi's grin consumed his face. "When I read about the fire I thought it would not hurt to come and see if you were interested in being a detective again. We have an opening and Major Serrao was in favor of the idea. I just thought you would like to know that that option existed. I was not sure how moving back to the Big Island would work out between you and Lisa, but maybe . . ."

"Is Jack still there?"

"Yes."

"Have you replaced Amaral?"

"Yes. With an old-timer, like me. Maybe you know him. Haanio. Detective from Oahu. He had been there twenty years."

"Yeah, I think so."

"His wife died. I am not sure of what. He does not talk about it. He needed a change in scenery. All his children are grown and moved to the mainland."

Ben said he was sorry about Detective Haanio's wife.

Tobi nodded once. "Well?"

"It's Harry's job, isn't it?"

Tobi didn't have to answer.

"When do you have to know?"

"For you . . . anytime. For a body that washed up at Kealakekua Bay . . . tomorrow."

———————

"I have a feeling this is a little like the last supper."

Ben put down his fork and moved closer to the table. He cleared his throat, suddenly realizing that it was becoming a preamble to most of their conversations. "Lisa, first of all . . . I *do* love you. And as far as what you said about you being too pushy . . . well . . . I think that was the case before, but it's not now."

Subconsciously Lisa's hands, which had been clasped together, separated slightly and her fingers extended. They assumed a praying position.

"It's more me than you, Lisa. I need some time to sort things out. But believe me, it's not that I want someone else, or that I don't want to see you, it's . . . it's just that I'm not comfortable with my life. I have to enjoy what I'm doing and in the right environment, then maybe I can settle down, and feel right about myself. I want you to be part of that, but not until I find myself. Damn! This sounds like Sausalito slapstick."

"Not too much excitement running a retail shop, is there?"

He hesitated and then shook his head.

"And the fire has given you an opportunity, hasn't it?" she asked.

He laughed uneasily. "You're not accusing me of starting it, are you?"

A broad grin crossed her face. She seemed happy, but it lasted only a moment. The grin evaporated as quickly as a Hawaiian rain shower. Ben reached for her hand and grasped it firmly and rubbed the back of her fingers.

"Benny the Torch," she joked weakly trying to lighten the mood.

His smile narrowed and a few quiet seconds passed. "I care about you. It's just that I've got to change my life. I want to be with you, but not until I've decided what to do with myself." He tilted his head to one side. "Do you understand what I'm trying to say?"

"I do."

He cleared his throat again. "I talked to Tobi today. He came over to see me." He paused to gauge her reaction.

"He did! How is he?"

"He . . . he offered me my old job back. I have until tomorrow to decide."

Lisa moved back in her chair. She was stunned. It had happened too fast—even too fast for her.

"Lisa, let's face it. I miss the excitement and challenge. When I quit before, it was because of what they did to Tobi. But I missed it. I'm not a retail man. I'm not a restaurant man. I'm not an artist. I'm not wealthy. And if you're not one of those, then the Islands are a tough place to live, at least for me. But being a cop . . . a detective . . ."

"I understand that it appeals to you. And don't think for a minute that there's something about my ego that won't let me marry a detective. It's just that the Big Island might as well be a million miles away if you're there and I'm here."

"Look, Lisa. After a couple of months, we'll both know how we feel. Me about the job. You about me. If we still care for each other as much, then we'll work out the logistics. Either you'll transfer to the Hyatt Waikoloa . . ." Ben put up his hand before Lisa could say anything, " . . . or I'll arrange a transfer back here somehow. If we want to be together, we'll find a way." He searched her eyes. They weren't gleaming.

"Why couldn't you apply for a position here, now?"

"There probably isn't an opening."

"But you didn't check."

Ben leaned forward and reached for her hands. Lisa placed her hands in her lap.

"I guess I haven't been entirely honest with you. I'm not sure I'd really transfer back. First, I'd try like hell to convince you to come to the Big Island. Maui's gettin' a bit too crowded for me. It's changed in the last few years. Maybe the Big Island will change, too. But not for awhile. Who knows, maybe one day we'll end up in Pago Pago."

There was fire in her eyes. Ben swallowed uncomfortably, realizing he should have told her the truth about Maui from the start.

"*You'll* end up in Pago Pago!" Abruptly, she got up, threw her napkin onto the table, and stormed out of Longhi's. She never looked back.

He sat there with a dumb look on his face. He felt everyone's eyes upon him.

At least the waitress was a pro. She handed him the check so he could pay quickly and get the hell out of there.

Two hours later he was sitting on a flat lava rock, four thousand feet up on the gentle slope of Haleakalā, a few feet from his grandmother's burial place. He missed her more than ever. He wanted the benefit of what she could teach him about his heritage. That was what Tobi had been talking about. Being sensitive to nature, to people, to the things that you shared the land and the sea with. Hawaiians respected their environment. They took only what they needed to survive so it would survive as well.

Ben asked for his grandmother's advice and waited for an answer. He heard the wind howling between the crevices in the rock, but other than that, there was silence. He shivered and held his arms close to his body. He remembered all the times she wanted to tell him things about the old ways, and he had said, 'later,' and hurried away to play ball. Maybe now, he was too late.

He stood and faced the small fissure where years before he had come with his mother to put his grandmother's bones to rest.

There were tears in his eyes.

5

THE LAST TWO YEARS WERE behind him, disappearing from view behind Haleakalā. He smiled, thinking of his grandmother. Minutes
later the entire western coastline of the Big Island filled Ben's view and
soon they were over the Kohala coast. Beneath him, he hoped, was a
fresh start. It was funny how a twenty-minute plane ride could take you
to a new life—or back to an old one.

He heard the landing gear lock in place and felt a shudder as the Aloha
737 began its final approach to Keāhole Airport. As it descended from
the northwest, the early morning sun sparkled against the left side of the
fuselage. Below, the black lava welcome mat extended for miles, first with
the resort hotels—Mauna Kea, Mauna Lani, the Ritz, and the Hyatt Waikoloa—and their lush golf courses snaking through the lava flows of the
1800s. Farther south, plumes of dust billowed skyward where huge
earth-movers were paving the way for another luxury resort. That gave
Ben a feeling of discomfort. Looking east, the terrain gradually changed
into a gentle brownish up-slope that eventually disappeared into the
clouds, which in turn obscured the Big Island's two massive volcanoes.

Nine months previously Ben had made the same flight. To help his
friend Harry, to be a detective again—for one more case. And the day

before, he had accepted Tobi's offer to rejoin the Kona police force. Swift Benny's would not be rebuilt. He was done with the retail world. All he had brought with him were some clothes purchased the day before, his bike, and the insurance check that was folded in half and tucked inside his breast pocket. He patted it every few minutes, drawing some comfort from the knowledge that he could make a down payment on a small house and buy a few furnishings.

Lisa had driven him to the airport. The final embrace had been long, but their had been space between their bodies.

———

Detective Jack Cooper met Ben at the gate. They collected Ben's bike and drove toward police headquarters a few miles south on Highway 19, named after Queen Ka'ahumanu and nicknamed 'The Queen K.' The highway also served as the route for the Ironman Triathlon. The thought made Ben feel better. He was home.

"So how you been, Coop?" Ben asked.

"Not bad. Still tryin' to get over the Dagdag affair, but basically back to normal. It's been real quiet since last October . . . at least until this body washed up."

"Might just be a boating accident," Ben offered. "August is a month of sudden storms."

Jack inhaled deeply and squirmed in his seat. "Yeah, there was a storm that night, but one thing's wrong. The man's left eyelid had been cut . . . sliced through, in fact . . . and Ken doesn't seem to think a fish could have done such a neat job. Or, if it was caused by the coral, then the area around the guy's eye would have shown something else . . . some small cuts or scrapes. Something . . . bits of coral. But it was clean as a whistle."

Ben thought about that for a few moments. "How was he dressed?"

"Not a shred of clothing on him."

Ben raised his eyebrows. "Any jewelry? What about a ring?"

"Nothing." Jack shifted his weight—it took a few seconds. "All we know is the guy was Japanese, somewhere around seventy, and probably about five-six."

"Probably?"

Jack swallowed hard. "Tobi didn't give you a lot of details, did he?" Ben shook his head.

"His legs were gone below the knees. Sharks did that for sure."

Ben sat back in his seat. His elbow came to rest on the arm rest and his chin in his palm. "Nothing else?" he asked quietly.

"Nope."

They mostly rode in silence for the next few miles. Every few minutes, Jack threw out a question. 'The fire? Lisa? How does it feel to be back on the job?' Ben provided short, to-the-point answers. Jack's eyebrows went up and he shifted his eyes between the road and Ben when Ben explained about Lisa.

Soon they reached the turnoff for police headquarters. Jack hung a left and headed up a slight incline on a freshly paved asphalt road as black as the lava just to the north. The building was a quarter of a mile up the road on the left. It was almost four years old and hardly exotic. The structure was basically two squares connected by a smaller rectangle. The building ran east to west and had vertical blinds on all the windows, shut to keep out the heat and sunlight more than for security. There were separate main entrances on the western side, one for **FIRE ARMS and RECORDS**, the other for **COMPLAINTS**. Both glass doors were trimmed in drab blue-gray. The roof on the connecting wing was flat. The main structures had slightly pitched roofs that were covered with light gray corrugated metal. The four sections of each roof met to form a rectangle at the top. They looked like sentry towers, but simply housed the air conditioning compressors. The public parking lot on the southern side was hot, reflective blacktop and was separated from the facility by crushed coral, bleached white from the sun. The landscaping, which had been sparse the last time he'd seen it, looked much better. The trees had filled out and others had been planted. Maybe there was hope for the building that was usually described as being 'across from the landfill.'

As they crossed the parking lot, Ben thought about Jack and wondered how the Dagdag ordeal had changed *his* life. He'd lost weight—maybe thirty pounds—putting him near two-ten. His pants were pressed, his aloha shirt was new, and it wasn't as flamboyant as the ones Ben remembered from before. And, by God, he was wearing socks. And they matched. Maybe that had something to do with Jack being able to see his feet after all these years.

"You been exercising?"

Jack beamed. "Uh huh. Three times a week and Drysdale's is about outta business . . . my bar tab's no more than ten bucks."

"We'll have to get you into the Ironman next year."

Jack rubbed his hands together in mock anticipation.

Minutes later they were seated in Tobi's office. It was medium-sized, twelve by sixteen, and efficient looking. The police-issue furniture was gone. When Tobi became Captain, he found he spent much of his time in his office. The metal-gray color was too much for him to bear. He brought in his own furnishings. None of the men took offense—just the opposite, they loved to be called into his office.

His *koa* desk was bare except for a gold pen and pencil set, a blotter that looked new, and a neat stack of manila file folders. The matching credenza supported a black glass vase that held three trails of dendrobrium orchids. And supporting the coffee table's glass top was a huge, brass elephant with a flat back and head. The walls were decorated with three Japanese paper prints—one of a white nightingale, another of a red-headed crane hiding in the reeds, and the largest, a pool of carp. Outside, a lone sandalwood danced in the window frame.

Tobi sat forward in his desk chair, hands clasped and resting on the desktop. Ben sat on a small love seat. Jack was wedged into an armchair.

Tobi looked pleased. "It's good to have you back, Detective Mc-Millen."

Ben nodded. "Looks like we've reassembled the team." He choked inside—sorry he'd said it like that—immediately remembering that someone was missing. He could tell that Tobi and Jack were thinking the same thing.

Tobi cleared his throat softly. "First things first. Your office area . . ."

"I'll take Harry's."

"Are you sure? We have another."

Firmly. "Harry's."

"Okay. Second, see Joyce. She has some forms for you to fill out. Then you will need a physical. While you are at the hospital, spend some time with Ken. He will tell you everything he has so far."

Ben nodded once more. "What about a car?"

Jack said, "I think they've got a white Suzuki jeep you can borrow until you buy a vehicle. I'll check with Joyce."

Tobi leaned backward. "Ben, I want you to work on the body that washed up. We have no ID. Maybe it was an accident, maybe not."

"Any Missing Ps filed?"

Tobi answered. "One. A woman."

"Jack told me about the slit eyelid."

"It is not much to go on," said Tobi, "but Ken said he would have more test results this morning. The man's stomach was basically intact. Maybe he will find a clue there."

Ben stood. "You don't think it was an accident, do you?"

Tobi shook his head. "Old men do not swim late at night in the ocean, especially in a storm."

"What if he was a fisherman?"

"We found no boat. And none is reported missing."

"You checked Maui . . ."

"Given the size of the storm . . . every island."

Ben spent the next hour completing payroll and insurance forms, signing for the jeep, renewing past acquaintances, and generally getting a feel for the station. He looked for Millie Kalehua, the Major's assistant, but found she had the day off. Millie had always been Ben's dear friend. Depending upon what he needed, she was a grandmother, mother, or sister.

He had held off the trip to Harry's old office for last. Now he stood transfixed in the doorway. The room was spotless, almost antiseptic smelling. The walls were bare, freshly painted in muted gray that matched the overcast coloring of the rest of the building. There was a standard-issue desk, credenza, filing cabinet, and two side chairs. An empty blotter was centered on the desktop. They had tried to make it look new, but to Ben it looked abandoned, but with Harry's personality forever buried in the walls.

Ben walked over to the window and opened the Levolor blinds. The view was hardly breathtaking. A gradual slope that led up to the foothills was covered with patches of long, dried brownish grass. Brown rocks lay strewn everywhere. A single baby palm, staked to the ground, was the only thing that let him know he wasn't sequestered in eastern Colorado. All was silent except for the hum of the air compressor on the roof—and the beating of Ben's heart. He closed his eyes. He could see his friend's tortured face. He could smell burning flesh. Ben pressed his palms against the warm glass and stared.

Thirty minutes later, Ben pulled up in front of Kona Hospital. The hospital was a two-story structure. White cement and salmon stripes covering the support beams. The foliage in front was plentiful. The parking was not.

As he made his way to the pathology lab in the basement, more memories of last October filled his head. Questioning the husband of the second victim, Philipe da Silva a philandering realtor, whom Ben had suspected at the beginning. Then his thoughts shifted to Janis Duerson, the hospital psychologist, who had helped profile the serial killer. The beguiling woman whom he'd been involved with twice. Most recently it had been a one-nighter, nine months before. Lisa had known. He wondered how she had found out. Women's intuition, he supposed—or the veneer of a man's guilty face. He wondered if it still mattered to her.

Approaching the lab, his mind traveled across the street, to the building that housed Janis's office. Visions of a huge spider's web flashed in his brain. He pictured himself being lured into the center of that web and rolled into a tiny silk ball for safekeeping, for a rainy day's entertainment.

Ben quickened his pace and kept his head down.

Near the end of the corridor were the pathology offices and labs. The door was open and he stepped inside. Some of the labs—toxicology, microbiology, chemical—were to his left, offices to his right. The autopsy room and morgue were at the end of the hallway, hidden by a small labyrinth of corridors. Within seconds the scent of formaldehyde hit him. Since the lab secretary was gone from her station, Ben proceeded to the first office. As he approached, he heard Ken Asumura on the phone. Ben stopped and stood in the doorway.

Ken swiveled in his chair, beaming broadly when he saw Ben. He motioned him inside and raised a single finger, signifying he'd be finished soon.

"Okay, fine. I'll be there at ten . . . right. Right. Okay. Thanks." The hospital's chief pathologist hung up and stood, hand extended. Ben and he were old friends. They greeted each other warmly.

"Back for good this time?" asked Ken.

Sitting, Ben gave him a thumb's up. "Looks like it."

Ken was wearing a white lab coat, smartly creased and spotless. It contrasted with his natural dark coloring and jet-black hair. He was thirty-six, four inches shorter than Ben, and had been at Kona Hospital eight years, coming directly after finishing his residency at Leahi Hospital just north of Diamond Head on Oʻahu. Ken was one generation removed from being pure Hawaiian. His mother, who lived in Pāhoa in the Puna District, was a *kahuna lapa ʻau,* a practitioner of Hawaiian folk medicine. And that presented an interesting dilemma for Ken. Although his University medical training was extensive, his *ʻohana*—family—medical training was stronger. He referred more people to his mother than to the hospital's care.

What Ben liked about him was his work ethic and his sense of humor. He was thorough and insightful. A team player. They were good friends and had spent a lot of time together—fishing, biking, running—before, when Ben was a Kona detective. All the detectives treated Ken like one of the boys.

Ken reached for a manila folder and handed it to Ben. He gave Ben a minute to study it before he spoke. As he began, Ben closed the folder and placed it on Ken's desk.

"The body was in bad shape. Both legs severed at the knees. His genitalia gone. His entire left arm and right hand were torn off. Definitely a shark. The tear marks were conclusive, but I also found three teeth. Good-sized, a blue probably. Six to eight feet, I'd say."

"Is that what killed him?"

"There was water in his lungs and some plankton, but you'd expect that. The key test is the amount of sodium in the heart."

"Explain."

"The left side of the heart receives oxygenated blood from the lungs . . . and water, if it's present. If you measure the sodium electrolytes in both the left and right sides and if the count on the left is considerably higher, then the ingestion of salt water probably caused the imbalance. The electrolyte count *was* much higher in the left. Medically, he drowned. But the shark attack probably caused it."

"Could have bled to death," Ben stated.

Ken nodded. "Could have."

"What about foul play before?"

Ken scratched his chin. "No way to tell. There was a relatively small slit across his left eyelid. There were some microscopic pieces of coral embedded in the wound. I found them this morning."

"Yeah, Jack said it was clean."

"I thought so yesterday. Other than that there are no lethal marks. No blows to the head. That in itself is remarkable, since he must have come across the reef. But, I suppose he could have skimmed across the top."

"So if someone dumped him, there's no evidence of it."

"Dropping someone overboard a few miles out has always been a good way to hide murder. Especially in a storm. So many things can happen. Sharks. Drowning. Hit your head on the coral. Heart attack brought on by the sheer terror of the whole ordeal. Hey, it's remarkable when a body makes it all the way in. What's left after the sharks can easily get hung up in the reef for days. By then, the reef fish clean you off and your bones sink to the bottom. Rough seas stir up the ocean floor, cover your bones, and you've disappeared."

Ben swallowed uncomfortably, then stood and walked to the doorway, and peered out. The lab technicians were busy with samples and charts. "No way to fingerprint him, right?"

"Not without fingers."

"How long was he in the water?" asked Ben.

"Not more than twelve hours . . . but we do have one revealing test result that came back this morning." He produced another piece of paper and handed it to Ben. "I noticed his arms seemed stained, darker than the rest of his exposed skin. We found a residue in the crease of his left elbow and the same thing all over his right forearm. The salt water didn't wash it off, so it must be something he came in contact with regularly, over a long period of time."

Ben gave the lab test a quick look. He prodded, "Go on."

"It's a combination of coffee berries and macadamia nuts."

"Well, shit!" Ben's expression brightened. "That's something. You think he was a farmer south of town?"

Ken nodded. "The outer skin of a coffee berry isn't as oily as the bean itself . . . same holds true for the shell of a mac nut . . . the nut's real oily but not the shell. So for someone to show signs of the oils, he must have lived with them every day for a long time. Had to be a picker or a farmer."

"Let's go have a look at him."

The morgue was not Ben's favorite place. It wasn't the unsightly gun-shot wounds, nor the twisted limbs, nor the bloodied depressions from the puncture wounds produced by a knife. He'd seen all that many times. It was the cold, white pallor that covered the victim like a suffocating film. The hidden terror beneath the skin. It was the silent screaming of someone trying to tell him who he should be after. But the words lay trapped inside forever.

Naked on a cold aluminum bed. It didn't get any more final than that.

Ben faced the stainless steel wall. There were four compartments. Each door had a small rectangular holder for an ID card. Only one was present. It was on the first door. Laminated, it contained space for the name, age, sex, height, weight, and approximate time of death. Ben squinted.

```
JOHN DOE ( JAPANESE )
70–75
MALE
5'6"?
140–150?
12:00 A.M.—08/01/90 [approx]
```

It was unusual to see a 'question mark' after the height.

One of Ken's assistants, a young Hawaiian with short black hair and beefy cheeks, slid open the drawer and pulled out half a body with a tag hung around its neck.

Ben grimaced. This one was the worst. The man looked like bait. Even his genitals were gone. Ben straightened up and took a cautious breath, as if he were afraid to inhale the smell of death.

"Not a pleasant sight," said Ken.

"It never is. Got a probe of some sort? You don't mind . . . do you, Ken."

"Go right ahead."

The pathologist's assistant handed Ben a foot-long metal instrument shaped like a tongue depressor.

Ben held it gingerly at first, then tightened his grip. First, he bent back the victim's right earlobe. He found nothing behind it. Then he lifted the man's right arm and checked the armpit, parting the matted hair with the edge of the probe. There was nothing. "Anything on his back, Ken?"

"No. We went over him thoroughly. No scars, no previous surgery."

"Which eyelid?"

"Left," said Ken.

Ben saw the slit. It was purplish now, the color of a vein, and tiny. It looked like a small razor blade cut, puffy at the edges. He walked around the aluminum guerney and pushed back the man's left ear. Nothing. He didn't have to lift the man's arm. All that remained was a torn shoulder joint, ripped to shreds by a ravenous shark. But then something caught his eye. He bent closer. At first it had looked like a curled hair. But upon closer examination it looked like a small number, like a tattoo in the man's armpit.

Ken came forward. "You see something?"

"Yeah. Come here. See that. It looks like a *three*." A tattoo of some kind just sticking out where the hair ends. Using the probe Ben pushed back the man's underarm hair. To the left of the *three* was a *seven*. "There's a number here. Maybe a serial number. Can you shave it right now?"

"Sure." He turned. "Tommy," Ken said to his assistant, "roll him in . . . on the double."

Once they were in the autopsy room, Ken took a scissors and trimmed the hair in the man's armpit close to the skin. Carefully, using a pair of tweezers, he placed some of the hair into a small plastic bag and marked it. Then with an electric razor he shaved the armpit. When he was finished, Ken vacuumed the man's armpit and the stainless steel table and handed the minivac to Tommy.

"Looks like we missed something big. Sorry, Ben."

Ben waved him off.

Ken squinted. "A tattoo . . . dark green ink. It's a five-digit number. Five-oh-five-seven-three."

Ben stepped closer and looked for himself. Then he wrote it down.

Ken nodded and Tommy stepped forward, covered the remains, and carefully slid the body onto the gurney and pushed it toward the cold locker.

Ben leaned against the wall. "The first thing that comes to mind is a number for a prisoner of war. The Germans did that. Did the Japanese?"

"No idea."

"Looks like I've got two clues. A coffee farmer with a mysterious tattoo. That's two more than I started with."

"Later this morning I'll try to do something with the tattoo. Maybe I can determine the kind of ink. I've got to tell you, I've never had a case where a tattoo is involved. I've seen plenty, but they weren't important to the analysis. I'll have to send this to Honolulu."

"Don't spend a lot of time on it. It's the number that's important, not the ink."

As they left the autopsy room, Ken's wristwatch beeped three times. "I've got a meeting. Anything else?"

"Got a photo of his face?"

"Eight-by-ten black and white okay?"

"Fine."

Ben followed the pathologist back to his office. "How many coffee farms do you think there are?"

"Unfortunately, there are hundreds. All small family businesses spread out over South Kona."

Ben shook his head and sighed.

As Ben drove north on Ali'i Drive, he passed Kailua Pier, the site of the start of the Ironman. He pictured himself at the water's edge wearing a yellow Budweiser swim cap, dancing nervously in the sand, waiting for the start. Deep breaths, shaking his arms and legs to stay limber.

A small grin formed on his face. For the first time he realized he would be training on the actual Ironman course itself. That had to help. He made up his mind to resume training right away.

He tried not to think of it as Harry's office, but *his*. He was sitting at *his* desk in *his* chair, looking at a map of the South Kona District. Kona coffee country.

The area south of Kailua from Keauhou farther south to Ho'omau Ranch had 2300 acres of coffee trees spread over more than six hundred small farms. Coffee was introduced to Hawai'i in the early 1800s when Chief Boki, returning from London with the bodies of King Kamehameha II and Queen Kamamalu—both had died of measles while visiting England—stopped in Rio de Janeiro and acquired a few plants. The rich volcanic soil and the climate—cool mountain evenings, a mild summer rainfall, cloud cover during the hot afternoons, and a dry winter—was ideal for the plants. The result was a superb coffee bean, treasured throughout the world. The harvest season was long, stretching from August to January. White blossoms appeared in the spring, giving off a fragrance similar to a gardenia, a close relative of the coffee plant. The flowering trees gave the entire South Kona District a veil of white for a few days until the berries formed.

Over six hundred farms. Ben shook his head and ran his fingers through his thick, black hair.

The other half of the residue on the man's skin had been macadamia nut oil. After asking one of the uniformed officers, he found out that many of the coffee farmers also grew macadamia nuts. Shortly after World War II, when world coffee prices headed downward, the farmers hedged their bets by supplementing their coffee business with macadamia nut trees. The market wasn't as big—world-wide, coffee was the second largest moneymaker, after crude oil—but mac nuts mainly grew in Hawai'i and Central America. And you could count on the stability of the price.

Ben dug a little deeper and found that there were five major coffee mills. He'd start his questions there.

Then he sought Tobi. He found him in the Major's office, discussing the case load with Major Serrao.

Louis Serrao was full-blooded Portuguese, born in Oporto in the shadows of the drug traffic district. Raised there. Policed a beat there. He was thirty-five and divorced, with fourteen years of service, when his partner was killed—stabbed by the housewife he and his partner were trying to save from her crazed husband. A half hour after the funeral, Serrao resigned, took his savings, and headed for Hawai'i, where he had relatives. The fishing charter boat he bought sank in a storm six months later. The last insurance premium for the boat was two months overdue. The policy had been cancelled. The next morning he was in Honolulu police headquarters filling out an application for detective. A week later he had his shield. And eighteen years later he made Major in the Kona District.

Today he had a fresh haircut and a sparkle in his eye.

Serrao stood and leaned over his desk. "Hey, Ben. Funny how things work out, heh? Welcome to the payroll."

"Major." He shook Serrao's meaty hand.

"Have a seat," said Serrao. "We're just getting to your case. Find out anything at the hospital?"

"Yeah. The guy probably worked on a coffee farm." Ben explained the coffee and mac nut residue engrained in the man's skin. "I'm going to see if anyone at the mills recognizes the guy. I've got a photo. It's a bit messy, but I think someone should be able to ID him."

Tobi smiled. "Good."

"There's something else, Tobi. Maybe you can help."

A nod.

Serrao hunched forward and placed his elbows on his desk.

"We found a serial number of sorts tattooed in the guy's armpit . . .

like the kind you've seen on someone who's been in a concentration camp." The surprised, serious look on Tobi's face drew him to a stop.

Serrao asked, "Well?"

The Captain of detectives folded his arms across his chest. His eyes moved slowly to the Major, then to Ben. "How many digits?"

"What? Oh, five. 5–0–5–7–3."

"He was not a prisoner of war. The man was an agent. Part of the Japanese Secret Service."

Ben straightened up. "A spy?"

Tobi nodded. "From World War II."

"That was fifty years ago," said Serrao. "It must be a coincidence."

Ben stood and angled toward to the door. "If he was murdered, it's no coincidence."

6

HEADING DOWN 'THE QUEEN K.' Back on the job.

To Ben's right—the *makai* side—the turquoise Pacific sparkled in the midday sun. As far as he could see, the water along the Kona coast was calm. The only signs of surf were small breakers near shore and a few frothing whitecaps far away on the horizon. The storm and high winds of the past few days were far to the northeast, approaching the California coast. Above the sea, dozens of red-tailed and white-tailed tropicbirds glided effortlessly, skimming across the water, piercing the glassy surface with keen eyesight as they looked for small fish that had ventured beyond the safety of the reef.

On the *mauka* side was the gradual slope upland—the ancient base of Mauna Loa, one of the Big Island's two active volcanoes. Near Kailua the foothills were green with foliage—above the foothills, tall brown and gold grass magically grew out of the bed of black lava. Higher up, slow-moving gray clouds licked the slopes of Mauna Loa.

As he passed Palani Road, which led to downtown Kailua, visions of the past crept into his head. Friday night at Drysdale's. The four detectives—Harry, Jack, Amaral, and himself—planning the weekend around a table of empty pitchers. Game fishing was the favorite. They had gone many times, and even when they returned to the harbor empty-handed, the camaraderie of a day at sea had made it well worth the time. But the thought of it evoked memories of the previous October and made Ben shudder when he recalled the fire that had engulfed the boat. His skin tingled all over as he remembered the flames melting away the smile of a maniacal killer.

It occurred to him then that the fire hadn't ended there. It had pursued him, taking *Swift Benny's* in the process. What was next? Was it a symbol of something else suspended in the shadows? His thoughts shifted to Lisa. Vaguely, her face appeared ahead on the road, like a watery mirage. Her expression seemed anxious. Abruptly, her face evaporated when the sun ducked behind a cloud. He remembered her fragile smile when they had parted a few days before.

He shook the image out of his head and concentrated on the roadway. At Palani the Queen K had become Highway 11—the Hawai'i Belt Road. It had no other name that he knew of. Ben thought surely there was some high chief or chiefess who hadn't been honored who was deserving of the remembrance. The Belt Road sounded too cosmopolitan and too constraining, like the Beltway around D.C.

His stomach grumbled. Ben checked his watch. It was just past one and he realized why he felt so light-headed. As he scanned the roadside up ahead, he remembered Mitchell's. He swung right off 11, taking a narrow street that dipped south and within a short distance intersected with Ali'i Drive. Backtracking, heading north on Ali'i for about a mile, Ben spotted the Keauhou Shopping Village on his right, turned, headed up the smooth black asphalt rise, and pulled into an empty space under the partial shade of an ironwood tree. He got out of the Suzuki Sidekick, reached for the photo folder that he had placed on the small back seat, tucked it under his arm, and walked across the parking lot toward Mitchell's. Suddenly, he stopped and gave the building a hard stare. Was the Dagdag case still haunting him? Luring him back to familiar places? Mitchell's had been the scene of the fourth and last murder. He took a deep breath and continued walking.

Mitchell's occupied the northwest corner of the shopping center. With its Spanish-style roof tiles, stucco walls, broad wooden beams, and the sparkling Pacific clearly visible across the road, the Keauhou Shopping Village resembled a spacious Mediterranean villa. Besides Mitchell's there were two art galleries, several up-scale clothing shops, an expensive jeweler, a book shop filled with volumes of Hawaiiana, and across the plaza from Mitchell's was Drysdale's Two, a contemporary version of Drysdale's 53, which was located in the Kona Inn Village Shopping Center a few miles north. Drysdale's Two—another familiar watering hole. He and Harry had spent many evenings there, watching ESPN on the wide screen and downing drafts.

Immediately, a prominent new sign caught his eye. It was hanging from a post by the entrance to the restaurant. Handcarved out of *koa*, it was round, at least four feet in diameter, with a raised sculpted marlin in the center. **Mitchell's** was etched across the top in a semicircle, and below the arched words, **Since 1215.** Squinting, his face yielded a myopic, puzzled look for a few seconds. Then Ben shook his head, grinned, and walked inside.

Mitchell's was a sizzling place at night. A refined singles dance club, upgraded from the days of disco. The floor was a mosaic of white tile squares with aquamarine diamonds in each corner that gave the place the atmosphere of a Parisian night-spot. Scattered about, with no apparent pattern, were small octagonal tables with aquamarine tops and chrome pedestal bases. Ice cream parlor chairs surrounded the tables. The ceiling was painted black to hide the electrical conduits, air ducts, and exhaust vents. All the ceiling fans were at rest.

The bar was thirty feet long, faced with white Formica. It had an imitation marble top with a cushioned armrest—dark aquamarine—that ran the length. Behind, a framed mirror covered the wall. Five liquor license decals were affixed in a jagged row near the bottom of the glass. Glass shelving held the liquor and a pyramid display of over forty brands of beer. Hundreds of glasses, all shapes and sizes, hung from slotted racks above the bar.

There were two entrances, one at each end of the building. The dance floor was to the right and rear with a circle of multi-colored lights framing it from above. A raised stage to the left was filled with amplifiers, speakers, tuners, microphones, and a nightmare of tangled cable.

It was twelve-thirty. Mitchell's never really had much of a lunch crowd. Now there only were two couples at one table by an open window, enjoying the *K Coast* pizza that was Danny Mitchell's specialty, and Danny himself, polishing the chrome railing that ringed the display of beer bottles.

"Hey, Danny. How's it going?"

Danny turned toward the voice, narrowed his eyes, and then broke into a broad grin when he recognized Ben.

"Damn! Haven't seen you in a while." Then his expression soured slightly. "Not investigating another mur . . . crime, are you?"

"Nothing that you should worry about. Just stopped in for a bite to eat and thought maybe you could help me out with some information."

They shook hands and then Danny extended his arm, motioning to a stool at the end of the bar.

Ben walked over, sat, and placed the photo folder on the bar. "Just a cheeseburger and a Pepsi," said Ben, folding his arms and resting them on the bar.

Danny raised a finger, leaned against the kitchen door—it opened a crack—and called out Ben's order to an invisible cook. "And hustle, George, we gotta V.I.P. out here."

Ben smiled. "I expect you'll be seeing a lot of me."

Danny was confused. "You said no crime."

"I've moved back. I'm a Kona detective again."

"Hey, that's great, but I thought you loved your surf shop. What gives?"

Ben explained the fire.

Danny shivered, obviously thinking about *his* place burning down. He came around the end of the bar and sat on the stool next to Ben. "So you're a full-time cop again. What are you working on?"

"Before we get into detecting, what's this bullshit . . ." he pointed toward the entrance, " . . . since twelve-fifteen on the sign?"

Danny laughed. "Simple. When we first opened five years ago, it was a quarter after twelve." He smacked his lips. "Cross my heart." He crossed his heart.

Ben shook his head and looked skyward. "Save this guy, Lord."

Danny chuckled and shrugged his shoulders. "Believe it or not, you're only the third person who's asked."

Ben grinned at him, but after a moment his expression changed to serious. "All right, a little business?"

"Shoot."

"A few days ago a body washed up south of here at Kealakekua Bay. Old Japanese guy. Sharks got him."

Danny made a grim face. "Not an accident?"

"Don't know. Right now I'm just trying to ID him. The pathologist found the residue of coffee beans and mac nuts all over his arms, at least on what was left of them. I remember you saying you'd worked the farms up and down the coast before you bought this place. I'd like to know if there is . . ."

The kitchen door opened and a big Hawaiian, wearing a blue bandana tied around his head, stepped out holding a platter. It was hard to tell if he'd forgotten the burger. The plate was covered with fries. He placed it on the bar, nodded, and returned to the kitchen without a word. V.I.P.s didn't seem to impress him.

Danny got up and went behind the bar. He filled a glass with ice and then shoved it under the Pepsi spigot. Ben thought about their first meeting nine months before.

Danny Mitchell was thirty-one, about Ben's height, blue eyes and dirty-blond hair—straight and medium length. He'd lived on the Big Island after dropping out of UC - Long Beach midway through his sophomore year. He had bought the dance club with money saved from working the coffee, mac nut, and fruit farms that choke the South Kona coast. A look at his arms and chest showed that Danny had been an athlete who was still in reasonably good shape. A glance at his stomach revealed that he spent a little too much time behind the bar. Ben couldn't exactly pinpoint what it was about Danny that made him feel comfortable. But he believed he was one of those people who after the first five minutes you knew you could trust.

Danny flipped the lever, wiped the bottom of the glass, and turned toward him. Ben got back to his question. "Is there any central place where coffee growers sell their beans?"

"In a way." He placed the Pepsi next to Ben's plate.

Ben took a few sips, then reached for the ketchup bottle, lifted the top on his burger after shoveling the fries to one side, and shook out a big blob of ketchup.

"Although we supply the world with Kona coffee, it's not as organized as you might guess. There are literally hundreds of small farms . . . and I mean small, like two or three acres each. They've been handed down since the eighteen hundreds, mainly by families descended from the earliest Japanese immigrants. It's a family operation. They hardly ever hire outsiders. There used to be several big coffee mills and even some full-time buyers, but now the farmers in the northern areas bring their bags to the Co-op. The ones in the south just leave their bags by the side of the road, and an old truck picks them up and brings them to one of the remaining mills. I don't know how *those* guys transact business and agree on prices, but that's the way it operates."

"How many mills are there?"

Danny scratched his elbow. "Four or five, I guess. There's Bay View, Bong Brothers, Superior . . . ahh . . . Kona Kai . . . maybe a couple of others."

Ben jotted them down. "If the guy was an old Japanese, would he live north or south?"

"Probably south . . . most of the northern farmers are new and they're *haoles*. The Japanese up this way were bought out in the last five or six years. The only old-timers left are near Ka'ū. This guy was probably one of the originals who leaves his coffee by the side of the road."

Just to be thorough, Ben extracted the picture of the victim from the folder he'd placed on the bar. "Ever see him?"

"Looks pretty bad," said Danny, furrowing his brow.

"Nobody looks good dead. Especially after eight hours in the water."

Danny shook his head. "Not exactly the kind of guy that comes in here."

Ben slipped the photo into the manila folder. "What do you suggest I do?"

"Well, to save time, I'd try a few of the farmers and see if they can help. I'm not sure anyone at the mills will recognize him if he left his bags by the side of the road, but you could try them next. Farmers that are neighbors must know each other pretty well. The coffee grows for twenty miles down the coast starting from Captain Cook. Maybe if you hit one or two farms every five miles or so you'll have some luck. But I'd concentrate south."

"Looks like a long day."

"It doesn't get dark until eight-thirty."

"Great. What about the mac nut residue? Anything significant?"

Danny rubbed his chin. "Don't think so. I think there were a few years after World War II when the coffee crop went to hell, or at least the market did, and the farmers planted mac nut trees to supplement their income. They've kept small groves going ever since. I bet most of them have nut trees."

Ben nodded—it confirmed what one of the police officers had told him. He absentmindedly stared at his lunch. Then he said, "Where'd you pick up all this stuff?"

"I read. Hawai'i fascinates me . . . especially the old stuff . . . the culture, the traditions. What it was like before."

Ben nodded once more. He was interested, too. The memory of his grandmother saw to that. He wished he had spent more time with her.

"Be careful back there," Danny warned. "You might come across some Kona Gold growers and they don't take to strangers snooping around, especially if you're the police."

Ben frowned at the thought of marijuana growers jeopardizing the safety of the Islanders. He'd heard rumors about some bad things going on up there. People missing. Gunfire. But he couldn't remember anything ever being substantiated.

His stomach grumbled. He speared a few fries.

After fifteen minutes of small talk and a promise to go fishing in a few weeks, Ben left and headed south for Captain Cook.

A few miles south the cliff on his left became almost vertical. Immediately next to the road the steep bank was covered with flowering hibiscus and plumeria. Only a few protruding formations of lava were visible. Higher up the rock wall was a thick maze of dark shadows with random patches of bright green where the morning moisture still glistened in the afternoon sun. Light reflecting from the broad, glossy foliage made sunglasses a necessity. Ben adjusted his as they slipped down his nose. Then he let his body rest against the seat, fingers drumming on the steering wheel, a tune, if you can call it that, whistling through his lips. He never whistled in public and he only sang on deserted islands.

Early afternoon. There wasn't much traffic on the road. Checking out the mills in the northern part of South Kona, from Nāpo'opo'o to Hōnaunau, he had brief conversations with one of the Bong brothers, a nice lady at Superior, and the burly manager of Kona Kai. His last stop was Bay View Farms, a combination farm and mill, set on a flat plateau overlooking Kealakekua Bay. The owner, who was the only one to offer a cup of coffee, didn't know the old man in the photo. Like the others, he suggested that Ben try the more remote farms farther south.

He passed the post office at Keōkea, a small stone building that sat on a ledge at the intersection of Highways 11 and 160, overlooking the bay about a mile to the west. A large white egret perched on the pinnacle of the roof, extending its neck, practicing its mating routine. Ben stopped suddenly, made a U-turn, and pulled into the post office parking lot. The bird flew away. Ben watched it until it disappeared into the network of foliage on the *mauka* side of the road. Then he turned and headed into the post office. He didn't believe there was regular mail delivery down the coast. Maybe the old man came in for his mail. Maybe a postal clerk could ID him from the photograph.

A minute later he returned to his jeep, dejected. Not everyone received mail on a regular basis.

About a mile farther south he came across his first burlap bags of coffee. They sat in a heap by the side of the road, shaded by a monkeypod tree. Ben angled over and cut the engine. He hurried over to the three bags.

Each had a single marking—a four-inch black circle with a big script *Y* in the center. Next to the bags was a glass jar. Danny had mentioned that the Co-op driver left a receipt in the farmer's jar. He looked around. Down the slope, toward the water, he could see a house, but it was at least a half a mile away and surrounded by a flat grassy meadow. No coffee trees in sight. Danny had said most of the coffee farms were on the *mauka* side of the road. Ben did an about-face and was confronted by the sheer, camouflaged mountainside. He looked back up the road down which he had just come. No driveway. No dirt road. Not even a footpath. He got back into his jeep.

After few hundred feet, he passed a sign announcing the village of Keālia, and shortly after he came to a badly chipped white gate blockading a rutted roadway that led up the hillside. Minutes later, after opening the gate and closing it behind him, he was driving slowly up the steep, winding grade. It was another world. For the first few hundred feet, there was nothing but deep shadows, with only a glimmer of sunlight. Soon he noticed that the trees had changed from a tangled jungle. They were arranged in neat rows ten feet apart, each tree about fifteen feet high. He leaned his head out of the window and sniffed for coffee, but picked up nothing at first. A few trees still sported tiny white flowers, blooms several months late, but most were loaded with burgundy-colored berries. There was a mild fragrance in the air. He couldn't place it, although it was quite pleasant. Then, as the grade flattened a bit, he smelled smoke. Cautiously, no more than five miles per hour, he crawled forward. A vision appeared in his mind. Marijuana farmers with shotguns pointed directly at his chest. His lips became dry and the jeep suddenly felt cramped. After another thirty yards there was a ninety-degree bend, and as he came around it, Ben spotted a squat farmhouse with a flat roof. He stopped the Suzuki. There was a gun locked in the glove compartment. He debated, but left it there. He got out, remembered to take the photograph, and then quietly closed the door.

As he approached the house, he saw a thin line of smoke coming from a leaning smokestack. It was quiet. Dead leaves on the forest floor muffled everything. All he could hear was his heartbeat. Near the front screen door was a huge gong. It was at least five feet in diameter and suspended from a rope. The rough hemp was knotted above a hole in the top of a square frame that surrounded the gong. A single four-by-four post, neatly jointed into the bottom of the frame, had been driven into the ground. As he came within a few paces of the antique gong, he noticed it was rusted around the edges and encircled with spider webs.

Not much call for mustering the troops up here.

At the two front corners of the house were large redwood catchment barrels. Most of South Kona relied on rainwater for bathing and washing. Curved wooden downspouts with broad leaders ran from the roof to the tops of the barrels.

He jumped when someone tapped him on the shoulder.

An old Japanese man, shoulders stooped, with a spaced, toothy grin asked, "Are you lost?"

Ben cleared his throat twice. "No. Sorry to disturb you. I'm Ben McMillen." He offered his hand.

The old man bowed.

Ben bowed awkwardly as he retracted his hand. "I'm a Kona detective. Can we talk for a few minutes?"

The man eyed him for a few seconds, then he nodded and extended his arm, inviting Ben into the farmhouse. Ben smiled and walked toward the door. As he was about to step inside, there was another tap on his shoulder, and a quiet reminder. "Shoes." Ben knew better, but the aura of the old farmhouse had enveloped his conscious. He slipped off his Rockports. The old man shuffled out of his sandals and placed the wide woven basket he had been carrying onto the seat of an old porch chair. They stepped inside.

The interior of the house was not what he expected. An intricate system of latticed *koa* and silk paper completely covered the walls. The paper was an egg shell white, grainy and translucent. Miniature drawings were painted on many of the panels. Looking around, Ben saw that the farmhouse was divided into three sections. To the right was a kitchen, jammed with hanging utensils, including a huge, blackened wok. Embers glowed in the belly of a wood-burning stove as the mountain breezes slipped through the open windows and were sucked up the smokestack.

The center space served as a common living area. One low table and thin mats were the only furnishings, except for a painting of a river filled with tall reeds that hung from one of the walls. A bright red bird with a slender, curved black beak was perched on the tallest of the reeds. It seemed so real that Ben expected it to fly away as he came closer. To the left, in the bedroom, Ben could see the corner of a sleeping mat. But that was all. The rest was out of view.

"Come sit. I will get tea."

The tea was green, weak, and seemed stale to Ben. After a sip, he put the cup down and explained about the body that had been washed ashore. The old man listened with a blank face. Ben told him about the coffee and macadamia nut residues engrained in the victim's skin. Ben noticed that the old man's eyes were glazed. Ben took the photo from the folder and handed it to him.

"Maybe you recognize him?" Ben swallowed.

The coffee farmer stared at the photo for a long time. Ben studied him while he did so. He had a thin gray mustache and sharp, penetrating eyes that Ben guessed missed very little. The old man was dressed in worn khaki work clothes. A red-and-white bandana was neatly knotted around his forehead. His face was deeply tanned, his arms dark with what Ben assumed was coffee residue. With his head down the farmer said, "My name is Yoshio."

"Pleased to meet you, Yoshio. Do you know him?"

Yoshio shook his head. "I do not go out into the world. I only walk to the road twice a week with my coffee. My niece brings me the things I need." He took a deep breath. "I know only two men." He pointed left and then right. "The farmers who are my neighbors. He is not one of my neighbors. Yet, if he was a coffee farmer . . . like me . . . then he was my friend."

Ben inhaled a silent breath, sensing the old man's karma, as he did with Tobi. He watched him rub the photograph with the tips of his stained fingers.

"There are many farmers, right?"

Yoshio nodded, still gazing at the picture. "Many."

"How will I find this man's farm?"

"You wait by the roadside for Mr. Bennett."

"Mr. Bennett?"

"Winston Bennett. He picks up the bags. If this man owned a farm in this area, Mr. Bennett will know him. If not, he can direct you to the others . . . the other mill owners." He pointed south. "Someone will know him."

"Are you sure?"

Yoshio looked up for the first time since Ben had handed him the photo. He handed it back. Ben put it back into the folder.

"If this man was a farmer, then his bag will not be there. Someone will go up and see what is the matter. No one misses bag day."

Ben cocked his head. "Today bag day?"

Yoshio nodded and took a sip of tea. "Around here, Sunday, Tuesday, and Friday."

"What time does Bennett come?"

"I never stayed to watch."

"What does he look like?"

Yoshio shook his head. "Never met Mr. Bennett."

Ben gave him a puzzled look.

"He signs the receipt . . . Winston Bennett. My niece read it to me once . . ."

"Where is she now?" asked Ben impatiently.

"In school . . . on O'ahu." He beamed broadly. "She is at the University. She is studying aquaculture . . . how to grow food in the sea."

"When will she be back?"

"She visits every month. She was here last Saturday and Sunday. She helped me pick berries. I am very proud of her."

Ben thought for a moment. Then he took out his note pad. "What's her name?"

Yoshio told him.

"You have a phone book?" Ben asked.

Yoshio smiled broadly and hurried into the bedroom. He returned in a flash, his quickness belying his age, and handed Ben a brand-new phone book. After a few moments Ben found Bennett's number.

"Your phone?"

"No phone. Just book."

Ben gave him a frown and Yoshio grinned sheepishly.

With his tongue out, an old habit when he wrote, he copied Bennett's number. Then he thanked Yoshio for the tea and stood to leave, but stopped halfway and sat back down. "Two more questions. Did you live here during the war?"

Yoshio said, "Right here in this house. I was born here."

"If I told you the victim had a number, a five-digit number, tattooed in his armpit, what would you say?"

"I would say you shaved him to find it."

Ben smiled at Yoshio's humor and thought again how this man reminded him of Tobi. They even talked the same—no contractions. Few adjectives. Extra dry wit. "It means nothing to you?"

He shook his head firmly.

Ben thanked him, stood, and turned for the door.

Yoshio got up and cleared his throat. Ben stopped and pivoted. The old man pointed to the folder Ben had tucked under his arm. "Before you leave we go out back and pray for our friend." He got up and headed for the rear door.

Tobi would have requested the same thing. Ben followed the coffee farmer.

Later, he found a pay phone in front of a small general store a few miles farther down Highway 11. He let Bennett's phone ring a dozen times before he hung up. The phone book had listed his address only as Kēōkea, but gave no street name. Ben checked his map. Kēōkea was a small town a few miles north of Keālia. Finding Winston Bennett's house wouldn't be hard.

The house was easy. It was also empty. Bennett wasn't home and the mailbox was stuffed with mail and newspapers. The dwelling was small—three or four rooms at most. To say the dark brown wood siding was weathered was like saying lava was hot. It bowed every few feet and the water stains reminded Ben of the patterns on the handmade tapa garments his grandmother had worn at special ceremonies.

Huge fan palms surrounded the house and a single, thick hibiscus guarded one side of the dirt driveway. Ben stuck one of Jack Cooper's business cards between the screen door and the jamb after writing a short note on the back. He decided to go back to Keālia and wait next to Yoshio's bags of coffee beans.

He made the slow climb from the coast in ten minutes and pulled off to the side of the road a few yards from Yoshio's Friday harvest. He checked his watch. Four-thirty.

As he settled back into his seat, making himself as comfortable in the jeep as he could, Ben closed his eyes and thought about the old coffee farmer who had been washed ashore.

What would a seventy-year-old farmer be doing in a boat at midnight? If most farmers were anything like Yoshio, they would rarely venture into town, let alone go fishing in the middle of the night. Tobi and Jack said there had been a bad storm that night. So someone dumped him at sea. But why? What had he done? What did he know? What did he see? But most important, was he a spy?

Ben's head sank to his chest. He quickly snapped forward and squinted hard, trying to squeeze the tired feeling from his eyes.

Who was he? Why hasn't someone reported him missing? What if he wasn't on a boat? What if he was by the shore and was taken out by the undertow? Why didn't I ask Ken and Tobi about that?

He reached for his radiophone. It was dead. He checked the wires, but none of them were connected. The jeep was brand-new. It didn't matter. His questions could wait. He didn't want to miss Bennett.

Three hours passed. It became dusk. A faint quarter moon—it was *Kāloa Pau,* the twenty-sixth day of the Hawaiian lunar month—hung high in the sky as if it were watching the setting sun from offstage. The bags of coffee berries were still there. A ring of moisture encircled the bottom of each bag. Birds gathered high up in monkeypod trees, squawking madly, passing along the day's gossip.

Yoshio said 'no one misses bag day.' Well, this day someone had—the bag man.

7

TOBI LIVED IN THE SOUTH KOHALA DISTRICT on a small parcel of a vast ranch, a few miles from the intersection of Highway 19, which continued east to Waimea, and Highway 270, which looped around the coast to the Big Island's northernmost town—Hāwī. The view from the front of his property was dominated by the expanse of the Pacific a half mile to the west. The terrain leading to the sea was rough—mainly lava rock covered with wiry grass and scrawny shrubs. And on a clear day, he could see the rugged coastline of southern Maui and much of Haleakalā. Out back was his garden, with a running stream, flowers, and plants representing each of the Hawaiian Islands, a dozen carefully pruned bonsai, and an intricate system of multi-leveled decking. Beyond the lava-rock wall was a grove of eucalyptus about three hundred yards away, and beyond that was the ancient base of Mauna Kea.

Inside, the rich smell of teriyaki filled the kitchen. Vegetables steamed in an odd-looking wicker basket. Next to it, noodles resembling angel-hair pasta, but much darker, squirmed like baby snakes in a pot of boiling water. Strips of range hen simmered in the teriyaki sauce. Soft flute sounds came from another part of the house, classical and soothing, yet Tobi's face was serious, almost to the point of anger. A bottle of Fuji Beer, empty except for a layer of foam on the bottom, sat on the counter, inches from his clenched fist. Usually this was the most relaxing part of the day, when work was many miles away.

Outside, the tropical sun had transformed into a swollen, salmon-colored ball. It was suspended on the western horizon, poised to take its daily plunge into the darkening Pacific. Now, after a hot windy day, the trades were cool and gentle, and the clouds had disappeared from the upper reaches of Mauna Kea, revealing the dormant volcano's immense proportions.

The music stopped and Tobi snapped out of his sullen trance. The tension on his face eased a bit. He flicked off the heat under the noodles, grabbed a gray, insulated mitten, and held the pot over the sink above an aluminum colander and poured. After rinsing the noodles thoroughly, he dumped them into the pan with the strips of chicken. A minute later, he scooped up the pan and slid the chicken and noodles onto his plate. And after shaking the wicker basket so the water that was left fell into the bottom compartment, he added the steamed broccoli, snow peas, and red pepper to his dinner plate.

A minute later, with another cold beer under his arm, he settled onto a thin mat beside his dining table and began to eat, handling the pair of rosewood chopsticks as if they were extensions of his fingers. After tasting a little of each part of his meal, he remembered the music, got up, and exchanged Mozart's flute concerto for George Winston's *Autumn*. He didn't know why, but Mozart seemed to bring out the fury inside him. George Winston, on the other hand, made him feel at ease.

Tobi shook his head and returned to supper.

He sat and ate, pensive, wondering about the identity of the old man with the tattoo under his arm, the unmistakable mark of the Japanese spies who swarmed the Pacific Rim and the Hawaiian Islands during World War II. He knew of no way to trace him, except maybe a call to Tokyo. But to find a man from that long ago—it was almost fifty years since the last of the old school had been so marked—was next to impossible. He thought briefly about today's spies. They were a different breed—more interested in computer technology than military secrets. The Japanese left that for the Russians and the Chinese . . . a grin formed on his lips . . . and the Americans.

The question bothering Tobi was whether the old man's death was related to his past. Tobi had ruled out an accident. No boat was missing and the man wasn't a fisherman. He was a farmer. Tobi leaned back, chewed slowly, and closed his eyes.

Ten months since he had been recalled to the Kona police department. Ten months and no murders. But now there was one.

Like all the male Otakis, Tobi's hair thinned and grayed at an early age. But his smooth, tanned face made him look more like forty than fifty-two. Besides Ben, Tobi was probably in the best shape of any of the Kona cops. Each day, before dinner, he exercised strenuously, all without the aid of weights and machines, applying old martial arts techniques of conditioning. He ended the workout with a three-hundred-yard sprint up the hillside behind his house, stopping only when he reached the thick grove of eucalyptus trees that made up the rear border of his pie-shaped wedge of land.

Breathing deeply, inhaling the soothing herbal smell of the eucalyptus, he would walk back down to his house, anxious for a shower and dinner. Afterwards, he would read a week-old Japanese daily while George Winston or Liz Story played piano.

And each morning there was mental exercise. Waking at dawn, praying in the *heiau* he had painfully reconstructed with the help of an old Hawaiian farmer who was knowledgeable in the history of old temples. Tobi's place of worship had originally been built about 800 A.D. It had been a *heiau ho'oulu ua,* a temple where offerings were made to ensure rain. Sometimes he prayed for rain to fill his catchment barrels and for his running stream. But most times he prayed for wisdom, meditating in a mixture of Japanese and Hawaiian, two cultures that blended very well for him. Making his mind fit, discarding what was unimportant, sorting out and prioritizing what was of consequence. He'd solved many cases sitting before the rising sun, palms outstretched, with his eyes lightly closed.

For some reason, he didn't solve many at night, no matter how much he deliberated. Such was the mystery of his *heiau*. So now he couldn't wait for morning.

Tobi's single-story ranch house, which he built himself without the aid of nails or screws—just pure Japanese joinery, was set on a gentle slope near the southwest corner of the famous Parker Ranch. Cowboys right in his backyard. Inside, his home was not unlike the one Ben had visited earlier in the day, but more richly appointed—to Tobi it meant he had more junk. It was divided by rice-paper partitions inset into *koa*-wood frames. The delicate paper was decorated with small hand-painted letters and scenery of Japan—cranes and cattails, delicate flowers and colorful fish, and majestic mountains with snow-covered peaks.

In the left rear was the kitchen, simple yet contemporary. The front half of the house was a living room with low wooden furniture and hand-made shelves that held vases of dried flowers, other pieces of carefully chosen pottery, and many books and stacks of Japanese newspapers. Scores of awkwardly molded candles were scattered throughout, as was the lingering smell of incense. There was no television, but a new stereo receiver and CD player, and a Nakamichi police receiver. Propped in one corner of the main living area was a fifty-year-old hand-carved guitar, a gift from his father, who had taught him how to play slack key when he was a small boy. Tobi was a fan of the late Gabby Pahinui, one of Hawai'i's greatest slack-key guitarists.

The bedroom, in the right rear quarter, was simple as well. His bed, a sandalwood frame, was only four inches high, joined to a two-inch pedestal hidden from view. Floating. A gray and maroon comforter was neatly folded at the base of the bed. No pillows, just a silk sheet folded again and again until it was about two feet square, but only an inch high. A low sandalwood chest of drawers and a matching night table. A doorway in the rear of the room led to a long, narrow bathroom, traditional in the American sense, except for its spotless condition. Natural light filtered down from a curved bubble skylight in the center of the ceiling.

Keʻo, a white nightingale, began to sing. Tobi opened his eyes and smiled.

"You like George Winston, little fellow?"

Keʻo stopped at the sound of Tobi's voice and cocked his head, an inquisitive expression feathered into his small face.

"We have an unidentified victim, Keʻo." The nightingale hopped from the low perch to the higher one.

Tobi got up and carried his plate into the kitchen. He rinsed it and left it in the sink. Back in the living area he stood by Keʻo's cage and gently rubbed the feathers around the bird's neck. Keʻo titled its head to one side and closed its eyes. After a few minutes, Tobi sighed and went outside, into his garden behind the house. He sat on the edge of the main deck, facing west, watching the sun slide into the cobalt water.

What do we have? A man of Japanese descent. Eight to twelve hours in the water. No lower legs. No left arm. Right hand missing. Coffee bean and macadamia nut oil residues engrained into his skin from his wrist to his elbow. A hand laborer, a picker. Did he work for someone? Then someone will report him missing. Was it his farm? One of those old farmers with a few acres who keep to themselves? I suppose a neighbor would notice the lack of activity and report something. But not if he lived adjacent to a marijuana grower. They don't report anything to the police. One might even have killed him.

As the sun made its last appearance of the day, Tobi closed his eyes, hardly breathing, and visualized the tattoo. 5–0–5–7–3.

Maybe it was a date. May fifth . . . seventy-three. Tobi shook his head. He was kidding himself. The man was a spy. And if he was about seventy-five when he died, that would make him twenty-five in 1940, when Japanese spies literally crawled over the Islands, especially Oʻahu. In the morning he'd make a call to Tokyo. Maybe someone there would have an idea how to track down the mystery man. Maybe, in the mean time, Ben's search of coffee country would surrender a clue.

It got dark almost immediately, but Tobi stayed for another twenty minutes, until the cool night winds gave him a chill, and he retreated inside for a cup of tea. And then a prayer for his ancestors before retiring.

$\mathcal{8}$

THE PHONE RANG AS HE WAS CLEANING UP the breakfast dishes. Tobi wiped his hands and squinted through the sunlight filtering into his kitchen. The wall clock said six. Too early for good news. Good news could have waited until he arrived at work in forty-five minutes.

"Hello?"

It was Jack Cooper. "Tobi, we've got a report of a body."

"Where?"

"Nāpo'opo'o."

"What can you tell me?"

"Nothing yet. We just got the call five minutes ago."

"You go out. I will meet you in an hour."

It hit Tobi right away. Coffee country. Ben!

———

The coffee farm where the latest victim had been discovered was buried amidst the hills on a soil-rich plateau a few miles to the north of Yoshio's farm. Two squad cars were banked next to a row of guava shrubs. Two others, a maroon Trans Am, which was Jack Cooper's, and a white Kona Hospital station wagon, were parked along the dirt driveway. A center strip of tall grass covered both cars' rear bumpers. The station wagon had a small embossed sign attached to the driver's door: **Kona Pathologist.**

Tobi got out and walked past the parked cars, turning sideways to fit through the narrow opening between the Trans Am and the overgrowth of trees. A small farmhouse was visible off to the left. Huddled in front of it were three Japanese men. One seemed to be about Tobi's age and size. The other two, Tobi presumed, were the sons. They were all clearly agitated. Jack Cooper was talking to the father, but stopped as the father's head turned when he heard Tobi approaching. Tobi spotted the forensic team near the side of the house. They were taking plaster castings. He thought—*at least there are some clues.*

He greeted Jack with a grim face, but soon relaxed his mouth a bit when he realized from Jack's expression that the victim wasn't Ben. Up until then, he hadn't ruled it out, although he had tried not to think about it while driving down.

Jack wet his lips. "Captain, this is Tadao Fukada," his head then tilted toward the two young men, "and his two sons. The youngest," he pointed to the boy on the left, "found the victim."

Tobi bowed to the father, then walked over to the adolescent son, and put his arm around his shoulder. "Are you okay, young man?"

The boy nodded hesitantly.

Tobi gave him a fatherly smile. "I am Tobi Otaki. Tell me how you found him."

The boy swallowed. "I was picking berries. I saw his legs. I thought it was my brother resting." He smiled nervously. "He's lazy."

His brother gave him a nasty look and then turned away from his father's corner-of-the-eyes gaze.

"Go on," urged Tobi.

"I went to wake him . . . then I saw it was a stranger . . . then I saw the ring of blood around his neck. I ran to get my father." The boy's chest was still heaving like he'd just run a great distance, but it was his anxiety.

"None of you ever saw him before?"

They all shook their heads.

"What is your name?" The younger boy answered, "Kiyoshi."

"What time did you find him, Kiyoshi?"

"Right away. We started at five-thirty. We have school."

"And neither of you," Tobi eyes included the older boy, "heard anything?"

They hadn't.

The father spoke for the first time. "They are late. Can they go?"

Tobi nodded slowly. "Please do not talk to anyone about this. Not until I tell you it is okay."

The two boys nodded in agreement and walked away briskly, talking softly to each other. Tobi caught one phrase, ' . . . not lazy!'

"Mr. Fukada, do you have anything to add?"

"Tadao." He bowed. "No, I did not see anything or hear anything until my boy came to get me."

Tobi turned to Jack. "Do you have the old man's picture?"

"Right here." He handed it to Tobi.

Tobi put his left hand on Tadao's shoulder and handed him the photo. "It is not a pretty sight, but this man washed up near Kealakekua Bay a few days ago. Do you recognize him."

Tadao looked closely at the photo. "His face is so swollen." He squinted. "It is hard to tell, but I think no."

"Thank you." Tobi bowed.

The father bowed.

Tobi could see a question forming on Tadao's lips. "Yes?"

"Are these two men . . ." He didn't seem able to finish.

"That is what we have to find out . . . if they are connected."

They exchanged bows once more.

Jack said he was going to talk to the forensic team. Tobi went to view the body and told Tadao he'd be back in a few minutes.

The corpse was still perched against a macadamia nut tree. The man's head was hanging low and to one side. His eyes bulged. His mouth was open and his tongue impaled on his upper teeth. He'd bitten through it.

Contrary to the rest of the scene, his hands were clasped peacefully in his lap. The amount of blood was staggering. Most was dried, but some near the gaping slit in his neck appeared wet and somewhat shiny. To a degree, the cool mountain air and early morning moisture partly accounted for that. But mostly, it was because the man hadn't been dead very long. Tobi guessed a few hours at most.

The victim was Japanese, seemed to be mid- to late twenties. He was trim and his black hair was close-cropped. Tobi bent to one knee and studied the victim's face. Death's last expression always was revealing to him. If it was terror, the victim probably didn't know his killer. Shock or disbelief—they knew each other. This man's facial muscles were drawn back in shock.

Ken Asumura appeared. He blew out a deep breath.

Without turning around, Tobi addressed him. "What can you tell me, Ken?"

The pathologist knelt next to Tobi. "The blade of the weapon was heavy and extremely sharp. It severed everything. His head is barely attached."

"A sword?"

"That or machete."

"Any ID?"

Ken stood. Tobi followed suit.

"Nothing. If this one isn't a professional job, I'll resign. The labels on his clothes are missing but most important, did you notice his fingertips?"

Tobi gave him an inquisitive stare and then examined the man's hands, carefully lifting the man's light blue work-shirt by one cuff then the other. There was blood on every finger and both thumbs.

"The tips of his fingers have been shaved off. No prints."

Tobi cleared his throat. An empty feeling crept into his stomach. He stood and asked, "It tells us we could have identified him by his fingerprints."

"One would assume so."

"Any scars?"

Ken raised his eyebrows and shook his head. "None clearly visible."

"Any sign of the same residues we found on the old man?"

"No, but I'll have to do a few tests to be certain."

"Time of death?"

Ken pursed his lips. "Only a few hours ago . . . no more than four."

"Okay. Thanks. I will be at headquarters."

"You think they're connected?"

"Just like the Dagdag case . . . there are so few murders on the Big Island that when two happen so close together you must assume they are connected. And here, both were Japanese, both with some tie to coffee farms. They are connected."

"I'm all done here. I'll call later."

Ken turned and took two steps. But suddenly he stopped.

Tobi smiled, knowing that Ken instinctively knew there'd be more. "Oh, Ken."

The pathologist turned his head.

Tobi looked up at the sky and watched a hawk circling. Then he looked at the medical man. "Shave his armpits."

Ken gave him a broad grin. "I'll shave him from head to toe."

Tobi leaned against a coffee tree with his back to the victim. For awhile he watched Jack talking to a member of the forensic team. Then he reflected back on his early morning meditation. Nothing came to him. He added this second man to what he knew about the first man, and still, nothing magically materialized. Only the certainty that they were somehow connected. *How? Were these two men related? Were all the workers on one farm murdered? Have we only found the first two?*

Jack approached, interrupting Tobi's thoughts. "Nothing much except the footprints. Cowboy boots."

Tobi's eyes narrowed. He pursed his lips. "Cowboy boots?"

"There's boot prints all over. Forensic guesses the murderer wasn't too heavy. The earth is soft but the heel print only goes in about a quarter inch."

Tobi rubbed his chin. "Parker Ranch?"

"Maybe, but we're a long way from Waimea. I asked Fukada if many of the farmers around here wore boots. He said a few."

A door slammed. They both turned around. Ben was heading toward them, walking briskly, eyes darting back and forth as he sized up the scene. He stopped five paces away. Suddenly, there was complete silence. The birds were hushed in the trees. The hawk had disappeared. The trades stopped blowing and the sun edged behind a cloud. All three of them shivered, sharing an eerie feeling.

Finally, Ben spoke. "Another coffee farmer?" He rested his hands on his hips.

Tobi folded his arms across his chest and rocked slowly on his heels. "This one may not be a farmer."

"This can't be another serial killer, can it?"

Tobi bit his lip, thinking. "I think not. Not a serial, anyhow. But there are two connections." He swept with his right hand. "Coffee." He paused. "And both were Japanese. Too say nothing of the timing . . . they are only days apart."

Jack copied Tobi's stance. "Maybe there's some sort of feud goin' on. Maybe there's a fight over some land."

Tobi shook his head. "I do not think so. The families up here have lived together for generations. They are friends. Their fathers, grand-fathers, and great grandfathers were friends. They do not fight with each other. It is an outsider."

Jack said to Ben, "There are cowboy boot prints all over."

Ben thought about it for a few seconds. He looked up. The movement of the hawk caught his eye. It had reappeared. Then he looked at both men. "Maybe it's one of the marijuana growers. Yesterday, when I stopped at Mitchell's for lunch, Danny warned me to be careful snooping around up here. You think maybe something has happened between the coffee farmers and them?"

"These farmers keep to themselves," said Tobi. "The only reported trouble with the marijuana growers has been hiking tourists who stumble upon one of the weed fields. Once, maybe ten years ago, there was a murder . . . I cannot remember about what . . . but mostly they just run people off with angry shouts or a raised shotgun."

A moment's silence.

"Who found him?" asked Ben.

Jack answered. "One of the sons. I don't think there's much more to get out of him."

Ben pointed to Tadao Fukada who was leaning against a porch support, watching them in earnest. "That the father?"

Tobi said, "It is his farm. He knows nothing except what his son told him."

"Let's have a look around." Ben started for the farmhouse.

Tadao Fukada eyed them closely as they approached. His left foot pawed nervously at the ground. With his faded, stitched-up outfit, close-cropped hair, and dirty face, he looked like a refugee.

Ben extended his hand. Fukada bowed.

Ben had the brown folder tucked under his left arm. He reached for it and started to open it.

"We already showed him a copy," said Jack.

Ben put it away. "Can we look around inside?"

Fukada gave him a puzzled look. "No one came inside."

"I know, but something inside may tell us why they chose your farm. It'll only take a few minutes. And we won't disturb anything."

"I have very little."

Ben didn't comment.

Tobi and Jack followed him inside.

The farmhouse was one large room, divided by rice-paper walls, similar to the farmhouse Ben had visited the day before. Except this one had no personality. In that respect it matched the owner. The walls were bare—no artwork—and the kitchen contained only a few cooking utensils. The inventory took only a matter of minutes. Tadao confirmed nothing was missing.

Now they stood outside. Ben's hands were back on his hips. He turned and faced Tadao. "Do you know a man named Winston Bennett?"

The farmer nodded.

"Do you know what he looks like?"

He made a big circle with his arms. "Heavy man. Tall. He smokes a pipe."

"How tall?"

The farmer shrugged.

"Taller than me?"

"Yes. Much." Then Tadao placed his palms six inches apart. "This much."

"What about his face?"

"It is round and red and he is . . . he is . . ." Fukada was struggling for the right word. Finally, he turned to Tobi for help and said, "*Hageta.*"

"Bald," interpreted Tobi.

"And a red . . ." Tadao patted his upper lip with his fingers.

"Mustache?" Ben concluded.

Tadao nodded.

Ben asked, "When was the last time you saw him?"

He swept his arm in a semicircle above his head. "A few weeks ago . . . down by the road."

"Don't talk about this."

Tadao bowed.

Ben did as well, but abruptly.

They were near the mac nut tree that supported the body.

"Who is Bennett?" asked Jack.

"He picks up the coffee beans. They call him the bagman. There are five or six mills from here to Pāpā. I think he works for one around here . . . but I haven't had time to check it out. I figured he might know most of the farmers and could identify the old man. But a funny thing. He wasn't at home and not all the coffee bags were picked up yesterday. Judging by his mailbox . . . he hasn't been home in some time."

Jack asked, "You don't suppose he's met up with some trouble as well?"

"I'm going to head out there after this."

Tobi was thinking, but not talking.

Ben stared at him. He guessed Tobi was wondering about the same thing.

Was Bennett the killer?

They walked around for twenty minutes, looking for signs of activity. Other than the cowboy boot prints, they found nothing.

As they stood next to their vehicles, about to part, Ben agreed to check in around three. He was going after the bagman. Tobi had some other business and Jack promised to get with the Hilo District to see if its computers could make other connections between the two victims.

Then Ben climbed aboard his jeep, turned the ignition key, and let out the clutch. After he had gone forward no more than twenty feet, he stopped short and stuck his head out the window.

He yelled back. "Tobi. Have Ken check his armpits."

"Good idea." Tobi winked and waved.

9

BEN TURNED OFF HIGHWAY 11 and headed toward the water. A half a mile from the roadway, along a steep, twisting road, was one of the coffee mills. It sat on a bluff surrounded by dense foliage on three sides. The rear of the old structure overlooked the southern end of Kealakekua Bay. In the distance were several small houses, surrounded by rows of coffee trees. Deep green, shiny leaves loaded with burgundy berries.

Ben was beginning to think that this place might tie everything together. It was near Fukada's farm. It was close to where the body had washed up. He thought maybe the first victim hadn't started out at sea. Maybe he had been dumped in the bay at low tide—even from behind the mill. Then swept out a few miles and propelled back in when the tide turned, as last Sunday's storm had gained intensity.

He sighed. Then again—maybe it was a long shot.

The building was tall—three stories high. Vertical boards of weathered *koa* ran all the way up to the corrugated metal roof, some planks more than thirty feet long. On the northern side of the mill, tons of light brown beans, spread across large mesh screens, dried in the Kona sun. There was a beat-up pickup truck parked near the side door. Old. Very old. Early sixties. He thought the paint looked red, but it was hard to tell. The hauling bed was stacked with 100-pound bags of coffee berries. The driver's side door was badly smashed. There was a crack in the windshield that snaked across the surface, resembling a bolt of lightening. Farther back, there was a rusted flat-bed truck. It looked like it had been abandoned during World War II, except the oil stains on the hood looked fresh. The license plate was covered with dried red dirt.

Overhead, smoke filtered slowly from a round metal chimney, but there was no other sign of activity.

Then Ben picked it up. Someone was whistling. He walked up a dirt grade that ended in front of a pair of huge barn doors. They were open, secured by rope loops knotted through eye-rings attached to the structure itself. The whistling came from within.

It was dark inside except for a half dozen exposed bulbs hanging high overhead. Near the beams, where they were strung, they were brilliant, but the area near the floor was almost black. Then the stench hit him. He expected the aroma of fresh-ground coffee. A glance left, out the back door revealed the source—a huge pile of berry skins that had been removed by a pulping machine. Rotting in the sun, the mound smelled like a mixture of manure and vomit. He held his breath.

The whistling stopped and a voice called out.

"Over here, young feller."

Ben smiled and walked slowly toward the man, wishing his eyes would speed their adjustment. He almost bumped into the whistler.

"Whoa, there. Let's not run me over." The man laughed. His voice had a southwestern twang and sounded raspy.

"Sorry." There was a moment of silence. "I'm Ben McMillen . . . Kona detective."

There was a hesitation Ben could sense, then, "Howdy. Pleased ta meetcha." The man raised his hand—a half-hearted wave—instead of offering it.

"Can we go outside and talk." Ben desperately needed fresh air. When the man opened his mouth, Ben saw his teeth. In the dim light he wasn't sure if the man was grinning or sneering.

A small chortle escaped from the whistler's mouth. "Sure 'nuf."

Outside again, it took Ben's eyes a few seconds to reverse their adjustment.

The man had the same trouble. He headed for the shade of a leaning ironwood tree. Ben followed, rubbing his eyes, taking time to think about his questions.

When he could see, Ben began studying the skinny, dark-skinned man. He wasn't sure if what he saw was natural coloring or stains from coffee. The man was only about five-five, but his shoulders and arms were muscled, and veins bulged from his skin. He was wearing a well-worn, medium-blue T-shirt rolled up to the elbows, faded jeans, a straw cowboy hat, and cowboy boots. Ben stared for a few seconds at the man's feet. Easily under a hundred and forty pounds, this man's boot print wouldn't be deep. When he looked up, he saw the man's tattoo. It appeared to be a pair of snakes. But Ben dismissed the tattoo after thinking about it for a few seconds. Actually, if the man hadn't had a tattoo, then Ben would have been suspicious. This man seemed to be the tattoo type. The type who has a few swigs of warm Southern Comfort before he goes out, and dabs a few drops behind his ears.

Suddenly the man seemed friendly. He extended his hand. "Jeremiah Furbee. People call me Jay."

Ben shook his hand, then spied a log close by, walked over, and sat. Furbee followed Ben's lead.

Ben took out the photo of the old man and gave it to Furbee. "Recognize him?"

Furbee studied the photo, squinting after awhile, but eventually shook his head and handed it back. "Dead, huh?"

Ben nodded. "The pathologist found residues of coffee berries and mac nuts on the man's arms. We assume he owned or worked on a coffee farm."

"Probably did, I reckon. But there's hundreds of 'em . . . from here to where the highway turns east."

"That's why I thought checking the mills would be better," said Ben.

" 'Cept he looks Japanese. Us millers don't see mucha them guys. They do things the old way . . . jest leave their bags by the side of the road." He looked over his shoulder at the dilapidated mill. His gaze returned. A sour expression filled his face. "Used to be they all was Japanese . . . and maybe a few Chinese. Now there's only a few left. Down south . . . try there. That's where all the Japanese farmers are. They keep to themselves."

"Do you know a man named Winston Bennett?"

"Yep, sure do. Say," he drawled, "ya know, he's missin' . . . come ta think of it."

"Missing?"

"Worked these parts over thirty years. Never missed a day durin' my time. But he missed yesterday. He's missing. I hadda take the swamper around myself. Damn pissed about it, too."

Ben furrowed his brow and narrowed his eyes. "Come to think of it?"

Furbee shrugged. "Hadn't thought much about it . . . 'till you asked."

"But he was here the day before?"

"Huh?"

"When was the last time you saw him?"

"Last Tuesday. Bag day for us is Tuesday and Friday."

"I thought you said only the Japanese farmers leave their bags by the side of the road?"

"Yep, that's right. But the others, we drive right up to the farmhouse. Those are the people I know. The Japanese are from Bennett's old days . . . old customers of his. I'm told he used to be a broker, but he got tanked too often and got canned. Now he just drives the swamper," he gestured in the direction of the rusted flat-bed, "and helps around here."

"You don't have a list of the Japanese farmers?"

"Nope." He pointed to his head. "In Bennett's head." He took out a blue bandana and wiped his brow. "But, I'll tell ya something, those guys are good pickers. They do four bags a day. Most of the others do two, maybe three. Better beans, too. Them Japanese take care of their trees. They prune 'em some special way."

"Bennett married?"

Furbee's eyes watered and he started shaking. "Damn! That's a good one. Shit, he drinks. Snores. Must weigh two-fifty. The only thing he doesn't do is bathe."

"Any friends? Somebody he hangs around with?"

More laughter. "Weren't you listenin'? I said he doesn't bathe. Who'd hang with 'im?"

"What about you? What do you do?"

"Sheeeit, son . . . I work the damn mill. Since '76. Ain't made a dime yet, but who's countin'?" He grinned. His teeth that had appeared white in the dark mill clearly showed brown tobacco stains in the sunlight.

Ben decided on another approach.

"You see any strangers around in the last week?"

"Nope."

This was going nowhere. Ben's eyes narrowed. "What about the marijuana farmers?"

The man's smile disappeared.

"What about them?" Furbee asked warily.

"Anything unusual happening? Any in-fighting . . . that sort of thing?"

Furbee stood. "Don't know nuthin' 'bout anything illegal. If yer done, I got work to do."

Ben eyed him for a few seconds, then handed him a card. "If Bennett shows up, have him call me."

Furbee took the card without comment and hustled off.

Ben watched him retreat. As Furbee disappeared inside, Ben saw him crumple the card and throw it into an old oil drum.

While swinging the jeep around, Ben memorized the pickup truck's license number. The miller was hiding something. Ben's mind raced, thinking about the marijuana farmers. Wondering what they were really like. Pondering if he had just met one.

He checked his watch. It was almost ten. When he was out of sight, he pulled onto a rutted side road, overgrown with ferns and tall grass, and stopped. First, he jotted down the license number before he forgot it. Then he waited ten minutes, expecting, or at least hoping, that Furbee would come zooming by, panic on his face. But it didn't happen. Finally, at ten-twenty, Ben gave the steering wheel a frustrated jab with the side of his clenched fist, started the engine, and drove away.

He guessed it would take three or four hours to check out the rest of the mills. He needed to ID the old man before he spent much more time on Furbee. But someone else could be checking him out now. So when he made the highway and was heading south, he reached for his radio-phone. He halted mid-way. He'd forgotten it wasn't connected. He made a mental note to have it installed as soon as he got back to headquarters. Then with one hand one the wheel, he jotted down *radio* so he wouldn't forget again.

––––––––––––

Since Bennett's house was on the way to the second mill, Ben decided to stop by. The small cottage looked the same as it had the day before with the addition of one more newspaper jammed into the mailbox. The card he'd left was still wedged between the front door and the frame. This time, when Ben got out, he spent some time walking around the house. The yard was overgrown with weeds and wildflowers. Nothing in the backyard revealed recent activity. For all he knew, Bennett hadn't been there in months. Except Furbee saw Bennett on Tuesday, or at least that's what he said. A small enclosed porch caught his eye. The screen door was warped and partially open. Ben walked over, gave it a yank, and was about to step inside when a big yellow cat came running out. It brushed Ben's leg and darted into the bushes behind the house. He turned and gave it a nervous smile.

Inside the porch he found a water dish, stacks of old newspapers, and a deep-sea fishing rod stashed in one corner. He walked over to the back door, held the handle for a few seconds, and twisted. The door wasn't locked. He swung it open, stepped inside, and found himself in the kitchen. He called out Bennett's name—somehow that made it less like an illegal search.

It was warm inside and musty smelling. Because of Furbee's description of Bennett, he expected a mess, but the kitchen was spotless. Nothing on the counters, save one glass mug. No dirty dishes in the sink and the floor had been recently waxed. The other rooms were a different story. Drawers were open, clothes thrown about. The bedroom closet was open and more clothes were heaped inside, on the floor. Ben had never seen so many pairs of shoes. His practiced eye quickly discerned that the place hadn't been ransacked. But someone *had* left in a hurry. Either Winston Bennett had a sudden urge to go on vacation, or he was on the run.

In the living room was a small desk. On top were letters and bills. The bills were the normal ones. Phone. Sears. Hawai'i Electric Light Company. The letters—there were two—both from London, England, and from the same woman. Postmarks a month apart. The most recent was two weeks old. He read them both. They were from an aunt, so it seemed. And they held no clue as to Bennett's sudden disappearance. Ben refolded them and replaced them in their envelopes. One he put back. The other, the one with the most current postmark, he stuffed into his pocket. Then he stared at the desk. Both drawers were locked—a credit card opened them in a second. Nothing but financial records. Mortgage, a loan from First Hawaiian, a Sears charge card purple from the carbons. What was more important was what was missing. There was no appointment book. And there was nothing business related. No list of coffee farmers. No receipts. Not even a paycheck stub from the mill.

Before he left, he found a small paper bag and carefully picked up the unwashed mug by the sink, pressing his thumb and forefinger against the inside of the glass. Gingerly, he dropped it into the bag. No harm having it checked for prints. As he was about to close the door, he spied the wall phone and was tempted to call headquarters. But he decided against it. He had entered illegally—not that it was a big deal—but he figured it was best not to use Bennett's phone and leave proof that someone had made a call when Bennett was away.

The cat was back in the porch lapping water, no longer afraid of the stranger. Ben bent and stroked its neck a few times. The cat closed its eyes and arched its back, claws sinking into the cheap oval rug that covered most of the porch. Ben stood, said 'good-bye' to the cat and then headed for the jeep, thinking about the cat's water. Thinking Bennett hadn't been gone too long. Or that the porch roof leaked and the cat was smart enough to push his dish underneath.

The second mill on his list was near Yee Hop Ranch, five miles south of Bennett's house and about three miles inland along a bumpy road that paralleled the path of the 1950 lava flow. There were three men working the mill. Ben told them he was a Kona detective. No one recognized the old man in the photo. Ben decided, as he had before with Jeremiah Furbee, not to discuss the murdered man they had found earlier that morning. He wanted a few more facts before he started asking questions on that one. He did ask about Winston Bennett. All three men knew him.

The foreman of the mill—a Spanish-looking man around forty, six feet tall, with a Maui Lager midriff—remarked, "You mean that old drunk? Yeah, I know him. Other than bein' a loud-mouthed sunnufabitch, he's okay. Why ya wanna know?"

Ben explained that he thought Bennett might be able to identify the man in the photo. Then he told them that Bennett missed bag day.

The three men exchanged puzzled glances.

The foreman said in a quieter tone, "You don't think anything happened to him, do ya? I was only kidding about him being loud-mouthed. . . . All in all, he's a good guy. Look, he never missed a day of work in his life. Hung-over, maybe, but he always showed up. Always full of funny stories."

Ben shrugged his shoulders. At the same time he was wondering why Furbee made Bennett sound friendless. "What about this guy Furbee that he works for?"

Glances again, although this time their eyes clearly showed contempt.

Ben pressed. "What do you know about him?"

The foreman glared at Ben. The other two men stared nervously at the ground.

"Well?"

"He's hardly a coffee miller. Were you there? Did you see that place? It's gonna fall down one of these days. . . . Maybe he'll be inside when it does."

Ben's tongue was between his lips in his 'think-how-to-ask-it' pose. "If he's not a miller, what is he?" The foreman shook his head.

Ben deliberated for a moment, then he stared at the other two. The taller one looked up. "We gotta get back to work." With that, they all walked away briskly, with their hands in their pockets.

Ben cleared his throat. "Kona Gold?"

They all stopped dead and turned. The foreman's lips stiffened and he nodded once.

"Are you afraid of him?"

Just stares.

"Maybe of someone he works for?"

The foreman's expression gave him his answer. Ben eased up, knowing that nothing more was to be said. He handed the man Jack's card. "Call this number if you see Bennett."

Grim-faced, the foreman gave Ben another nod.

Coming out of the hills, he headed south once again. Almost immediately, he spotted a Hawaiian historical marker. The yellow, brown, and red sign featuring a helmeted warrior designated the road as Māmalahoa Highway. Ben smiled to himself. *Fuck the Belt Road! Highway 11 has a name.* Speeding by, he promised himself to look her up—assuming 'Mama' was a woman.

He was right about Furbee. He'd have the Kona Gold Boys—Jack Cooper called them the KGB—on Furbee as soon as he got back to headquarters. Next stop, 'Ōhi'a Mill, another four miles.

The sun was just short of its apex, but high enough in the sky to clear the trees that bordered the *mauka* side of the road. It suddenly felt hot and muggy, making it hard to concentrate. Ben was wondering about Winston Bennett. What was his connection? Why had he disappeared in the midst of two deaths? But in his mind Bennett had switched sides. From potential murderer to potential victim.

At ʻŌhiʻa Mill he found a little more activity than at the other two mills. He questioned everyone but no one recognized the old Japanese man in the photo. They reaffirmed what the first farmer, Fukada, and Furbee had told him. The Japanese farmers kept to themselves. They handled bag drops as if they were numbers runners. You made your delivery and headed back to your farm, minding your own business.

This time Ben remembered to ask for a phone, half expecting that there would be none, but he was directed to a small, dark office in the rear of the mill. The phone, a black, outdated rotary-dial model, was greasy with coffee residue, and its fabric cord was badly frayed. But it worked.

He hadn't seen an old rotary for some time. For some reason it brought him back to his home when he was a boy. There it sat. In the kitchen on a countertop that served as his mother's desk. He smiled and savored the moment. He hadn't thought about home, or about his parents, in a long time. When he thought about family, he usually focused on his grandmother.

His memory was interrupted as he misdialed twice. While he listened to the ringing on the other end, he visualized his grandmother sitting in the kitchen, making dinner, pounding taro into *poi* in an ancient calabash, snubbing the modern conveniences that surrounded her. God knows where she found taro in southern California. Suddenly, his thoughts shifted. He saw the old Japanese farmer being thrown from a boat. He saw sharks circling and the boat speeding away.

Who would want to kill an old Japanese coffee farmer? No one. Who would want to kill an old Japanese spy? Many.

Was his grandmother trying to tell him something? Hadn't one of her 'aumākua—she had had two—been the shark? He remembered the story that a shark, a mako he thought, had saved her grandfather's life. He'd fallen overboard while fishing. Sharks closed in. Gray reef and blues. A mako—*manō hae,* a fierce fighter—appeared and swam circles around him, creating a whirlpool, a barrier between him and the other sharks. Gradually, the mako headed for shore until her grandfather could escape. Only then did the mako turn and chase the other sharks away.

Was the old man not saved because he was a spy?

A male voice answered.

Ben cleared his throat before he could speak. The officer on the other end repeated his 'hello.' Ben asked for Joyce Ah Sing, the detectives' secretary. She picked up after a single ring.

"Joyce. It's Ben."

"Hi. I'm about to go for lunch, what's up?"

"When you get back, can you get a rundown on a Winston Bennett for me? He lives in Hoʻokena."

"Sure."

Ben could hear her scribbling something down. "Is Jack there?"

"No."

"What about Tobi?"

She transferred his call.

A few moments later, Tobi picked up. "How is it going?"

"I don't have much," said Ben. "I've been to two mills. No one recognizes the old man. People know Bennett, but not where he is. His disappearance is a bit strange. Seems he hasn't missed a day of work in years." He decided not to tell Tobi about his illegal entry into Bennett's home. That was better done in person, when Tobi could see his sheepish grin.

"Where are you?"

"ʻŌhiʻa Mill. On my way to Koa Mill. It's not far from here, but you know these back roads."

Tobi chuckled.

"Tobi . . . one more thing. There's this guy Jeremiah Furbee. Works at Nāpoʻopoʻo Mill. A few people I questioned led me to believe he's into marijuana. I've got a plate number."

"Go ahead," said Tobi.

"N-H-H-4-4-5. It's an old Ford pickup. Hard to tell what color. Used to be red, I think."

"Got it."

"Have the KGB check him out." Ben could picture Tobi's frown. He didn't like the nickname. "The other thing is that he was wearing cowboy boots and he's kind of runty."

"Your English is improving," joked Tobi.

"How's diminutive sound?"

"Better."

"Anyway, Forensic might want to take a few plaster casts."

"Okay."

"Tell them to approach carefully. He was the only one there when I went . . . but it wouldn't surprise me if he has a shotgun handy."

"Okay."

"Anything from Ken on the second guy?"

"Nothing that helps," Tobi answered. "No coffee or macadamia residue. I doubt the guy was a farmer. In fact, his hands were pretty soft . . . hardly any callouses."

"Tobi, do you think there's any connection between the coffee farmers and the marijuana growers like Jack suggested . . . like a feud of some sort?"

"I can find out."

"How?" asked Ben.

"Every drug operation has a kingpin, even here. I'll talk to her."

"Her?"

"Her." Tobi hung up.

Ben's puzzled face stared at the phone. Out loud—"You know her?" *Her?*

Koa Mill was boarded up. It looked like it had been shut down for a long time.

It was almost five o'clock when Ben reached Headquarters. As he headed for the side entrance he checked off three cars. Jack Cooper's, Tobi's, and the Major's. It was meeting time.

After a stop in the bathroom, and then to the Evidence Clerk's office where he dropped off the glass and letter, he headed for Major Serrao's office. As he approached he could smell the Major's cigar and he could visualize Tobi's discomfort. He chuckled to himself, picturing Tobi's prune face—upturned nose, wrinkled brow, and narrow eyes almost closed.

They acknowledged Ben's entrance with expectant stares. Ben gave them an innocent look. "Sorry, guys. No miracles."

"What have you got?" asked Serrao.

"Not much." He relayed what had happened at each of his stops. He saved Winston Bennett's house and his quick survey for last.

Tobi shifted his chair, trying to dodge the inescapable cigar smoke. "You broke into Bennett's house?"

"The back door was open," he answered with a guilty grin.

Tobi nodded, annoyed. Serrao said nothing.

"He left in a hurry. Or someone forced him to leave. I've got Joyce checking him out and I hope I have his prints on a glass . . . plus a letter from an aunt. Don't know what that'll reveal, but who knows?"

Serrao nodded. Jack sat quietly, staring out the window.

"I sent Forensic out to Nāpoʻopoʻo," said Tobi. "They reported back an hour ago. No one was there. They were going to wait another fifteen minutes, have a look around, and lift the boot prints. I sent two officers with them . . . just in case."

"Okay, gentlemen," said Serrao. "Any ideas?"

Ben looked at Tobi. Tobi signaled him to go ahead. Out of the corner of his eye, Ben caught Jack Cooper's hulking frame. Slouched in the corner on the Major's couch, Jack's mind seemed elsewhere. His head alternated from resting on his chest to jerking up. Resting was winning.

"He was murdered," stated Ben, arms outstretched for emphasis. "From what I've seen up in the hills, those farmers' lives are bounded by their property lines. They're as unassuming as they come."

"But ours was a spy," reminded Tobi.

"Right . . . I was getting to that. By the way . . . anything on the tattoo?"

"Not yet. That one may take some time. Chances are we will end up with nothing."

Ben continued. "Being a spy means he's much more likely to have been involved in something illegal . . . something that got him killed. Maybe there's a connection with the marijuana farmers. This guy Furbee makes me think that. That's one angle and we'll check it out. But since our mystery man *was* a World War II spy, who's to say that hiding in the hills, playing the role of a small coffee farmer, isn't a perfect cover? I don't think it's coincidence that an old spy washed up onto the beach. Old spies have something to hide until the day they die." He paused for effect. "We've got two possibilities, here. Two very different ones. One is drugs. The other is espionage."

Serrao relighted his cigar. Tobi coughed. Serrao gave him a frown, looked at the cigar, and reluctantly placed it in his ashtray. He pushed around the ashes for a few seconds before letting it go. "Okay, Ben. Tell me what a seventy-year-old spy spies on, and tell me where the second guy fits in."

"The second guy's a new spy, one from the nineties, without a tattoo. The old guy didn't retire at the end of the war. He's smart, knows the Pacific like the back of his hand. Maybe he's a key link in the network. We live at the crossroads of the Pacific. There must be hundreds of things worth spying on." Ben sat back in his chair and folded his arms across his chest. When he felt Tobi's penetrating eyes, Ben relaxed a bit and placed his hands on his knees and gave them both a shrug. "Tell me something better."

Tobi smiled. "The old man went fishing in a small, unregistered boat, one too small for the high surf. He was swept overboard. The man we found at Fukada's farm buys Kona Gold, got into an argument with the marijuana growers, and they took him to a coffee farm . . . to cover it up . . . and murdered him."

Ben countered, "That makes them unconnected and we all agree that's unlikely. And what about the fact that his fingertips were shaved. That's professional. That's what spies do."

"No," said Serrao. "That's what the mob does."

Ben leaned forward. "You telling me organized crime is getting into the Kona operation? I don't buy it. It's too small."

"Ben has a point there, Major," Tobi stated flatly.

Serrao glared at Tobi. "How do you know?"

"I checked a source," he answered simply. "No mob."

Both men stared at Tobi for a long time. Jack sat up, paying attention.

Tobi stared right back. It was obvious that that part of the conversation had ended.

Serrao eyed his cigar, then he resumed his staring at Tobi. Finally, he said, "So who killed the second guy . . . another spy?" He asked it sarcastically.

Ben was still wondering about *Her*. He'd bring it up with Tobi later.

Joyce knocked on the door. Jack waved her in. She entered quickly, like an intruder.

"This is Bennett. I'll have Furbee a little later or first thing in the morning." She handed Ben a manila folder and left. She was blushing a bit.

"Thanks, Joyce," he said to her retreating figure.

"Anytime, Ben," she said over her shoulder.

Serrao snorted a few times. "You know she has the hots for you, old boy."

Ben grinned and opened the folder. He skimmed it. Winston Bennett's only offenses were drinking related. Two barroom brawls. Driven home numerous times completely tanked. And one DUI two years before.

"He seems to be a drinker, but not much more." Ben got up, handed the folder to Tobi, and walked over to the window. Outside, most things were brown for lack of rain.

Ben turned. "What did Ken find on number two?"

It was Tobi who answered. "The second man died instantly. His jugular was completely severed. Nothing more on the weapon. A sword or machete is still the guess. Ken believes that his fingertips were peeled off with a razor. As I said before, there was no coffee or mac nut residue."

"What about other stuff? Under his nails, on his feet?"

All eyes shifted to Jack since he had talked with Ken. "Just some small scratches on his arm," answered Jack. "Probably from the bushes."

"What'd they look like?" asked Ben.

"Actually, they were like sets of parallel lines."

"How many together? How long?"

"Four, I think," answered Jack. "A few inches."

Ben faced the window once more. Something intrigued him. He thought of Bennett's yellow cat. Looking outside, he said, "Like cat scratches."

Jack—"Huh?"

Ben spun around quickly and headed for the door. "I'm going to the hospital."

Serrao stood. Hands on hips. "Maybe you will share your illumination with those of us in the dark."

Ben turned. He could see Tobi understood immediately, that he had run across a cat somewhere in his investigation.

Tobi said, "No cats at the Fukada place."

"Bennett has a big yellow one. And maybe some of the old man's coral scratches are a bit too symmetric." He ran out and sprinted down the hallway, grinning to himself, thinking about Bennett and the second victim.

But why didn't Bennett's cat scratch me?

Ben's smile disappeared.

10

"YOU'RE RIGHT, SAME PARALLEL SCRATCHES. They're not as deep, but that might mean the cat was friendly to the old man. But my guess is that it's the same cat. They were at the same place at some time."

Ben expected to feel elated. All he could muster was a grim expression. "Bennett's cat, but no Bennett. He's the only one who might know something, and he's disappeared. But then again, all I've got is Furbee saying Bennett might know our mystery man. He could be lying. Hell, he could be trying to frame Bennett."

Ken Asumura didn't respond.

"You're thinking it could be someone else's cat," said Ben, somewhat deflated.

"I can probably tell if it matches . . . length, depth, distance apart . . . that sort of thing, but I'll have to try to get it to react the same way. I imagine a cat can use its claws many ways. This is a long shot . . . what my mother used to call 'spearfishing in the dark with your eyes closed.' I'll check it out because we have nothing else. But this is really grasping."

Ben nodded, then glanced at his watch. "I'll have someone bring in Bennett's cat." Ben thought—Not much progress for such a long day. "I guess I'd better let you get home."

"I've got some other stuff to finish up. By the way, Honolulu hasn't got anything on the first victim's tattoo. They said it's old. They don't expect they'll be much help."

"Like I said, the ink's not important. Tobi's checking with some agency in Tokyo on the number. Maybe that'll give us a name."

Ken gave him a hopeful look.

"Talk to you tomorrow."

Five minutes later Ben was back in his white Sidekick, headed north on Highway 11. He reached for the radio, realizing as his hand was halfway there that he'd forgotten once again to get it fixed. He'd call Tobi when he got home. Then he remembered that *he* didn't have a home. Only patrolman Keli'i's apartment for two weeks while he was on his honeymoon in San Francisco. He wondered when he'd have time to look for a house and decided to call a realtor in the morning.

His thoughts turned to the two victims.

If they were working together, then did the same person kill them? Probably. Then why was one dumped at sea . . . so the body wouldn't be discovered . . . and why was one left in plain sight? Was the killer surprised the second time and had to flee? Not likely. Not at two or three in the morning in the middle of a coffee field.

Just as the night before, a salmon-colored sun hung low over the Pacific, but Ben hardly noticed. There were no clouds except in Ben's mind. The ocean was calm. Ben's mind was not.

If they weren't working together, did the second guy kill the old man? Then who killed him? Either way there's a killer out there. I've got to find out who the old man is. We're not going to find out the identity of the second victim . . . not without IDing the first.

The sun disappeared from sight. Not until then, when dusk nearly covered the Pacific, did Ben instinctively look to the west. He saw nothing but an empty pink sky.

Keli'i's apartment was small. One bedroom and a combined living room and dining room. A dark one-lane kitchen that was in need of a window. Unlike Ben's old apartment above *Swift Benny's,* it was neat.

He had slept there the night before—his first day back on the Big Island. It seemed much longer than that to him. He thought about that. To a detective, everything seemed much longer when there were few clues, particularly when a second victim appeared on the scene before the first victim was put to rest.

He called Tobi. A dispatcher connected him to Tobi's radiophone. Tobi was halfway home. They talked for a few minutes. Ben saved his questions about *Her.* Face to face was better.

A shower was the next order of business. He stripped, quickly knocked off a set of twenty-five sit-ups and headed for the bathroom. For the first few minutes, he leaned against the shower wall, motionless, letting the hot water run over his head, washing away the tension while he wondered if the one thing he hated about police-work would get the better of him. The frustration when the pieces didn't fit together right away. Then, as if by video magic, Lisa's face appeared in his thoughts. Although it materialized for only a fleeting moment, that was long enough for him to see the 'I-told-you-so' expression in her eyes. Ben closed his eyes, lightly at first, then tighter. Her image was replaced with thousands of tiny red dots, moving slowly, like something far away in the galaxy. Then the dots swirled faster and faster and disappeared into a black hole like water down a brand-new drain. Was the vision of Lisa predicting where his career was headed? Where she wanted it to head?

He reached for the soap.

After drying off and slipping into a pair of royal blue cotton pants held up by a frayed drawstring, he padded into the kitchen and stood in front of the refrigerator. Ben hoped Keli'i had left something edible behind. He peeked inside as if he were pulling to an inside straight. His prayer wasn't answered. The refrigerator was empty save for an orange, a Tupperware container of sliced pineapple—so ripe it was brown—and a loaf of seven-grain bread that looked a bit puffy. Still, all that didn't diminish his appetite. Performing a quick about-face, he headed for the bedroom for a shirt, and shoes, and then left for Mitchell's, just down the road.

It was eight. Already Mitchell's was getting more lively. The place was three-quarters filled, although some of the older people were gulping hot coffee and looking a bit frantic. They seemed nervous about the nighttime atmosphere and wanted to leave.

There was no room at the bar, so Ben chose a table for two, near the door. A waitress appeared before he had time to pull up his chair.

"Hi, handsome. What'll it be?" Her free hand went to her hip and her hip cocked.

"A Beck's Dark and a menu."

"Be right back."

Ben watched her until she disappeared behind three guys who were at the bar near the cash register. Looking around the room, he saw that most of the tables were occupied by couples, some alone, some paired. He didn't see any singles. Everybody had somebody. Right then he missed Lisa. He couldn't figure out if that was good or bad. There was no time to think about it—the waitress was back and her meter was running.

"Want me to pour?" she asked in a hurry.

"Go ahead. I *do* look like I'd spill it . . . don't I?"

She took a long look at him. "I didn't mean *that*. Some guys like a head on it," she paused, "some guys like it poured slowly," her tongue rested on her lips for a second, "down the side."

Ben gave her a wry grin. She handed him the menu and said she'd be back in a minute. He watched her again as she flirted with a thirtyish guy at the bar and sold him another drink.

She was back again. Ben decided on swordfish.

He was halfway through dinner when he felt a hand on his shoulder. "Hey, Ben."

Ben chewed faster so he could reply. A few seconds later a muffled 'hi' came out. He swallowed and took a sip of beer. "Sit down, Danny. How's it going?"

"Good. We'll pack'em in tonight. Good band."

"Wet T-shirt night?"

"No way."

"Just kidding."

"How's the case working out?"

"Nothing new." Ben decided he shouldn't discuss the second murder. Tomorrow, when he had more on the latest victim and a photo, he'd talk to Danny. The second man was a more likely candidate to have been in Mitchell's at one time or another. "I hit all of the coffee mills and two farmers. They *do* keep to themselves. You know a guy named Winston Bennett?"

"Bennett. Shit, names are tough. What's he look like?"

"Big. Six-two and heavy. Say, two-fifty. Bald."

"British accent?"

Ben raised his eyebrows. "I don't know. Maybe. It's an English-sounding name."

"I think I know him. Been in here a few times . . . not recently though. Had to throw him out once. He was drunk and creating a disturbance. Made a pass at some guy's girl. We've never had a real fight in here . . . believe it or not . . . but once you do, the place changes."

"When was that?" asked Ben, forgetting about his meal for the time being.

"Musta been six or eight months ago."

"Ever seen him since?"

"Nope."

"Know anything about him? Anything at all?"

"Nope."

"Was he with anyone?" Ben asked.

Danny shook his head but it was easy to tell that his raised eyebrows and empty grin meant 'don't really remember,' not 'no.' "What's this Bennett guy got to do with it?"

Ben tasted the lemon butter and licked it from his lips. "He's what they call a bagman. Picks up the beans."

"Berries," Danny corrected. "The beans are inside."

Ben closed one eye and pulled his head back. Then he smiled. "Okay, Mr. Expert, berries. He works for the mill in Nāpoʻopoʻo."

"He was alone, best I can remember."

"What about a guy by the name of Furbee. Jeremiah Furbee."

Danny laughed. "That's his name?"

Ben nodded.

"Nope. Never heard of him. Who's he?"

"Runs the Nāpoʻopoʻo mill. Foreman or something." Ben shrugged his shoulders. "And . . ."

"And?"

Ben took a deep breath and let it out slowly. "Might have something to do with the Kona Gold trade. In fact, this whole thing might have something to do with it."

"Like I said before, be careful up there. There's stories of people just disappearing."

Danny got up, turned a chair around and straddled it, crossing his arms in front of him.

"What do you know about the marijuana?"

"Whaddaya mean?" Danny leaned back. His arms remained folded across his chest.

"I never worked vice, so for openers, who's in charge? I heard it was a woman."

"I've heard that, too, but I don't know her name. You hear mostly rumors about what goes on up there . . . and not a lot of detail. I know the serious guys are in Puna. A few in South Kona, but Puna's where the bigger farms are. They call it Puna Butter over there."

Ben didn't say anything. A far-away look bound his face. He wondered how much Tobi knew about this woman. Why was Tobi being so close-mouthed? He had a lot of questions, but somehow no energy to ask. Frustration was setting in.

After a few moments of silence, Danny said, "Gotta go, Benny-boy."
He patted Ben on the back.

"Okay. Take it easy."

"Good luck."

"Yeah."

Without so much as a drumroll, the band blasted into *Crocodile Rock*.
Every table emptied and the dance floor filled. Ben decided to stay for a
few songs and then get some sleep. Soon his left foot tapped and his
fingers drummed the tabletop. He was reliving some time in the past,
when things weren't as complicated and all he had to do was worry about
himself. He realized those days were gone forever.

The music was so loud he didn't hear her at first. She leaned over and
shouted into his ear a second time. "Dance?"

Before he could say no, she grabbed his hand and pulled him from
his chair.

They hardly touched except when their section of the dance floor
became so crowded that everybody seemed to rub every body. Then you
had to pay attention to keep your toes intact. Each time they came together the woman pursed her lips as if she were evaluating an answer
he had given. Once Ben felt her breasts against his chest. He couldn't
help himself—he grinned. She winked.

She was pretty, with sparkling, attentive eyes. Her long black hair was
frazzled, but it looked good, as if she'd been careful as to how it frazzled.
She was a few inches shorter than he was and he guessed she was around
twenty-five. Ben pegged her breasts at thirty-six. She smiled when his
eyes returned from her chest. He smiled back, but felt uncomfortable.
He knew this would happen. Meeting someone. He just thought that two
days away from Lisa was a little too soon. He hoped Lisa was home in
bed. Alone . . .

After the first number, the band immediately rolled into a slow tune
and the woman was in his arms before the saxophone player had time
to wet his lips. But not before she wet hers.

"My name's Marguerite."

"I'm Ben. Ben McMillen."

Don't call me Maggie."

Okay, Maggie.

Her head nestled against his shoulder and her body pressed against his. Ben could tell she had closed her eyes.

And when the lead singer crooned the last few bars, Marguerite said, "Okay, Ben . . . let's hear your best line."

"Let's hear yours."

Tiptoes to his ear. She told him.

Ben felt fortunate it was dark. Otherwise, he was sure she would see a crimson tone sweeping across his face.

Later, driving back to the apartment—alone—Ben smiled to himself, proud that he hadn't succumbed to the temptation, but also remembering Detective Amaral's best line. 'Check your oil, ma'am?' He laughed out loud.

He stood beyond the *lānai* in the wet sand, watching the moonlight dance on the water. His gaze reached past the reef to a point where he could visualize the old man being dumped into the sea. He squinted. *Who was the other man on the boat? Were there more than one? Was one of them the second victim?*

The sound of a car passing the front of the apartment brought him back. Although it was late, it was time to begin training. The urge to accomplish something was too great.

Ben went inside to change into his running shorts and New Balance roadsters. Ten minutes later, after warming up with stretching exercises, he started out, heading up the entranceway toward Highway 11, which he remembered had a name, Māmalahoa. He pictured a great chiefess, frocked in feathers and plumes. He wondered if she had been an enforcer of the *kapu* system, or a temptress. Had she sat by the side of Kamehameha the Great? Had she shared his bed?

What was your line, Māmalahoa?

Certainly nothing as brazen as Marguerite's. Saying it to himself, his cheeks burned. Both sets.

Running. Running was his favorite. The swim was okay, although it was impossible to avoid swallowing salt water, which in turn, meant coughing for the first few miles of the bike ride. The bike ride was a pain in the ass. But even though the marathon sapped all his energy, there was something about running that made him feel enthusiastic about the whole ordeal—the Ironman Triathlon. Almost two and a half miles in the swells of Kailua Bay, one hundred and twelve miles by bike across the hot, black roadway that stretched along the Kona and Kohala coasts, knifing through the lava fields and the plateau of ranch lands. And finally, the marathon—twenty-six point two on the shimmering Queen K, surrounded by lava beds that soaked up the heat of the sun and kept it near the ground.

It was ten now and the highway was deserted and dark. The night breeze cooled Ben's skin as he began to stretch out his stride. He'd decided on a six-minute pace and five miles. He'd also made up his mind that he'd concentrate on training and keep the murders out of his mind. Not an easy thing to do when there was no one else to talk to and when darkness had taken away the scenery, so he stared ahead at the moon, studying the detail of its surface, imagining what it would be like prancing around up there.

He missed his old running shoes. These new ones needed some work and he thought he felt a blister forming on his left heel. If it got much worse, he'd have to stop. A serious blister, if it broke by itself, would curtail his running for several days. But a small bubble could easily be lanced with a sterile needle, the fluid drained, and the skin left in place, giving the new skin time to mature.

He passed a mile marker on the side of the road. Grabbing his wrist and pushing the LIGHT button, he checked his time. Two miles in just under twelve minutes. Good pace. He felt fine. For a split second he thought about Marguerite.

A cloud covered the moon, diverting Ben's attention to the ocean. He couldn't see it, but he could hear the surf. He imagined the coastline snaking south to the point where the Polynesians first landed. *Ka Lae*— South Point. He tried to picture their expressions, their exhilaration, when, after a month of sailing by the stars and sun, they came upon another paradise almost identical to their homeland, but much newer. They came from a land of atolls, crescent-shaped land masses that were the remnants of the rims of great volcanoes. Before them was 'a great mountain,' later translated to Mauna Loa.

Ben wondered if they understood anything about the evolution of the land. Of the Pacific hot spot that created the chain of Hawaiian Islands. When they landed the Island was alive and spewing lava. They had a goddess and a legend to explain it. Pele—the fire goddess—was un-happy. Her lava represented her wrath. He wondered if any of them doubted her power.

Did they understand that the black-sand beaches had been formed from the lava cliffs by the pounding surf? That the rain had broken down the lava into rich soil? That offshore the coral of the huge reef was being nibbled by parrot fish, who in search of food, digested tiny bits of the reef over and over again, eventually turning parts of the reef into broad, silky beaches? Did they know that a new seamount was forming to the southeast over the bubbling hot spot located under the Pacific plate? That the birds that had arrived, some on their own power, some propelled by savage winds, had carried seeds from which the plants grew. That other living things had floated ashore, and that some seeds had been blown inland by the wind to form the rainforest that developed at the base of the volcano and on the fertile windward side of the island?

That a few million years later the rainstorms, the wind, and the relentless pounding of the sea would cause the downhill slide to a crescent rim, then an atoll, and then it would all vanish beneath the sea?

Did they know that in a few million years there would probably be more islands to the southeast? Did they care? Would there be people left to inhabit them? Would there even be a planet in a million years?

He guessed their gods and goddesses and legends were far better than reality.

Three miles. Halfway. Ben turned around.

He felt the blister but he convinced himself that it was small and would not be a problem. He was gliding now, what every runner, every cyclist, every swimmer tried to achieve. Effortless motion with the same fluid rhythm. Ben breathed in through his nose, slowly, deeply. Then out through the oval he formed with his mouth. He could feel his heart beating, not racing. So far no cramping, but he didn't expect any on such a short run. He kept his hands and fingers loose and flexible, except for his thumbs which he pressed against the sides of his forefingers. The moon reappeared over his shoulder and the roadway lightened a bit. He couldn't help it—he started thinking about the case.

Both men were Japanese. One . . . let's say . . . seventy. The other twenty-five or thirty. Two generations separated. Where they related? Grandfather and grandson? Great uncle and nephew? Who was their enemy?

He didn't like that one. *If they're related, and if they had a common enemy, then they would have spent a lot of time together. Wouldn't the second victim show signs that he, too, worked on a coffee farm?*

If they're not related, then, did the second victim kill the old man? Why?

Ben's face was etched with frustration, realizing that not knowing either identity made it impossible to guess.

The old man was a spy. That stuck in Ben's mind. *What might that mean? Does it have anything to do with present day? Shit . . . it was fifty years ago! He couldn't still be a spy, could he?*

He shook his head, then held his wrist, and pushed the LIGHT button once more. Five miles. He increased his pace thinking—*Winston Bennett . . . Winston Bennett . . . Winston Bennett.*

Soon he was back at the entrance to the apartment complex. When he reached the last bend in the driveway, he slowed down, and then stopped running, shifting to a brisk walk. He passed the building that housed Keli'i's apartment and headed for the water. It was a quarter mile away. Ben began to jog. When he reached the shore, he quickly stripped off his shirt and kicked off his running shoes, bursting the blister on his right heel. "Damn!"

But he quickly forgot it and raced toward the ocean and dived in. In a few seconds he was headed straight out, gliding once more, stretching his tired back muscles. After a few strokes, the sting of the salt water on the blister disappeared. He swam for three minutes. Then stopped and treaded water as he peered farther out. Where did you come from, old man? Then he heard something and peered into the darkness. Suddenly, it seemed as if the entire horizon had turned silver. Ben swam a little farther out. He stopped, transfixed. A short distance in front of him the water rippled and he saw thousands of fins breaking the surface. At first he was scared. Then he realized there were far too many for it to be sharks. The stream of fish funneled by for more than a minute. Ben was mesmerized. The ribbon of yellowfin tuna seemed endless. From his vantage point he could only guess at its width. Finally, when they passed, he kicked toward shore, gliding once more, making believe he was one of them.

Sitting on a flat lava rock, resting, with his knees bent and his head buried between his legs, Ben closed his eyes. As his breathing slowed, his thoughts returned to the two victims. His mind churned through the other clues. Cowboy boots. Kona Gold.

He had to find Winston Bennett.

And maybe it was also time to pay more attention to Jeremiah Furbee.

11

NOT A SOUND. NOT MUCH LIGHT EITHER. It was chilly and moisture hung heavily everywhere.

Tobi knelt by the tree where the second victim had been found. Over his left shoulder the first rays of morning light filtered through a tiny opening in the thick foliage. His fingers played with the rich earth, feeling for something left behind, something overlooked. Every few minutes Tobi glanced toward the farmhouse, making sure there was no sign of activity. He wondered if Fukada and his sons took Sunday off. Or at least slept late. Although he had every right to be there looking for evidence, Fukada had every right to know he was there. For now, with so little to go on, Tobi decided everyone was a suspect. Who was to say Fukada and his sons weren't lying? Better that they not know he was there.

Tobi moved forward, still squatting, probing the soil.

It took fifteen minutes but finally he was convinced that nothing had been dropped near where they had found the body. Tobi stood. It was lighter now and the silence was broken by a solitary dove, cooing what Tobi knew was the jungle cry everyone identified with the tropics. *Coo-cooh ooh-ooh . . . coo-cooh ooh-ooh.*

He had tried to teach it to Ke'o, but Ke'o would have none of it. Nightingales obviously held themselves above doves.

The clearing between the trees was no more than ten feet wide. Tobi patiently scanned the area, trying to visualize the direction from which the killer had come, carrying the unconscious man. Ken Asumura had found a deep bruise at the base of the victim's skull. He and Tobi agreed that the man had been carried to the farm unconscious, placed against the coffee tree, and then his throat was slit—his neck nearly severed. The finger tips had been shaved last. That part was a guess, but it didn't really matter.

Fukada's three-acre parcel was crescent-shaped, with short flat ends. Three other farms bordered it. The front acre—thick forest—ran down to the highway. Jack Cooper had talked to the farmers on each side. The farm in back was abandoned. Neither neighbor had heard or seen a thing. Access to their farms was by dirt road. There were two. One ran along the outside of the farm on Fukada's left and looped around, dead-ending where the farm on the left and the one in back abutted. The farm to the right was accessed by a road that ran almost parallel to Fukada's about two hundred yards farther south. If the killer and his victim had come by either of those routes, forensic would have found tire marks. Few cars, if any, ventured from the highway. There were no tracks. Tobi wondered if the killer had carried the man from the highway. It was possible, but unlikely. Three hundred yards uphill with a hundred and fifty pounds on his shoulder and no boot prints. He sighed and walked farther into the grove of trees.

If the killer had come through the forest that separated each farm, it would be almost impossible to trace. Footprints do not leave a permanent impression on a hundred years of dried leaves. Tobi guessed the mat of the forest floor was at least a foot thick. He was right.

He wasn't looking for anything obvious. The Kona forensic team was good. But he also knew that you never found everything—there was always something left behind. He retraced his steps back to the tree. There was blood on the bark. Lots of it. Now it was brown, a much darker brown than the tree bark.

The sun found a space between two ʻōhiʻa trees. He blinked a few times—the glare on the wet leaves made it hard to see for several seconds. Tobi looked at his watch. It was almost seven. He guessed Sunday was a day off.

Tobi decided it was time to pick a path. He ruled out everything but the main road, straight in. The possible, but unlikely, path. If that were it, then the killer had parked down below, partially hidden, but close to the highway. Just like he had. The killer had not walked up the dirt road, but next to it, in the tall grass. If there was something to find, it would be there.

A light went on in the farmhouse. Tobi heard Fukada waking his sons. "*Maki.*" Firewood.

Tobi hustled out of sight just as the eldest son stumbled out the front door and headed toward the coffee trees. Tobi waited until the boy was out of sight and then he started walking along the dirt driveway. He was lucky. He only had to check one side. The other was carved into a rocky bank that made using that route impractical. He walked slowly, eyes straight down, focused on the ground, ears alert, focused on the farm-house. He hadn't gone more than fifty feet when he spotted a brown clump nestled in some tall grass next to an exposed ʻōhiʻa root. It looked like a clump of wet wood mulch. Bending, eyeing it closely, he brought his face within inches of it and smelled. Closer. The unmistakable scent of tobacco. The killer had been chewing. The strain of the climb uphill with an unconscious man on his shoulder required total concentration. Breathing would have become difficult. The physical exertion, sucking and blowing air through his mouth. Tobi could visualize him spitting it out. Then he wondered if it belonged to Fukada. No. Fukada would have no reason to walk anywhere except on the driveway. Quickly, Tobi extracted a small evidence bag from his back pocket and a small pocket-knife from his front. As he scooped the chew inside the clear plastic bag, he started to think about cowboy boots and cowboys and Parker Ranch.

The Big Island has as diverse a climate and landscape as anywhere on earth. Leeward, dry sun-drenched lava beaches extended from South

Kona up the coast to Kohala. The interior is covered with moonlike expanses of black rock stretching from the ocean all the way to the top of the twin wombs of Hawai'i—Mauna Kea to the north and Mauna Loa to the south. Yet there are thick rain forests windward—on the northern and Hilo sides—smack in the path of the moisture-laden trade winds. South of Hilo, around the southern tip, there are both old and new lava fields of the Puna District. The most recent ones are from Kīlauea. A small volcano in comparison to the Island's other two volcanoes, but currently the world's most active—its most recent eruption has been flowing on and off since 1983. Recently, it destroyed the town of Kalapana and added hundreds of acres of coast line where the Pacific had ruled for eons. Here and there are isolated pockets of forest known as *kīpuka,* where the lava has spared the plant life, forming an oasis of greenery that, if given enough time, will reseed the lava fields and create useful land.

South Kona is rich and fertile—fruitful lands that house the coffee and macadamia nut farms.

And in the western shadow of Mauna Kea is Parker Ranch, over two hundred thousand acres of cattle land. In the 1840s John Parker, an American, pioneered cattle raising on the Big Island. With Kamehameha III's blessing and assistance, Parker's ranch grew and prospered. Today it is the largest individually owned cattle ranch in the United States. It gave Hawai'i its cowboys—ranch hands from Mexico who came to Hawai'i in the 1800s to ride and rope and ride herd on the vast ranchland, bringing with them all the tradition and flavor of North America's cowboys. They called themselves 'espanol' and the Hawaiians translated it to *paniolo.* They became a colorful fixture—bandanas, broad hats, denim jackets.

And boots.

And chewing tobacco.

———

It took Tobi an hour and fifteen minutes to reach the town of Waimea, the gateway to Parker Ranch. He'd come up 180 just north of Nāpo'opo'o, then inland along 190, the northern section of Māmalahoa Highway. On the high ridge that Highway 190 followed, he had time to think.

At some point, victim one had been with victim two. Ben had surmised that and Ken's analysis had confirmed it. Funny—scratches from a cat. But whose cat? Victim one had been a spy. Maybe he still was when he became a homicide victim. The killer could have murdered them both. But also, victim two could have killed victim one. Did that make sense? Two killers? One dead. It would explain the different methods. But nothing explained *why*.

Parker Ranch. Had he been hasty? Nothing said everyone who wore boots and chewed tobacco worked on Parker Ranch. Some orchid growers in Hilo probably wore boots. Who said they didn't also enjoy a chew?

Two bodies—no IDs. He needed a brand on the boot and maybe the brand of the chewing tobacco. Maybe Ken could find something else in the tobacco.

Waimea was a sleepy town. On Sunday morning before nine it appeared catatonic. It was clean and quaint, and recently, when the current owner of Parker Ranch decided to let tourists tour and browsers browse, new retail establishments had filled in all the available spaces downtown. Waimea would soon wake up.

Tobi sped past all this, and when he was a mile east of town, he turned right onto Mānā Road, past a corral of fine-looking quarter horses, and headed for an area called Palia'ali'i. After five miles, he reached an unmarked dirt road, a road he knew well. At the end, near a point called Pu'u 'Ōhi'a, at an elevation of 3500 feet, was a small ranch house. Built by hand, like his, the exterior was more than eighty years old, fashioned from eucalyptus logs and mud, with a lava rock chimney. The round windows looked strange, but no stranger than the man who was sleeping inside on his day off.

Tobi got out of his car after the dust settled. When he was away from the dirt drive, he took a deep breath of air, which was mildly scented with eucalyptus. There was a huge grove off to his left. From where he stood he could see most of Mauna Kea, except for the last thousand feet, which was covered with dark gray rain clouds looking ready to burst. Tobi knew they wouldn't—not until afternoon. He headed for the ranch-house.

Moments later, he knocked on the door and heard Walker grumble. He hadn't seen Walker since he'd rejoined the Kona police force. He turned the knob and stepped inside.

"Some cowboy."

Walker opened one eye. It appeared to Tobi that Walker liked what he saw because he opened the other. "Well, I'll be," he said, sitting up, wearing red long johns with buttons all the way up the front of his barrel chest. Walker swung his legs around and bounced up, hand extended, jerked it back with a laugh, and then bowed politely.

Tobi bowed and waited for Walker to speak.

Walker was one of Parker Ranch's two foremen. He handled the ranching end of the operation. A man named Kenny Okala was in charge of the tours and the Visitor's Center, the ranch's newest and fastest grow-ing business. *Pussy business,* Walker called it. Tourists belonged by the pools of the resorts. And as far as Walker was concerned, the resorts belonged somewhere else, as well, anywhere but *his* island.

Tobi only knew Walker as Walker. If he had another name, it was his secret. He had been born on the ranch in 1930 and hardly ever left it except to visit his mother who was in a nursing home in Hilo. Tobi didn't know her condition. Walker kept things like that to himself. But Tobi figured it was serious. He could see it in Walker's eyes from time to time. Sometime soon, there'd be a funeral—casual dress and donations to the Hawai'i Tropical Botanical Garden. One thing he did know about Walk-er's mother—she was a long-time patron of the botanical garden.

Unlike the faint boot prints at Fukada's farm, Walker's would be deep enough to trip over. He weighed over two-forty and used to tease Tobi that when his cowboy days were over, he was going to beef up, and become the Island's first sumo wrestler. Tobi grinned, thinking about it now.

Then he frowned. He knew it was time for the bear hug. Walker opened his arms.

Somewhat painfully, after what seemed like an eternity later, Tobi sat and exhaled. Walker seemed to have gotten stronger.

"Captain, heh? Damn glad for you!"

"Thank you." A pained puff of air that wouldn't have made a candle flicker.

"What's your question?"

Tobi liked Walker. Liked how he got right to the point. He tried a slow deep breath before he spoke. "There has been a murder on the Kona coast. Up in the hills."

"Marijuana trouble?" asked Walker.

"A possibility." Tobi raised his hand so Walker wouldn't interrupt. "Also, an old man washed up at Kealakekua. We found scratches from a cat on the guy that was murdered in the hills. We found matching scratches on the guy we found on the beach. At first, we mistook them for coral cuts."

Walker whistled.

"There is more. There were boot prints at the murder scene." Tobi watched for a reaction. There was none. Walker hadn't made the connection yet—or he had a damn good poker face. "And this morning, when I went back to have a look around, I found a wad of chewing tobacco."

Walker made the connection. He sat on the edge of his bed and it creaked noisily with the addition of his weight.

Tobi kept silent.

"You think it might be one of my hands?"

"I suppose there are many on the Island who wear boots and chew tobacco. I imagine the highest percentage work here."

"True. What do you want from me?" Walker stood and went over to the stove, picked up a relic coffee pot, and shook it. The disgusted look on his face told Tobi it was empty. "You don't drink this stuff, do you?"

"Only when I am here," answered Tobi smartly.

Walker grinned and set about finding some beans.

While Walker was making coffee, Tobi asked his questions. "How many people do you employ?"

"Who wear boots? . . . Oh, I'd say about a hundred. They're the ones who work for me. And your next question is . . . how many chew? I'd guess maybe twenty-five or so . . ."

"What if I got you a brand of boot and a brand of tobacco, could we narrow down the suspects?"

"Sure . . . I'd haul all their asses into the office, have 'em take off their boots, and empty their pockets."

"Seriously?"

"Absolutely."

"I might be back." Tobi got up.

"Hey, no coffee?"

"Sorry, Walker. No time."

"You never stay long."

"That is what happens when you have two men who get right to the point."

Walker laughed heartily.

They shook hands. Tobi was glad Walker only bear-hugged hello.

———

Three hours later he was home, having dropped off the chewing tobacco at the hospital and stopping at headquarters. He wanted to see if there was a response from Tokyo on his request for information on the old man's tattoo. But there was no answer to his inquiry.

Jack Cooper was in his office, working on a burglary. Other than that, headquarters was as quiet as Tobi could remember. Even for a Sunday.

He was in his garden pruning a stubborn fig tree when the phone rang.

It was Ken. The tobacco matched on his second test. It was Scoal—Wintergreen. The boot print would take a little longer. There was an insignia on the bottom, but most of it had been worn off. What was left, even under a microscope, was hard to distinguish. They were getting samples of new boots from several suppliers on the Island. He hoped, they could match enough of the old pattern against the new one to make a determination. And Forensic hadn't been able to get a good cast of Jeremiah Furbee's boots. Too much crushed stone and soft sand.

Tobi seemed to be sleeping. Ben approached quietly to get a closer look. Tobi's chest moved up and down. He detected a slight snore as Tobi inhaled. Gently, he shook Tobi's shoulder. His friend's eyes opened immediately and his lips formed a small smile. "What time is it?"

Ben checked his watch. "Almost noon."

Tobi sat up and stretched, yawning, and shaking his head.

"Getting old?"

"Getting rest so I do not get old. Besides, I have to go in later."

Ben knelt gingerly and then sat on the floor.

"You look a little worn out yourself," Tobi said.

"I'm training . . . I biked up here."

Tobi nodded.

"I called Ken before I left. He told me about the chewing tobacco. What else have you got?"

Tobi inhaled deeply, purposefully, clearing his mind. "I went to Parker Ranch and visited with an old friend. When we have the boot identified, we can go back up there, and he will line up all the cowboys and we will have a look at their boots and their chewing tobacco."

"Like a random drug search . . . that'll go over big."

"Everything Walker does goes over big, but you follow his orders or you are history, as they say."

"Tobi, lots of people must wear boots and chew tobacco. They sorta go hand in hand."

"True enough, but the highest percentage of them work at the ranch."

"What about the spy angle?"

"I do not have any word from the people in Tokyo. Is that the scenario you still like best, Ben?"

"Yeah."

"What about the marijuana farmers?"

"That's in the back of my mind. After I bike back, I'm going to check on Bennett one more time. Then I'm going to find a Kona Gold farmer and question the hell out of him."

"Better not go alone," Tobi warned.

"I'll stop by HQ and see if Jack's around. I better get going. It's an hour and a half ride back and my muscles are starting to tighten up."

"See you tomorrow."

"Okay." Ben hesitated. He looked at Tobi. He could tell Tobi knew that he had yet to ask his real question. "Tobi . . . one more question?"

Tobi nodded.

"How do you know this woman who is charge of the marijuana trade?"

Tobi's smile indicated that he had been expecting the query. "I will answer that only for you. But we will discuss it once, now, and never again."

Ben nodded.

"Five years ago, I met her at Dorian's, at the bar. I was very depressed. It was the tenth anniversary of Leika's death. She came over and asked me if I was okay. I guess my eyes were red. We had a drink. Then dinner. We became friends. Later, when I found out what she did, I stopped seeing her. But we are still friends. Probably because we had gotten along with one another so well. I did not think that could ever happen with anyone except Leika. But it did. She said I was different. I treated her as an equal . . . something no one had done before. Now, I think she wishes she could quit. But some things are yours for life . . . once you start. If you choose wrong . . . some things are until death." He paused, biting his lip. There were a few moments of silence.

"And yes . . . I still love her . . . but I tell you . . . it will never be."

Tobi stood, gave Ben a faint smile and a wink of his eye, and shuffled into his bedroom.

Ben heard Tobi say, *"Wae aku i ka lani."*

He needed no translation. It was something his grandmother often repeated—'Let the selecting be done in heaven. Take life as it comes.'

12

B EN WAS PERCHED ON HIS TREK, admiring the view of the South Kohala coast that spread out before him. Magically, it seemed, tall grass
and small shrubs completely covered the rocky plateau. Hardly a trace
of lava was evident—although it was there, countless tons of hardened
magma. To the west, as far as he could see, the Pacific Ocean shimmered
in the afternoon sunlight. In the distance, a half dozen triangles of white
sailcloth skimmed across the water. A few clouds broke up the vast
stretches of blue above. To the northwest, heavy clouds obscured the
Island of Maui. Grimacing, he visualized the smoldering heap that was
now *Swift Benny's,* then tried to picture what Lisa was doing on her day
off. He placed her at the summit of Haleakalā, facing toward the southeast. The same clouds that obscured Maui from him blocked her view
of the Big Island.

At that moment, a cold shudder passed through his body. He felt as
if they were looking at each other.

He pushed off, wriggled his feet into the bindings, and began peddling. For starters, he stood high off the seat, churning, gaining mo-
mentum. The first part of the roadway leading from Tobi's house was
flat. But soon he was heading downhill as he would for the next three

miles, gliding. The bike was part of him. Maybe he was part of the bike. Ben rubbed the handle bars for good luck. He settled in, head down, back curved, the wind whistling through the small vent holes in his helmet.

The Trek cost two grand and about five hundred a year to maintain. It was painted bright yellow, and sleek lines of gleaming chrome trimmed the frame. The rear wheel always attracted attention. It was a solid graphite composite disc the same dimensions as a regular wheel but without spokes. It was a half inch thick around the perimeter and three times that at the hub. The surface of the disk was perfectly smooth. HED manufactured it and the wheel's surface advertised that fact.

The seat was high and uncomfortable looking. Ben often joked that the feeling of your butt rubbing across the firm surface was like impaling yourself on a trailer hitch.

But by far the most interesting part of the bike were the handle bars. They pointed straight ahead, curving and bending in just the right spots to accommodate the rider's arms. They enabled Ben to lean forward, low, in harmony with the frame of the bike. Aerodynamic—like a speeding bullet. With a sore butt!

Ben wound around a series of curves, braking a few times, although he tried to avoid it. Finally, he reached the highway and turned left, south toward Kailua. The road was straight, but hardly level. Up and down sweeping hills. The rises required the sustained burst of a sprinter—although it all looked and felt like slow motion. Down was like a toboggan run with no brakes. Two minutes of extreme exertion and twenty seconds of exhilarating rest.

The next twenty-one miles that led back to Kailua were equivalent to the sixth and last segment of the bike phase of the Ironman. When Ben competed in the Ironman he broke the bike component into six parts. Three up the Queen K and three back down.

Now, his muscles were a bit stiff—the half hour spent with Tobi had allowed lactic acid to build up in his muscles. Usually he took a long time cooling down after going thirty-five miles. But with Tobi, he had concentrated on the case, not his conditioning.

As the grasslands gave way to more stark patches of lava, Ben thought about the woman who had taken Tobi's heart. He wondered if Tobi was vulnerable to being tricked by a woman. Somehow he had never thought it possible—man or woman. But it had been Tobi, himself, who said, 'never believe that anyone is infallible. Always assume that everyone has their price.' Tobi was a man of infinite advice. Most of it was passed along in the form of Hawaiian proverbs and legends. Ben remembered the time Tobi had watched him training for the Ironman. He had been going through the motions. Tobi talked about the difference between someone who competes and a competitor, and told a story. It was about a small boy who was blind. In olden times, Hawaiians believed meeting a blind person was bad luck. The boy wanted desperately to be loved and respected, but without vision he thought it an impossibility. One day, an old *kahuna,* a high priest above the influence of the boy's misfortune, pointed out to him that one did not need to see to swim fast. He said you could derive *mana,* power, from your heart, if you believed. The small boy listened and became determined to be a great swimmer. Among Hawaiians, excellence in water sports commanded much respect. The boy swam and swam, and over time he developed into a good swimmer; not a great one, but good. But when the swimming contests were held, he always finished first. Tobi had asked Ben if he knew why. Ben had just stared. Tobi had smiled and said, 'It was because he had no fear of the others. He just swam as hard as he could. Others, more powerful swimmers, would glance at the competition and become worried. Their strokes stopped being smooth. They let their minds control their bodies.' Tobi went on, 'Your training allows you to compete, but your mind makes you a winner.'

Ben's thoughts came back to Tobi and the woman. Did Tobi have a weakness? A failing? The man Ben held in the highest esteem, who believed there was a difference between being a man and being human? Like the American Indians, the Hawaiians revered great human beings, not great men.

One by one he passed the major resort hotels. First the Mauna Kea, then Mauna Lani and The Ritz, and eventually, the Hyatt Waikoloa. He hoped the Hyatt held something special for him. He hoped that Lisa would transfer there. As he thought of her, he dipped his head under the wind and glanced over his right shoulder in the direction of Maui. Two unsolved murders. It was getting to him.

Twenty miles gone. Fifteen more.

After a hot shower, followed by an eye-opening minute standing under ice cold spray, Ben felt refreshed, ready to head into coffee country. But this time looking for a marijuana farmer.

The Suzuki Sidekick's engine roared with the turn of the ignition key. Before he put it into gear, Ben opened the glove compartment and took out his handgun. It was a 9 mm Smith and Wesson, something he had thought he would never see again. But Major Serrao had saved it and given it to Tobi. And Tobi had asked him to carry it. Although regulations required that each detective carry one, concealed under a shirt or strapped to an ankle, Ben had always kept his locked in his glove compartment, and he hardly ever took it out. Except for once, with the KGB. He was told that when they went crop dusting, they went in armed.

Ben checked the clip—it was fully loaded. He replaced it, closed the compartment, and shifted into first. As he headed out of the apartment complex, he switched on the radiophone and tested it. It worked. He'd asked Joyce Ah Sing to have it installed, not really believing that someone would get to it before Monday. It was a pleasant surprise and he felt a little relieved.

As he drove south, the threat of rain increased. The sky was filled with dark gray wispy clouds that had floated down from higher elevations, covering the hillsides. The sun—a radiant yellow ball—still sparkled to the west although it was much lower in the sky. It gave everything an eerie look as its light reflected off the water and illuminated the otherwise dark undersides of the clouds. The sea breeze picked up as well, and Ben wished he'd brought a jacket. But that would have been hard to do—the fire had claimed his only windbreaker.

On the small back seat of the jeep was a thermos of coffee—black. Also, a powerful but small flashlight, a pair of hiking boots he had borrowed from Keli'i's closet, a hiking map of the area that he had picked up earlier in the day, and a small walkie-talkie that fastened to his belt. It was set to the same frequency as his car radio. He probably wouldn't be near the jeep much of the time.

When he saw the sign announcing Kēōkea, Ben took a planned detour—Winston Bennett's house—not that he expected to find him there. He turned down the familiar dirt road and shortly came to the overgrown driveway. Bennett's mailbox was still jammed with newspapers and mail, but there was something different. There was a pickup truck parked in the driveway. A light blue, late-model Toyota. He pulled up behind it, blocking any escape.

Before getting out, he eyed the glove compartment for a few seconds but left the gun where it was. He reached for the photo of the first victim and tucked it into his waistband behind him. Then he got out. His feet made a crunching noise on the gravel walkway. At first, he ignored the sound, but he soon stopped, realizing that he knew little about Winston Bennett. Maybe he was connected to the marijuana business. Another thought struck him—maybe it wasn't Bennett's truck. He sneaked a quick glance over his shoulder back toward his jeep, thinking again about his gun.

Deep breath. He hitched up his pants.

Ben moved onto the porch. Step by step, floorboard by floorboard, creak by creak, he approached the front door. It was partially open. He knocked softly on the frame, but didn't wait for an answer. Turning the handle, he opened the door, and stepped inside. It was dark and musty smelling—just as before. No one was in the living room and no sounds escaped from the other parts of the house. He went over to the desk. A set of keys lay there—they hadn't been there before. And an airline ticket.

From the folder Ben could tell it was from a Hawaiian Air flight to Honolulu—**HON**; **277**; and **46** were written in the appropriate boxes for *Destination*, *Flight No.* and *Gate*. Ben glanced around quickly and then opened the ticket folder. The receipt was still there, though barely legible. But he made out that the ticket was for W. Bennett for a round trip to Honolulu leaving July 31—the day before the body of the old man was discovered—and returning August 7. Ben checked his watch dial.

Today.

He looked at the ticket. The arrival time was smudged and hard to make out. It appeared to be **1:13p**. He replaced the ticket receipt and put the folder on the desk underneath the keys. Then Ben tiptoed into the bedroom. It seemed a little neater and there were two new suitcases, both on the floor by the closet. Ben checked them. They were empty.

He heard a noise coming from the direction of the kitchen. It sounded like something had been knocked over. Quickly, on the balls of his feet, Ben moved down the short hallway, stopping by the kitchen entryway just in time to spot the cat slipping through the unlatched screen door leading to the back porch. Ben knew he had closed it the day before. A fast scan of the kitchen revealed that someone had been cooking. There were two saucepans in the sink, and on the nearby counter, a frying pan with food stuck to the surface. A six-pack carton was next to it, ripped open, like someone had been in a hurry. Three dead cans were farther back on the counter lined up against the backsplash. The smell of stale beer grew stronger as he approached the counter.

Ben suddenly froze. Another sound. At first he couldn't identify it, but it definitely came from the back porch. A rhythmic noise. Someone breathing heavily. Someone snoring. After a few seconds, Ben relaxed his guard, as he pictured Winston Bennett asleep on the porch, loaded down with beer.

He peeked outside. He was right.

It had to be Bennett. The man just looked too much at home.

He took up the entire rattan loveseat. His hands were folded and resting on a huge stomach. Legs crossed at the ankles, sinking into an old leather hassock. He was completely bald on top, but he had thick, bushy hair over the ears. Ben could see that it also grew down most of the length of his neck. A red mustache was almost lost on his face, except when he inhaled and his upper lip folded down. Ben guessed he weighed over two-fifty and was more than six feet tall. He was wearing a pair of cotton twill pants held up by suspenders and a gray T-shirt with a picture of a breaching whale on the front. Looking at Bennett, Ben wouldn't have been surprised if under the whale the shirt had carried the caption— *Actual size.*

He stepped closer and shook the slumbering giant. Bennett squirmed and dug himself deeper into the loveseat. Ben gave him a poke in the ribs. The man grunted and slowly opened one eye. His jaw drooped and he craned his neck, obviously trying to bring everything into focus.

His head wobbled as he spoke. "Who the hell are you?"

Ben smiled. "Detective McMillen . . . Kona police." He waited for Bennett's response.

"You don't say. What am I . . . illegally parked?" Bennett grinned like a child.

Ben tried to keep a straight face. "I'd like to ask you a few questions."

"Say . . . I know you. Aren't you a Kona cop?" Bennett roared. The loveseat creaked as his stomach shook.

Ben wondered if he'd really been sleeping. He seemed much too alert—drunk, but alert. "Look, I realize you've had a few and this is your house and I don't have a search warrant. You can throw me out if you want. But I'm not here to give you a rough time . . . just a few questions, that's all."

"Spoken like a true gent. Whaddaya wanna know?" He made no attempt to sit up.

Ben pursed his lips. "Where were you last week?"

Bennett answered directly. He didn't seem so drunk now. In fact, he was dead serious. "I was on O'ahu." He looked at the floor. "My sister died." Then he stiffened and looked at Ben.

Ben watched Bennett's eyes. He saw remorse and sadness. "I'm sorry."

Bennett grunted an acknowledgment. "Car accident, fuckin' drunk drrr . . ."

Ben nodded, realizing Bennett knew he was also describing himself. That seemed to sober him some more. "What was her name?"

"Alice . . . why are you here? What's this about?" He used his hands to push himself up and put his bare feet on the porch floor.

Ben reached behind him, extracted the photo of the old man, and handed it to Bennett. He remained silent.

Bennett looked at the glossy for a few seconds, then leaned closer, squinting. His lips parted slightly. Then he looked up. "What happened to Ahi? Is he dead?"

Ben tried to hide his elation, but couldn't. "So you know him! He was a coffee farmer?"

"He's dead, huh? Poor old guy. He was a hard worker. Everybody else manages two or three bags. Ahi always put out four. How did it happen?" Bennett wet his lips and eyed one of the empty beer cans on the floor.

"He was found on the lava, washed up in Kealakekua Bay. The sharks got him."

"What!" Bennett seemed angry. "That's horseshit! He never went down to the water. His best friend drowned some years back. He never went near the water after that." He stood with some effort and started pacing. Then, abruptly, he turned. "When did this happen?"

"We found him last Monday," answered Ben.

"Somebody killed him."

"He never went near the water . . . you're sure?"

"How can I be sure? But, I'll tell you . . . I'd be damned surprised!"

"How long have you known him?"

"Long, long time." His eyes glazed a bit. "Maybe thirty years. Damn good man. Damn good."

"What's his last name?"

"Ishizu."

"Spell it."

Bennett spelled it.

"Bennett?"

Bennett seemed to be thinking deeply about something. "Yeah?"

"What did you know about him?"

"He was a coffee farmer. They all keep to themselves, but Ahi, well, Ahi seemed different . . . like once he'd been out in the world. The others are born in the hills and they stay there forever. He was different. Shit!"

"But what do you know about him? Where did he come from? Any relatives?"

"Nothing about him personally. I can't help you."

Now it was Ben's turn to pace. He weighed what Bennett had said. If Ahi was a spy, then he'd have kept his past to himself. Bennett's words—'out in the world'—stuck with Ben. But he decided to keep his spy question for later.

"Where's his farm?"

"Way down the coast. He's the only one I dealt with down there."

"Why's that?"

"He has a lot of mac nuts. I'm the only one who'll buy 'em all . . . so I take his beans, too. That area used to be my territory. We kinda stuck together." Bennett's eyebrows raised. "I forgot. He's got a granddaughter. She visits him once in awhile . . . maybe twice a year."

"What's her name? What's she look like?"

"Never met her. Forget her name. I didn't talk with Ahi much. Most of what I'm telling you is something . . . well, something you just feel. Thirty years is a long time. You get a feel for a person's personality, even if you only see them from time to time and exchange a few words. It's like mutual respect . . . you know what I mean?"

"Thirty years and you never met her? . . . Come on."

"Never met her, McMillen." Bennett said it vehemently.

Ben stared at Bennett, who walked over, picked up the cat, and stroked its head. Ben believed him. "Where'd you say his farm is?"

"Hoʻomau Ranch. Just before the Old Mama Highway turns east."

"Old Mama?"

"Māmalahoa."

"Who was she?"

"Who was who?"

"Old Mama."

Bennett gave him a strange look. Then he shut one eye. "Beats the hell outta me." He placed the cat on the love seat.

Ben eyed the cat.

Ben got detailed directions, asked Bennett not to leave the Island, offered his condolences again—this time he added Ahi—and then started to leave. But he remembered two things and faced Bennett once more.

Bennett had picked up the cat again and was stroking its chin.

"What about this guy you work for?"

Bennett sized up Ben for the first time. "Been snooping around, huh?"

No answer was required.

"Furbee's an asshole."

"A marijuana asshole?"

"Yeah . . . a marijuana asshole. I hope you blow his doors off."

"But you work for him."

"I was here before him, and I'll be here after him."

"Where's he live?"

Bennett told him.

"One more thing. Has Ahi Ishizu ever been here?"

"Dumb question."

Ben face flushed. "Look . . . I haven't totally leveled with you. There's been another murder. The man was found at a coffee farm near Nāpo'opo'o. He had scratch marks on his arm. Came from a cat. Ahi had the same marks. I was guessing it was your cat."

"Ahi had cats . . . strays that is. Two or three hung around there, as long as there were mice about."

Ben was glad to hear it. It made more sense.

Bennett added, "And you weren't leveling with me because you were hoping I'd slip up and say something that indicated I knew about the other murder."

"It crossed my mind."

"Well, uncross it."

The Hoʻomau Ranch area was about twenty miles south. Ben sped down Māmalahoa Highway. He radioed headquarters on the way and left a message for Tobi. It was brief: Found Bennett. Seems clean. Old man's name was Ahi Ishizu. Owned farm in Hoʻomau Ranch . . . and a cat. On my way.

He also asked Forensic to meet him there as soon as possible.

His foot pressed the accelerator farther down and he shifted the new jeep into fifth for the first time.

Bennett's directions were to follow the signs to the Hoʻōpūloa Church Monument, go a quarter of a mile past, and then take the first left. The first left turned out to be a dirt road bordered by dense foliage on both sides. When Ben came to a side road with a white gate he turned left again, downshifting all the way to first. The road was rutted beyond belief. Up a gradual slope, around a wide bend—almost a hundred and twenty degrees to the right—then straight for two hundred yards. A small farmhouse was directly ahead. Ben drove up and stopped within a few feet of the front porch. He noticed, off to the left, the same type of gong that he'd seen in front of Yoshio's house. This one too was rusted and encased in spider webs.

Two catchment barrels hugged the front corners of the farmhouse. Attached to the left side of Ishizu's home was a *furo*. The *furo* served as a bathhouse. It was built over a three-sided cement curb about ten inches high, with a smokestack in back. The tub, made from redwood, was three feet high and about four feet square. The roof was fashioned from copper sheets secured to posts that extended a few feet beyond the top of the tub. A fire under the tub heated the water. Coffee tree prunings served as firewood. Ben peered inside. A stagnant film covered the water—the only movement, two flitting waterbugs playing tag. He backed off and surveyed the rest of the property. About fifty feet beyond the farmhouse, shaded by the rim of the forest, was an outhouse, the exterior green with moss.

The house was in good repair though it seemed quite old. Several of the planks on the porch were new, as were the front steps. There were flowers planted along the length of the porch, mainly ginger plants. The blooms were red and pink and white. They looked like large, elongated, elegantly painted pine cones.

And on the first porch step was a skinny gray cat. As Ben bent to pick it up, the cat ran into the woods. Ben stood and tried the front door. It was locked. He walked along the front of the house, jumped off the side of the porch, and headed for the back door. It was locked as well.

Before checking for an open window, Ben took a look around the back. There was a small clearing near the house. Then rows of macadamia nut trees. Beyond that were coffee trees stretching as far as he could see. Everything was neat. The rows perfect. There were weeds beginning to grow, because Ahi had been gone for a week.

All the windows were tightly shut. But Ben spotted the outline of a small door a few feet above the ground, right next to the fireplace. It had a flat wooden handle. He walked over and opened the door. Inside was firewood, neatly stacked. As quickly as he could, he emptied the wood bin. He had guessed right—another door. It would be latched, but not locked. Ben crawled into the bin on his hands and knees and pushed against the door. The latch gave on his second push, and the smoky, mildew smell from inside hit him smack in the face. He scrambled inside.

There was a single large room, just like the other farm houses—paper screen dividers between the kitchen, living area, and a small bedroom. And there were paintings everywhere. All scenes of Japan. Except one, a large rice paper mural that hung on the rear partition of the living area. It was Hawaiian. A volcano smoking in the background. The perspective was from the ocean, looking toward the land. At the water's edge there were huge billowing steam clouds where a fiery reddish orange lava flow met the sea. On either side of the steam clouds were palms. It looked like the lava had carved a path of fire right through the middle of a large grove. Everything else on the land was black and the sky was a deep gray, except for a few streaks of yellow where the sun's rays tried to pierce the ashen clouds.

Then Ben saw the broken chair. And the ropes. And finally blood stains everywhere—on the ropes, the chair, the floor. This was the spot were Ahi was killed. Or at least where someone had started the process. Forensic could worry about typing the blood, dusting for prints, and vacuuming for other specimens. He was sure Ken Asumura would find an exact blood match with the man who had washed up at Kealakekua Bay. And probably a set of fingerprints that would have matched those of the second victim, if his fingertips hadn't been shaved off.

But the first victim had a name now and Ben had to find out more about him.

He started in the bedroom. Taking out his handkerchief, he opened the drawer of the night table. There were letters in their envelopes, all neatly tied together with a purple string. He pulled at the bow. Then barely touching the edges, Ben flipped through them. All were from the same person. Someone in Sapporo. Everything was written in Japanese except for the addresses on the envelopes. But the sender's name gave him no clue as to whether the letters came from a man or a woman. He brought one to his nose. There was a faint smell of something sweet, but no strong perfume, nothing to indicate they had been written by a woman, but he guessed they were from Ahi's granddaughter. The one on top was the most recent. The postmark was July 15. Checking back, the letters seemed to be monthly, all around the middle of the month. He'd let Tobi translate them. There was nothing else in the drawer except a pair of nail clippers. He didn't touch them. He expected Forensic would take samples from them as well.

The chest of drawers contained clothes. Again neat. Everything in its place.

Under a pile of work shirts there was a photograph of a young girl. Late teens, Ben supposed. Dark hair. Beautiful face, perfect complexion. Ben extracted the photo from the frame and read the back. The processing date was June 1979. He wondered if the girl in the picture had written the letters. If so, then why wouldn't Ahi have had a more recent picture? Still, he was sure it was the granddaughter Bennett mentioned. He nodded to himself, visualizing the living room. There were no other photos that he remembered. Had the killer taken them? It seemed odd. Was this young woman part of the mystery? He kept the photo.

The clothes closet was spotless. Ben checked all the pants and shirt pockets. Nothing. Normally that would be unusual, but he guessed Ahi was a fastidious person, so it didn't surprise him as much.

In the living room he found a small bound ledger on top of a writing desk. The entries were simple. Deposits from the mill. A list of payments. The electric bill. Groceries. Nothing much else except a change purse containing a few rolled-up dollar bills and two nickels, and next to the ledger, a small burgundy notebook. Ben opened it. The book contained Ahi's poems. After skimming for a few minutes, he turned to the last entry. Ben read it. And again. Then, after thinking about its meaning, he carefully removed the page, folded it in half, and put it into his pocket.

So Ben waited for the Forensic team to arrive, sitting on the floor, arms around his knees, staring at the broken chair. *Who tortured you?*

He had no answers, but he had come to one conclusion.

Marijuana farmers are out. They have nothing to do with this. Ahi Ishizu was once a spy, and somehow, after all these years, it caught up with him. What did he have or what could he possibly have known that would be so important after all this time?

There was someone pounding on the front door. Ben was startled at first—the noise had broken his concentration. A voice shouted. "McMillen?"

He hadn't even heard a car pull up. He stood, narrowing his eyes as his gaze returned to the overturned chair.

What secret did you have, Ahi Ishizu?

Do you still have it? Or did they get it from you? . . . I think you still have it.

More pounding on the door. "Hey, Ben. Open up!"

13

A FTER EXPLAINING WHAT HE'D FOUND to the Forensic team, Ben went outside to check the surrounding area. He discovered that two farms bordered Ahi's farm. To the north, he found an old Japanese farmer who lived alone, was hard-of-hearing, and spoke little English. Ben couldn't communicate with him, but the man seemed unaware of Ahi's disappearance, further confirmation that the coffee farmers worked hard and socialized little. He decided to spare him the pain, at least until Tobi could explain it gently. South of Ahi's farm lived a family of five—fourth generation farmers—a man of fifty, his wife, and three daughters ranging in age from eight to fourteen. The man hadn't seen Ahi in days. Hadn't thought much of it, either. Hadn't missed his bags because the coffee harvest had just started—not everyone's berries ripened the first week. They'd had no trouble from the marijuana farmers, although they seemed somewhat scared when Ben asked. They asked about having Ahi's remains for a proper Japanese funeral. Ben said he'd be sure to get in touch with them when the body was ready for release, which probably wouldn't happen until the case was closed. Afterward, Ben walked east, away from the highway and the farms. Within a hundred yards he was confronted with a sheer cliff at least a hundred feet high. He walked along the base for a quarter mile in each direction. Best he could tell, the rock wall continued for some distance in both directions. He turned around and headed back.

Soon he was back on Māmalahoa, speeding north, having radioed Tobi to expect him in forty minutes.

Ben pulled into the parking lot at the same time as shift change. Men and women, some joking, all headed for the side entrance to the Squad Room, some to fill out daily reports, others to be briefed before taking on their assignments in the Kona District. Those with broad smiles, hunched shoulders, and dragging feet had just completed eight hours. The rest carried brown bags, walked briskly, and small smiles masked grim expressions. Not that it was a jungle, like New York City or L.A., but they had a job to do and sometimes it got a little scary. Just the week before, a patrolman had gotten beaten up and he was still in critical condition. He had tried to break up a fight in one of the bars and was hit over the head with a heavy chair. In real life, your head was broken, not the chair.

Ben nodded to a few officers and they nodded back. They were mostly new—only a few recognized him from three years before. He held the door for one woman officer and she gave him a strange look. Her mouth said 'Thank you'—her eyes said 'I can get it myself.' Ben hated that in women. He'd have held the door for a man. Men didn't take it as a sign of chauvinism. Why did women?

————

Tobi was bent over Joyce's desk, watching her as she was writing what she was hearing on the phone. Ben patted him on the back. Tobi looked up and asked him to wait in his office. He said he'd be there in a minute. Ben went to the break room, poured a cup of coffee, stared for a second at a glazed donut that looked like an orphan before he decided to leave it homeless, and walked back to Tobi's office.

Tobi came in a few minutes later, holding a sheet of paper, which he promptly handed to Ben. After Ben was seated Tobi said, "That's what we have on Ishizu. Not much more than you can get out of a phone book."

Ben read the profile. Name, age, address—no phone number, no social security number, no tax returns, State or Federal, no bank accounts, no fingerprints on record. Didn't own a car. Didn't have a license. And no criminal record.

No known relatives. There was a note on the bottom of the page that there was one other Ishizu. He lived on Kaua'i, but wasn't related.

"Looks like a spy's profile, if I ever saw one."

"You ever see one?" asked Tobi.

Ben frowned. "No . . . not really. I'm surprised you found out *anything* about him."

"He voted regularly. His registration card says he was born in 1915. Lists his birthplace as Honolulu. But there is no record of it. I have no idea what he showed them when he registered. And I cannot figure out why he voted, unless it was part of his cover . . . proved to his friends that he was an American citizen. What did you find?"

"Blood-stained ropes and a chair on its side . . . and blood on the chair." Ben reached into his breast pocket and extracted the letter and the photo of the teen-aged girl. "I found these. They were the only personal things I found without making a detailed search . . . I didn't want to disturb things."

Tobi took the letter and photograph. "You and I will go out there first thing tomorrow. By then we will have Forensic's report and Ken's lab work." Tobi switched his attention to the photograph. He stared at it for awhile and then turned it over. Softly, Ben heard him say, "*Maika'i*." Beautiful.

"It's more than ten years old," stated Ben.

Tobi nodded once. Then he opened the letter and read.

Ben could tell Tobi was in deep thought, probably rereading many of the sentences. Probably picturing Ahi as *he* read them. Tobi pursed his lips. When he was done he stared out of his window.

Ben knew enough to remain quiet and to let Tobi speak first.

Tobi turned, a sad look in his eyes. "This letter says Ahi's sister has died."

"Who's it from?"

"His granddaughter."

"Is the return address complete?"

Tobi said it was. "We can track her down. She seems very devoted to him. Most Japanese have a special place in their hearts for their grandparents. She is planning a visit in two months. I guess she will come sooner. It is too bad."

"Where does she live?"

"Sapporo. She is a teacher. Grade school. Teaches English. The letter tells of some of her students and how smart they are. I will make a call. I doubt there will be anything back on her until tomorrow." Tobi paused to reflect for a few seconds. Then he asked, "What about the surrounding farms?"

Ben explained about the hard-of-hearing old man and the family of five. Then he described the rock wall that ran at least a mile or so north and south behind the three farms. After Tobi seemed to have digested it all, Ben asked, "Anything on Furbee?"

"I have a man keeping an eye on him. So far he has been at the mill or at home. He lives in a small cabin a few miles southeast of the mills . . . in the hills."

"Bennett told me. Is it near a marijuana farm?" asked Ben.

"Smack in the middle," replied Tobi.

Ben made a wry face.

"What is this man Bennett like?" Tobi placed his hands on his desk, after brushing some lint from his soft cotton shirt.

Ben rolled his eyes and frowned at the same time. "He's quite a character. Sort of a British redneck."

"Redneck?"

"Southern farmer . . . Alabama, Mississippi. You know, drives a pickup. Big beer drinker. Punctuates his sentences with a belch. That type. But at the same time, he comes off with the air of a gentleman.

There's some formality to him. I have a feeling he's a well-educated drop-out without much use for protocol."

Tobi looked disgusted. "Think he has anything to do with it?"

"I'm going to keep an eye on him, but I don't think so. He's no fan of Furbee's, which puts him on my side." Ben got up.

Tobi smiled. "You look tired. Get some rest. I will pick you up to-morrow at six-thirty. It will be too dark to find much tonight. Ahi Ishizu can keep his secret one more day."

Ben let out a long sigh. "Okay. I think I'll swim a little, grab some dinner, and then hit the sack."

"Any luck on a place to live?" asked Tobi.

"Haven't had a chance to look. Maybe in a few days. Think Keli'i's bride will welcome a house guest?" Ben grinned.

Tobi gave a quiet snort. "Oh, I forgot." He tapped his head. "Lisa called."

Ben perked up. "When? Any message?"

"For you to call after eight."

———

Ben tightened the chin strap on his helmet and then bounced a few times on his toes. He told himself that he loved his bike, but he was shaking his head, disbelieving. It gave him leg cramps and knots in his calves that lasted for hours. His hands would ache from clutching the hand grips. The hard seat. Ouch! He smiled to himself, realizing that he was just making excuses. The good bike riders didn't fight with their bikes. They relaxed, they glided, their bottoms barely glazed the seat. He stared at the yellow-and-chrome Trek. "Let's be friends, okay?"

The route he chose formed a triangle. Due north on Highway 180—a steep grade for the first two miles from sea level to about 1500 feet, then it flattened out for four and a half miles. The view over this part of Kona would be breathtaking. The entire west coast of the Big Island would spread out to his left. The Pacific, a hazy blue at this height, disappeared into the horizon, many miles away. Then he would reach Palani Junction, make a 270-degree left turn, and speed downhill, like an Olympic skier, for just over two and a half miles, bearing straight into Kailua. At the traffic light—the final leg of the triangle—he'd make another left and head south for five miles over fairly flat land, bringing him back to his starting point.

The arduous climb of the first two miles was hardly the way to become friends with his bike. The only salvation was that Ben had to stand almost upright, never touching the seat, to be able to peddle fast enough to make it up the steep grade. Halfway through, at about eight hundred feet above sea level, his calves and thighs started to burn, and a vein throbbed in his head, forcing his eyes partially closed. Soon it passed.

His stamina was good. He was breathing fast, but not hard, not strained. When he finally reached the plateau where 180 flattened out, he felt exhilarated. A panoramic view of the entire northern coastline was his reward. He thought about the Race for the Sun—a crazy competition on Maui that he'd almost entered on two occasions. From sea level just east of Kahului—the center of industry and farming on Maui's northern side—to the summit of Haleakalā, the house of the sun. Sea level to ten thousand feet, on a bike, with a winding, twisting road at the top, and curve after curve. The winner took more than three hours to accomplish the feat. Ben shook his head, thinking how thin the atmosphere was above seven thousand feet. The Ironman suddenly seemed more sane than it had before.

The flat ride gave him the opportunity to become friends with his Trek. Like an experienced horseman, he patted the bike's frame, and gave it a few 'atta-boys.' In a short time Palani Junction appeared ahead.

Just like the climb up 180 had been unfair, so was the sprint down 190. During that stretch, he kept the bike in tenth gear, but still it was easy. His odometer red-lined. The town of Kailua, always visible, was magically speeding toward him, like it was meeting him halfway. He focused on a small, white church spire. Minutes later, the spire had grown so he could see three bells hanging inside. Moku'aikaua—Hawai'i's first church.

The traffic light at the bottom was green. He braked so he could navigate the turn, and soon was on Highway 11, heading due south. This was a short training run, but one he liked. He believed the uphill climb would greatly benefit him later.

Sweat dripped from every pore as he approached the entrance to the apartment complex. Still, he was relaxed. The usual tension in his shoulders and leg muscles was there, but it felt different. More like exercise than strain. More than sixty percent of his Ironman time would be spent on the bike, and it was where he could improve the most. His swimming segment was close to that of the pacesetters. They finished the 2.4 mile swim in just under an hour. He could do a consistent sixty-five minutes. His marathon was two hours and fifty minutes—one of the best. But his bike time was almost two hours off that of the leaders. Now he had a new outlook toward his bike riding. The desire was there again. He was going to cut an hour off this year, and an hour off next. His body tingled with excitement as the vision of breaking the tape and waving to the cheering crowd flashed into his mind. Ben McMillen—Ironman Champion!

It wasn't until he was gliding through the water that his thoughts shifted to the two murders. And quickly, he focused on a new angle. *What if there's some espionage activity going on right now?* That made him think about the second victim. Clothes labels removed, fingerprints stripped.

What if he killed Ahi and then he was killed by someone avenging Ahi's death? Was Ahi a double agent? Had he been discovered and the second man sent to eliminate him? Was the third man Ahi's protection, Ahi's accomplice, only he arrived too late?

The swells in Kealakekua Bay covered his head and drowned out any more thoughts of double agents.

Ben thought about where he was. Without planning it, he'd come to the spot where Ahi was so roughly thrown ashore. Although the water was warm, goose bumps covered his body. His muscles ached and he felt cramps coming on. He'd have to abandon his swim and head straight for the lava beach. Just then, something wrapped around his leg—seaweed. But all Ben could imagine was the remains of Ahi's arms and legs.

———————

Since it was Sunday, Mitchell's wasn't crowded. The band had the night off. A music video was playing, but Danny had the volume down, so most of the patrons paid little attention to the pyrotechnics and gyrations on the wide screen. It was more family night for tourists, but a few singles roamed about with faraway looks in their eyes. None of them would stay long.

Ben sat near the end of the bar, away from the faraway looks. He was sipping his second cold Beck's; the first had disappeared in less than a minute as his brain encouraged him to replenish his burned magnesium.

Danny came over.

"Any luck on your case?"

"We've ID'd the old man. Coffee farmer from Ho'omau Ranch area. Just north of there. Problem is . . . we don't have a motive and we don't have a suspect. And . . . there's been a second killing down there."

Danny put down his wipe rag and sat next to Ben. "Can you tell me about it?"

"We found a man with his throat slit . . . on one of the coffee farms."

"Any connection?" asked Danny.

"More than likely. But I don't know if we have a common murderer, or if the second victim killed the first."

"Another beer?"

"Yeah, and I'll try one of those K Coast pizzas. A small one."

"Be right back."

Danny returned from the kitchen quickly, reached into one of the refrigerators, and pulled out a cold Beck's. He opened it and put in down in front of Ben.

"Thanks."

"Your K Coast will be out in ten minutes."

Ben gave him the 'okay' sign.

"You run into any of the Kona Gold fellas?"

"Just the one, I think . . . Furbee, the guy I asked you about the other day."

Danny smirked.

"Something slimy about that guy. You know the type."

"Run enough bars, you meet them all the time."

"He seems like a lowlife."

"You think he has anything to do with what's happened?" Danny asked.

Ben shrugged his shoulders. "First thing tomorrow . . . I'm gonna find out." Then he remembered that Tobi was picking him up at six-thirty.

Well, second thing.

"Ben, can I tell you something?"

"Sure."

"Ho'omau Ranch is where two tourists disappeared several years ago. Told their friends they were going hiking. The police found their rental Jeep, but not them. No traces. They just vanished."

"Jesus! You know, I was working here then. I vaguely remember it. It was Amaral's case. I wonder if it means anything?" Ben transported himself back three years ago, just months before he had quit. Nothing registered.

"Maybe people keep stumbling on something down there," Danny volunteered, "that someone doesn't want them to see."

"Maaaybe." Ben had a faraway look now. *Maaaybe . . .*

14

B EN WOKE LONG BEFORE THE ALARM. Immediately, he realized he'd forgotten to call Lisa. He squinted at the clock. Too early to call? *Maybe it's too late.* He called. After ten frustrating rings, he hung up. He stared at the phone for a long time, as if it were to blame. Where the fuck was she?

After fifty sit-ups, he went outside. There was a chill in the air and the first rays of sunlight had just edged over the mountains behind him to the east. He stood on the *lānai* with his hands on the railing as he watched the long-legged Black-necked stilts—*ae'o*—running around in the shallow water, feeding on small shore mullet. The Hawaiians actually called them false mullet or *uouoa*. When a mullet was speared, the stilt's head went back, neck straight and rigid, and the silvery fish disappeared down the stilt's long throat. One young stilt—possibly on his first fishing sojourn without mama—was struggling with an oversized mullet. Ben thought to himself—No! Don't!—but too late, as the inexperienced stilt found himself with a wriggling mullet caught in his throat. Ben could see the outline of the fish as it squirmed inside the stilt's narrow neck. Eventually, the mullet worked its way north and south, and slid down.

After the ordeal, the stilt sat in the sand, weary and dazed, but a little better prepared for the next time.

Tobi wasn't due for an hour, which was fine with Ben because he had plenty to think about. He was convinced that Furbee had something to do with the killings. And the only way to find out for sure would be to tail him—something Ben planned to do himself, relieving the man Tobi assigned. That was next, right after he and Tobi made a thorough check of Ahi's farm. First he'd check with Forensic about Furbee's boot prints. Then he'd see if Joyce had come up with anything more on his background. Then he would follow Furbee all day and night, if necessary. Something told him Furbee would screw up long before the sun went down. He also reminded himself to remember to ask Tobi about the hikers who had disappeared near Hoʻomau Ranch.

Ben sat on one of the deck chairs and put his feet on the other, crossing his legs at the ankles. His hands were clasped behind his head. He watched the early morning clouds far out over the ocean. They seemed stationary. There was hardly a breath of wind. But by midmorning they would find the warm shoreline and be sucked inland and upward, finally covering the upper slopes of Mauna Kea and Mauna Loa.

Back from the clouds to Furbee. *Why are two men dead? Does it have to do with spying . . , or Kona Gold? Is the marijuana trade so big that it's worth murdering for? Why create attention?*

Ben knew the Big Island marijuana growers had it pretty good. They were basically tolerated as long as things didn't get out of hand. Not something he agreed with—but that was the way it was. However, if organized crime had gotten involved, then what were the chances the business would remain small? Pretty slim, Ben guessed. In fact, maybe it hadn't been small for a long time. He'd heard about the formation of an Eradication Team, but hadn't had time to talk with them. Trained men repelling from helicopters, armed with sniper's rifles and machetes. Dropped smack into the middle of the weed fields. Maybe, finally, the Big Island would get serious, as long as the budget didn't get in the way.

Maybe finding the bones of two hikers buried in a marijuana field would put a little pressure on the bureaucrats.

He'd said it over and over to himself—*Ahi Ishizu was a spy. But was he? Is Tobi sure? Are there no other explanations?*

And if he had been a spy, had he still been active? What would a spy find to spy on buried in the hills of Kona?

He couldn't think of anything.

Did he travel? Was the farm his cover? Bennett indicated that Ahi had been a farmer for a long time. Did he do his spying after the growing season? Harvest or not, there still must be a ton of things to do to keep the farm in shape. Planting new trees. Thinning out old ones. Does the Japanese Secret Service, or whatever they're called, really have spies in Hawai'i? Probably not. So it must be something from the past. Something that started around the time of the Second World War. What secret could be so important? Could Ahi have exposed someone? Did that person discover the old spy's hiding place? Did he come after Ahi to silence him? After fifty years?

Ben sat forward, letting his legs slowly unwind, touching the deck.

Who was the second victim? Maybe he also worked for the Japanese Secret Service. Maybe he was on a mission. But then . . . who killed him?

The sound of the radio responding to the ALARM setting broke Ben's concentration. He took a deep breath, stood, and went back inside.

After shaving, he stepped into the shower and adjusted the Shower Massage to MEDIUM PULSE. Then he turned the knob into the red zone and settled underneath the hot jets of water, forgetting about murders and marijuana for the time being, letting the beating water work at the knots he felt in his neck and shoulders. He twisted his neck from side to side and back and forth. Gradually, he felt loose. He reached for the soap. As he washed his underarms, he thought about Ahi's tattoo. Up until then, he had felt sorry for the old man, murdered at sea, cast to the creatures of the deep. But the tattoo put Ahi Ishizu into a different category. He had spied against the United States. He probably had something to do with the attack on Pearl Harbor. Ben remembered being told of his uncle who had been killed in his sleep aboard one of the vessels anchored in the harbor that eventful Sunday morning. Ahi had been the enemy.

As he shampooed his hair, his thoughts turned to Lisa. He pictured her sleeping. There was a tiny, almost imperceptible smile on her face. He hoped it was him in her dream. They'd been separated only a week, yet the thought of losing her gave him an empty feeling. But what was he supposed to do? He wanted to be a detective. The job he wanted was on the Big Island.

. . . and she's not. I suppose I could have waited. Tobi would've kept the job open for me. I could have convinced Lisa to transfer if I'd given her more time to think about it. Instead I rushed into it like a teenager, impulsive, only thinking of myself . . .

He wondered how bad he'd screwed things up. He wondered if it was repairable.

But why didn't she answer the phone at five-thirty in the morning? Huh?

Ben dried off, left his hair wet, and padded into the narrow kitchen for some cereal and fruit. His standard breakfast when he was training consisted of a mixture of three dry cereals—Shredded Wheat, Oat Flakes, and Grape Nuts—with skim milk and a sliced banana. He also ate half a papaya, two English muffin halves—dry—and drank a cup of coffee with a little more skim milk, and a teaspoon of raw brown sugar. Morning and night he also took a vitamin—*Enhance*. He'd heard other triathletes talking about the supplement, researched it, and found that it wasn't a gimmick. He'd been taking two a day for the past three years. And he hadn't been sick in all that time. He didn't know if it was the Hawaiian climate, the triathlon training, his diet, or the vitamins, but he wasn't about to change any of his routine.

Tobi's horn bleated just as Ben finished the last of his coffee.

After they had driven a mile, Tobi asked, "Have you had time to train?"

"I've squeezed it in, but what happened to the good old days when we were done at five and if we wanted to see a murder investigated, we had to watch it on TV?"

Tobi frowned. "Things will settle down."

"Anything new?"

"At six-thirty in the morning? A new day, how is that?"

"I thought maybe Ken had called with something. I know he often works strange hours."

"No."

"Question. Danny Mitchell mentioned to me last night that two hikers disappeared in the area of Ahi's farm. Ring a bell?"

"I remember it. Three years ago. You think there is a connection?"

Ben raised his eyebrows but didn't answer. "What about the case?"

"They vanished. We found the Jeep. Amaral worked the case. We interviewed many people in the hills and came up empty. No traces of anything. Nothing. After a month we pulled him off and filed Missing Ps." Tobi shrugged. "And later, Amaral even checked to see if anyone filed an insurance claim on them. No one had."

"Hmmm."

Tobi began whistling and Ben thought about the hikers for a few more minutes before discarding them.

"Tobi, what do you think about the spy angle?"

Tobi stared straight ahead. "I think it plays a major part. I hope we will find something this morning that will point us in the right direction. There must be something in his house that links to his past. He was up to something, or he had something to hide. Old spies do not just turn up dead on the beach."

"What could he be hiding?"

"Someone's identity. Or maybe he continued spying after the war. There are millions of things he could have gotten into."

"Like drugs?"

"Like drugs, smuggling . . . he could still be a spy."

Ben loosened his seat belt a little. "I believe it has something to do with the Kona Gold trade."

It was Tobi's turn. "Hmmm."

Ben stared at his mentor for a few seconds. His breath swelled inside his lungs as he inhaled deeply. "Tell me more about this woman who runs the show. Not the two of you, just her."

Tobi looked at Ben out of the corner of his eye. "Her name is Michiko Higa. Hilo has a complete file on her. You can read it."

"Tobi, with all due respect, you seem . . ."

" . . . like I still care. I told you I do. But it is done." He sighed heavily. "We have nothing specific on her. Her name comes up from time to time. But she has never been directly associated with the trade. I know what I know because she confessed it to me, because . . . because she cared about me, I guess."

"It surprises me that we don't try to put a stop to the trade."

"If we get funding for an all-out eradication program, who knows. But chances are it will just start up again."

Ben felt himself becoming impatient. "What about a serial killer? Why bother . . . there's always be another to take his place."

"Ben, I did not mean it like that. What I meant to say was the trade is small in our district. It is not really that harmful. Puna is where the big growers are. That is Hilo's responsibility. If they get money and ask for our help, we will be the first to sign up. You may join, if you like."

Ben felt he was being placated. He shifted his gaze out the window, absentmindedly watching the scenery, catching glimpses of the shoreline when the foliage thinned. Thinking of something to say.

Tobi's fingers drummed on the steering wheel. "We have to focus on the more serious crimes."

"And you think marijuana is no more serious than burning incense."

"In fact, they are similar, and that is how the vast majority of the Kona folk use it. They grow three or four plants. We are not going to try to track all those down."

Ben's impatience became anger. "Marijuana is the first lab exercise. Coke is next."

They sat in silence.

Ben was confused. It was the first time his respect for Tobi was at issue. He tried to rationalize what Tobi had said. *Maybe there's something in the Japanese psyche attached to mild drugs.* He thought about the smell of incense in Tobi's home. He remembered that a few times, when it was especially strong, he had left feeling a little light-headed. *Maybe Tobi really doesn't think marijuana is much different. Maybe it was the woman? He ended the relationship. But he's still reluctant to do anything about stopping her. Is it indifference, or is it emotion? The Tobi I know would do something about it.*

"For the first time you wonder about me, yes?" Tobi braked slightly and the car slowed. "I have always believed that passive drugs, used in moderation, relax the brain, enable you to think more clearly. I use incense."

"What about marijuana?" asked Ben.

"No. Only incense."

"Did you ever?"

"As a boy. Did you ever steal a piece of candy?"

They remained quiet the rest of the way. Ben was starting to understand Tobi's position, although he didn't agree with it. He also didn't know much about Michiko Higa—but he intended to.

"Turn here."

Tobi took a left, slowed, and slipped the car into second gear as they crawled up the winding dirt road. The overhanging trees made it exceptionally dark and Tobi was squinting. Finally, he flipped on the headlights. At the top of the first hill, the trees thinned a bit, and a muted slice of the morning sun was visible above the crest of the hills behind Ahi's farm. Tobi knocked off the lights.

"It's around this bend," instructed Ben.

"Are you still angry?"

"I don't think so . . . but I'm going to check her out." Looking out of the corners of his eyes, he saw Tobi nodding.

"Is that your approval or a subtle warning?"

"Both."

Ben stared at Tobi. Tobi stared back. A smile broke through Tobi's lips. The corners of Ben's mouth widened. Then he laughed. Tobi grinned broadly and shook Ben's shoulder. "Check her out," he said. "But be careful not to fall for her . . . she is younger than you think."

A small snort from Ben.

They pulled up in front of the farmhouse and got out of the car. Sunlight filtered through the trees, casting beams of suspended dust all around. Narrowing his eyes, Ben could see the County of Hawai'i crime seal on the front door.

Tobi stepped forward, extracted a pen from his breast pocket, and scribbled something on the paper seal. Then he sliced through it with the tip of the pen, turned the doorknob, and opened the front door.

The smell was much worse than the day before. When they were finished, the Forensic team had shut all the windows and doors. Ben walked briskly to the windows above the sink and opened them. Tobi had already opened the ones in the bedroom. In a few seconds Ben could feel the air beginning to circulate.

The fireplace smelled of damp ashes. Forensic had sifted through the remains. The odor was strong and left a smoky taste in Ben's mouth.

Ben looked around. The chair and the ropes were gone. Drawers were open, but everything seemed neat, not ransacked. The men from the lab had taken their time.

Tobi said, "You take the kitchen and the living area. I will concentrate on the bedroom and the bath."

"Fine."

Ben started in the kitchen. His hands rested on his hips as he thought about potential hiding places. Looking for things Forensic might have skipped. After all, their job was to find evidence—fingerprints, loose dirt, hair, scraps of paper—not necessarily hiding places, places with lists of all the Japanese spies stationed throughout the Pacific Rim.

Ben walked around slowly, testing the floor, looking for wide seams, loose planks. Then he got down on his knees and examined the baseboard trim. It all seemed firmly in place and there were no telltale scratches or pry marks. Next he pulled away the paper screen partition.

There was nothing behind it, and the exterior wall of the farmhouse held no clues either.

He leaned on a cutting block next to the sink. He heard Tobi opening and closing drawers in the bedroom. Ben tapped the block. It was solid throughout.

He opened every kitchen drawer. Every cabinet door. He climbed onto the countertop and looked up at the vaulted ceiling. Wooden beams, an undergarment for the roof, left everything exposed. The tops of the cabinets were bare.

There was no oven to look into, but there was a refrigerator. It had been emptied. He checked the freezer and the ice cube trays. Nothing. Time for the living area.

"Any luck?" he shouted to Tobi.

"Not yet," answered Tobi.

Not yet . . . always the optimist.

He swept his tongue across his lips and entered the living room. It was sparse. There was one other chair that matched the one Ahi had been bound to, a squat *koa* table, old and worn, but still with a wax luster, and several floor mats and pillows. The pillows looked deflated, defeated. Ben saw that they had been carefully opened along their seams. Each pillow was empty except for remnants of the cotton fill. He checked the floor, walking each plank, looking for one that was loose. The workmanship was excellent. Not one creaked. He got to his knees and looked under the low table. Nothing taped to the bottom. He tapped the underside. No secret compartments.

Then he walked toward the back of the room and unhinged the room divider that faced the rear wall. Like the one in the kitchen, there was nothing behind it.

Tobi had finished with the bedroom. There hadn't been much. The desktop was clear. Forensic had taken all the letters and other papers. The sleeping mattress had been neatly slit and searched. A few clothes hung in the closet. Several pairs of work pants and shirts, looking very incongruous with the other remaining garment—a ceremonial robe.

Tobi searched the pockets of the work clothes. He found nothing. He spied some jars of paint and a few brushes on the closet shelf, and in the corner was an easel. On his tiptoes he reached and pushed the paints aside. There was nothing behind them. He took a jar and unscrewed the lid. Paint, brown, pretty new, not dried, but used. The rest were mainly earth tones, although there was a lilac and a pink. He bent and examined the base of the easel.

Tobi gazed at the robe for a few seconds, then he slid it off its hanger, and carefully spread it out on the bed, fanning the oversized sleeves. It was old, maybe very old. Pure silk and in good condition. The robe was yellow and red with black piping along the sleeves and running down the front. A wide red sash was tucked into one of the sleeves. Tobi patted the material from top to bottom, sleeve to sleeve. It would have provided an excellent place to hide a document, but there was none. Respectfully, he hung it back in the closet. He ran his fingers along the cloth one last time and shook his head in admiration.

He went to the center of the room, hands on his hips just like Ben. His eyes searched the ceiling. Then he walked to the exterior wall, unhooked the paper screen divider, and examined behind it. The space was bare.

In the bathroom he found a toothbrush and several glass bottles of herbs and parts of plants. He recognized all of them. Traditional medicines. Some to be combined with sea salt, hot water, and rubbed on aching muscles. Some for healing cuts. A container of *awa* leaves to be chewed for headaches. Another plastic container held a single piece of 'uhaloa root bark, probably one of the best-known Hawaiian remedies. It was used to cure sore throats. But none of these revealed anything special about Ahi. They were all common medicines, especially for a laborer. What it did mean was that Ahi probably never saw a doctor. One less person to know something about him.

There was no marijuana. Tobi thought about it . . . something *was* missing. He looked back into the bedroom. No incense. He wondered about that.

When Tobi came into the center room, he found Ben standing in front of one of the paper and *koa* frames that separated the living area from the bedroom. He was staring at one of the drawings.

"Find something interesting?" asked Tobi.

"These paintings."

Tobi stepped closer. "Very nice work." He bent forward and examined the Japanese letters on the bottom. "They're his." He glanced at Ben who was staring at the painting on the far right. "That one seems to have you mesmerized."

"It's different. All the others are scenes from Japan . . . best I can tell. This one's from here."

Tobi studied the painting for a few seconds. A smoking volcano in the background, a lava flow, looking real, looking hot, twisting through the jungle, ending up in the ocean in a cloud of steam. "There are volcanoes in Japan. Ever heard of Mount Fuji?"

"This is here. This is where Kīlauea's lava meets the sea near Kalapana. I've been there often. The place fascinates me . . . it's the only spot I know where the earth is still giving birth. And besides, look at the colors, they're more vibrant than those on the other paintings . . . they're not faded. This one's new."

"So?"

"Well, nothing, except it tells us something about him." Ben could sense that Tobi was smiling to himself. Knowing Tobi felt good when his protégé did some thinking—felt good when he talked about spiritual things like the earth giving birth.

"Tells us what?"

"That he's been there. That he left the farm. Maybe he *is* different from the other farmers."

"But he could have made it up. He could have seen it in a newspaper or a magazine."

"It's real," Ben said firmly.

Tobi nodded, going with Ben's conviction. "I found paints and brushes on the bedroom closet shelf. And an easel folded up in the corner.

"Anything on the easel?"

Tobi's lower lip was firm. He shook his head.

"I mean the legs . . . were they dirty?"

"No."

"You find anything else?" asked Ben.

"Nothing, except home cures in the medicine cabinet. Nothing special."

"I came up empty in here. Let's have a look out back."

Rather than break the seal on the back door, they exited out the front.

As they turned the corner and approached the backyard, they both stopped in their tracks. Ben's mouth opened and his eyes widened. He turned toward Tobi. His mentor was frowning.

There were holes and piles of dirt everywhere. More than a dozen. They walked over to the nearest. It was about four feet deep. Jagged lava rock was evident in the bottom. Tobi walked to another. Same thing.

Ben shouted. "They're all dug down to the lava bed." Ben knelt and whistled long and low. "Look, cowboy boot prints all over."

Tobi came closer. "They look the same as those at scene number two."

"They're close, but I think there are at least two sets."

Tobi's hands went to his hair and he stroked the sides a few times. Ben stood, hands on hips, a familiar pose.

"It would take at least two people to dig all this from the time Forensic left until now," said Tobi.

Ben's tongue was between his lips. He made a smacking sound. "I guess Ahi *was* hiding something. Do you think they found it?"

"If there were one or two holes, I would say yes. There are far too many. They were guessing."

"I counted nineteen."

Tobi stated, "Twenty. There is one by itself back there." He pointed.

Ben looked to the far end of the open area, forty yards away, past the mac nut trees, but before the first row of coffee trees. He saw a large mound of dirt.

A hawk cried out. Tobi shielded his eyes and followed its circular flight above the coffee trees. Soon another hawk joined it and they circled, letting out occasional squawks, maintaining the same height, but narrowing the circumference of their circle, until they were only a few feet apart.

Ben expected a fight, but then he realized, by comparing their sizes, that they were mates. And their heads were down fixed on the ground. They were focused on the twentieth hole. They seemed curious rather than preparing to strike.

Ben saw Tobi walking toward the solitary dirt pile. He followed.

There was a straw cowboy hat lying on one side of the mound. There was a small man with small boots stuffed into the hole. There was a cruel smile on his face. There was a neat bullet hole dead center between his eyes.

"From your description . . . with the exception of the bullet hole . . . I take it this is Jeremiah Furbee."

Ben was speechless.

15

I T DIDN'T TAKE AN EXPERT TO MATCH the bottom of Furbee's boot to
the boot prints they had found at the second murder scene. Ben and
Tobi recognized that right away. Still, neither spoke. Tobi was staring at
Furbee's face. His expression told much. Furbee looked as if he had expected his fate. His killer was someone he knew—and someone he did
not trust.

Ben watched Tobi until Tobi looked up, frowning. Just then, the sun
fell behind a huge dark gray cloud. Instinctively, they both looked over
their shoulders and stared at the eerie scene behind them. Mounds of
earth. Long shadows disappearing into the small craters that littered Ahi's
backyard. Even the forest birds, now silent, seemed to take notice.

Ben finally spoke. "Do you think Furbee killed the guy at Fukada's,
or was he just a witness?"

Tobi's eyes fixed on one of the holes. After a few seconds, they darted
to another. And then to another. Ben expected him to respond with
something revealing. What he got was a shrug of his mentor's shoulders.
"Does it matter?"

Tobi then knelt and examined the second set of boot prints around
Furbee's resting place. These prints were small as well, basically the sa-

size as Furbee's. The only difference was that the boot that made these impressions was new and a bit more pointed. There was no insignia, no special markings, on either the heel or the sole.

"Based on what you told me about Furbee, I think he was double-crossed. I think he and his murderer were digging these holes. I think they had an argument, and the other person killed him."

"But you *don't* think they found what they were looking for." Ben inhaled slowly, waiting for confirmation.

"Only if it was something small. See the boot prints leaving. The heel impression is no deeper. The person was not carrying anything heavy."

"What if it *was* something small?" asked Ben.

"People do not bury something small," Tobi answered with finality in his voice. He straightened up. "Ben, call this in. I will follow these boot prints." In a matter of seconds he disappeared into the coffee trees.

Ben trotted back to Tobi's car with visions of suspects, all blurs, whizzing through his head. There were no suspects, except maybe Bennett, but he didn't believe Bennett had done this.

He radioed headquarters.

He caught up with Tobi at the back of Ahi's property. The last row of coffee trees was followed by two more rows of mac nut trees and then an old lava rock wall in bad repair. After that, it was thick forest. The trail of boot prints ended there.

Without turning, Tobi said, "The person walked straight to here. I cannot follow the prints any farther."

"Forensic, two patrol, and Ken are on their way."

Tobi nodded, but he was still staring into the forest. "You said there's a family to the south. They didn't hear or see anything?"

"Right."

Tobi pointed to the other farm, north. "Does the old man understand sign language or read lips?"

Ben frowned. "I couldn't get much out of him yesterday. He seemed . . ."

"We go to see him now. No one else will be here for twenty minutes or more."

"And leave the body?" It was against procedure to leave a body unattended. Tobi thought about it for a few seconds. "We will be right back."

The old man smiled when he saw Tobi—a toothless grin. Tobi spoke in Japanese, slowly, exaggerating his mouth's movements. The old man had seen nothing. Not last night, not the night Ahi had been killed. Tobi asked him about Ahi. The old man spoke in halting Japanese. When he was finished, Tobi translated for Ben.

"They were friends for a long time. Ahi showed up just before Pearl Harbor was attacked. At least that is how I take it. He keeps referring to the time of 'many planes and ships.' His father gave Ahi a place to sleep and fed him. Ahi worked here until this man's father died. His father's will provided Ahi with the front three acres. This was after the many planes and ships went away."

Tobi asked if Ahi had owned a big radio. "*Rajio,*" he repeated. He got a shrug.

Ben was impressed with Tobi's subtlety. He was checking out the spy angle without asking about it directly.

When they made their way back to Ahi's farmhouse, two patrolmen were standing near the body. Both sported quizzical looks, probably wondering about the unguarded corpse, but neither said anything. Tobi greeted them and gave them instructions. One was to wait for Forensic, the other to search for caves in the cliff at the rear of the property. Tobi told the man who was to guard Furbee's remains that as soon as Ken Asumura arrived, he was to join his partner combing the forest and the area near the cliffs. He also told the second man to radio for some dogs.

Then he and Ben went back into the house. Tobi said he felt they had missed something. "Remember, Ahi was once a spy. We have to search with that in mind. This was a person who was used to hiding things. He lost his life because he was hiding something."

They exchanged rooms this time. Ben took the bedroom and bathroom. Tobi the living area and kitchen.

Ben sat on Ahi's thin sleeping mat. Slowly, he looked around the bedroom. Inch by inch. Thinking, imagining hidden trap doors in the floor, false bottoms in drawers. When he leaned back, arms extending to brace himself, he spotted a hanging painting that he had overlooked before. All the other paintings were done on the rice paper walls. This was the only free-standing—actually free-hanging—picture. He thought about it carefully, while trying to imagine what Ahi was like. After a few minutes, he decided this man was a lot like Tobi, and that if Tobi had something to hide, he'd hide it out it the open. Ben stood quickly. He walked over to the hanging picture. Batik, he thought it was called. A print on a piece of raw silk. One side was a watercolor of three irises in full bloom. He spun it around. The other side had three iris buds on a separate piece of silk. Then he held the artwork and positioned it so he was looking at it from the side. A smile crossed his face—two pieces of silk with some kind of mounting board between. He took out his pocket knife and cut the thin mono-filament line. He sat and then carefully peeled back one of the silk paintings. The matting board turned out to be a large white envelope. It had a waxy finish. Waterproof. A top flap was tucked inside.

"Tobi."

"Right here," he said as he entered Ahi's bedroom.

"Look at this." He handed the envelope to Tobi.

Ben watched as Tobi opened the envelope and removed five thin packets of paper money. The money was new, crisp. Hundred-yen notes. Each packet was about an eighth of an inch thick, bound with a thin paper strip, an official-looking paper band. There was Japanese script on the binding.

Tobi muttered out loud, "The Imperial Bank of Japan." He examined the top banknote. Ben took another packet and did the same.

Tobi sat back and exclaimed, "These are old . . . never been used . . . but very old. The date is 1939."

"Is this what he was hiding?"

Tobi counted the notes in one of the packets. After awhile he sat on the floor and crossed his legs. "This is not much money. Even for back then."

Ben held up the envelope and shook it. Two small photographs fell out. Ben looked at Tobi. They each picked up one. Tobi's print was in color. It showed the volcano scene Ahi had painted. Tobi informed Ben that the word for 'active volcano'—*kakkazan*—was printed in Japanese on the back.

Ben's was an old black and white, yellowed where it was supposed to be white. The edges were cut to form a fancy ridged border. The picture showed a large, light-colored stucco building in the background. Tall, majestic palms flanked four men who stood in front of a black Buick roadster, arms around each other, big smiles. Four Japanese men. All looked to be in their mid-twenties. The name of the photography studio was imprinted on the back in flowing ink. *Silver Moon Studio.*

Ben handed it to Tobi. "I wonder which one is Ahi."

Tobi studied the photo for a long time. Then he closed his eyes. He kept them closed while he spoke. "He is the second from the left. The one whose smile is most confident."

Ben asked his question once more. "Is this what they were looking for?"

"It does not explain the holes in the backyard. They were anticipating something big . . . like buried treasure."

Ben made a frown. "Buried treasure? Maybe they thought there was more money. Maybe over time, with exaggeration, these packets became a lot more."

"Maybe," said Tobi. "Maybe." He was studying the photograph.

Back at headquarters Millie Kalehua's arms reached out and Ben walked into her embrace. It was their reunion. She'd been away on vacation, visiting an aunt who lived on Kaua'i. It was her first day back at work since Ben's arrival.

There had always been a special bond between Ben and Millie. To

Ben, the Major's administrative assistant was a combination mother and adviser. She was obviously delighted to see him and held him tightly like any Hawaiian mother would.

After a few moments she stepped back, still holding onto his arms. "Let me look at you."

Ben smiled. "I'm all here."

"You look well . . . are you still training?"

Ben nodded. His mind raced ahead a little, preparing for the next question.

"And how is Lisa?" Millie asked.

He told her Lisa was doing fine. Millie was hard to fool—in fact, it usually wasn't worth trying—but she seemed to accept his response at face value. There'd be time to explain later. And then again, maybe there wouldn't be anything to explain. Maybe it would work out.

"You have to come for dinner. Morris wants to see you."

"I'd love to . . . just as soon as we wrap this up."

She stepped up an gave him a peck on the cheek, and instinctively, even though there was no lipstick to wipe, she wiped off his cheek with her fingers. "*Pōmaika'i.*"

"Thanks, we'll need it."

When Ben came in, Tobi was alone in his office. He was seated, elbows uncharacteristically planted on his desk, staring at the two photographs, paying the most attention to the one taken of the four men.

He looked up at Ben. "I know this place. It will come to me." He handed Ben an enlargement that had been made. "The year on the license plate of the Buick is 1938. I'm sure this was taken just before Pearl Harbor."

"So where is it?"

"It will come to me."

"What about the money?"

"Counted. Their were only fifty notes in each packet. Two hundred and fifty one-hundred yen notes. I had someone check out the value of a yen in '41. I could not remember. It was about twenty-five cents U.S."

Ben made a quick calculation. "That's only a little over six thousand dollars. Not much. Not usually worth three murders." Ben lowered himself into a chair.

"Not only that, these are probably worthless today as currency. They are old yen . . . not today's. The only real value might be with a collector. Even then, how much could they be worth? Believe me, they are not what the murderer has been searching for." Tobi's brow furrowed, a score of deep ridges formed on his forehead. "This building must be on O'ahu . . ." Just then a small smile turned up the corners of his mouth.

Ben sat forward.

Tobi pursed his lips for a second. "It is on the waterfront," he said. "When I was a boy it was . . . I think it was a cannery."

"Like a fish packing house?"

Tobi didn't answer. When he spoke, it was to himself, "No, that was the building next to it. An export . . ." he squinted, " . . . a trading company. Something like that. I wonder if it is still standing." Then he brought Ben back into the conversation. His gaze was firm. It seemed as if he was transporting himself back to Honolulu to the time when he was a boy. "I wonder what it was before the war?"

"Don't you know someone who'll know?"

Tobi faced Ben. "It was fifty years ago. We need someone who is at least seventy now . . . like Ahi Ishizu. Someone that old. I wonder if Haanio's parents are still alive." Tobi picked up the phone and pushed the intercom button.

A few minutes later Detective Haanio, the transferee from O'ahu, was in Tobi's office, nodding. "Both parents are still alive. My father worked the waterfront for many years, but he is almost eighty. If he does not remember, perhaps one of his friends will. I will call."

Ten minutes later Detective Haanio reappeared, a broad smile filling his face. "My father said it used to be the Japanese Trade Association building."

"Trade Association?" Ben was confused.

"It was supposed to be like an embassy promoting commerce and trade, but my father said it was the headquarters for Japanese spies as well. He said that after Pearl Harbor, they proved a few of the men were high-ranking members of the Japanese Secret Service."

"I wonder what happened to them?" Tobi mused.

Haanio shrugged. "My father didn't know anything else."

Ben and Tobi exchanged glances.

Tobi said, "Thanks, Haanio. Thank you very much."

Haanio nodded and left.

"Ben, it looks like you are on your way to Honolulu."

"Aren't you coming?"

"I should direct the team on the murders. You find out more about Ahi Ishizu. He holds the secret to all this. He was hiding more than photographs and five packets of yen."

Ben thought about the painting and the photo. They were similar, but Ahi hadn't painted the scene in the photo. The perspective of the painting was different—from the sea. "You know, that's something. The perspective of the painting is from the sea. Maybe the ocean wasn't so strange for him after all."

"I think he visualized it," said Tobi. "His easel showed no signs of having been outside, even though his paintings portray the land."

Ben's eyebrows arched. *Kalapana. That's where Kīlauea is flowing. There or Honolulu? Find out more about Ahi, or his painting?* But he let it go and his mind quickly changed focus. "What about his granddaughter? Any luck tracking her down?"

"We're working on it. The school she teaches at is in recess. And no one is at home."

"I hope she's okay."

"My wishes exactly."

———

"How are you?"

Lisa said she was fine.

"I called this morning . . . *early*. I guess you were out." Despite his best efforts, his tone was accusing.

"I slept at the hotel . . . we had a late meeting." She didn't sound at all defensive, only tired.

He softened his timbre. "I miss you."

Lisa didn't respond right away. "Do you, Ben? Do you really?"

"Of course, I do."

"I'm sorry. Your voice was kind of flat when you said it, that's all."

Ben cleared his throat. "I guess there's still some tension between us. Look, I just called to let you know that I have to go to Honolulu tomorrow. I thought maybe after I was finished, I'd fly to Maui and we could have dinner."

"When would you get here?"

Ben screwed up his face. "I don't know . . . maybe around five or six. If you met me at the airport and we went to Mama's, I could get back in time to catch the last flight . . . or I guess I could catch the first one in the morning."

"Call me before you take off. I'll be there."

His cheeks flushed. He had half-expected her to refuse. "See you tomorrow."

They each waited for something else to be said. After several seconds of painful silence, there was a polite click. Then another as Ben put down the phone.

But he had no clue whether she wanted him to spend the night.

16

Tobi had decided to send Haanio with Ben since the veteran detective knew most every police officer who worked for the City and County of Honolulu. Haanio's family was old O'ahu. Haanio was well connected.

So just past eight the next morning they disembarked from their flight from Keāhole to Honolulu. The plane had been less than a quarter full. Tourists clogged the inter-Island flights during the afternoons, after they checked out of their hotels and condos, headed for the next adventure. Now there were only a few dozen commuters and some others who'd spend the day shopping downtown. Ben and Haanio were met at the gate by Detective Paul Kalani. Haanio embraced him warmly. They exchanged a few words in Hawaiian, smiling. Haanio patted Kalani's stomach, which hung over his wide black belt. Then Haanio introduced Ben. The two detectives shook hands.

The Inter-Island Terminal was an L-shaped building attached to the main airport terminal by an outdoor walkway. It sat at the northeastern end of the airport and housed the two major inter-island carriers—Aloha and Hawaiian Air. A few smaller carriers also used the facilities—like

Princeville Air, which hopped back and forth between Honolulu and the Princeville Airport on the north shore of Kaua'i.

A stiff breeze blew as they stepped outside. The sky was clear overhead, gray in the foothills, and almost black in the mountains. Engine noise and jet fumes filled the air. People of all nationalities scurried about, overloaded with luggage. Those arriving were pale, tired from their flights, but smiling as they anticipated paradise. Those leaving kept a stiff upper lip as they waited in the check-in line, guarding their boxes of pineapples and papayas, headed for colder destinations. The arriving passengers craved eye contact. The jealous, departing ones avoided it.

As they walked to the car, Ben counted ten 747 tail sections protruding above the exhaust barricade that separated them from the international gate area in the main terminal. Ten jumbos ready for departure.

Kalani had double-parked directly in front of the inter-Island terminal. Haanio jumped into the front seat of the tan Camaro. Ben stretched out in the back. Instinctively, they each rolled up a window and sealed off the noise.

"Where to?" asked Kalani, pushing the AC button to MAX. "Downtown?"

Haanio turned around.

Ben leaned forward. "I'd like to run by this old Trade Association building first."

"It's a warehouse now," answered Kalani. "When Captain Otaki called, two of us went down there and looked around. But most of the managers and staff were at a productivity session at one of the Waikīkī hotels, so we didn't stay long. We did find out that it was shut down during the war, but sometime in the late '40s, it was sold back to the *new* Japanese Trade Commission. They've been there ever since. "

"That's good. We probably won't find anyone who remembers Ishizu, but they may have some old records stored away. It might even be better than the stuff downtown."

"Fine. We're on our way."

Detective Kalani pulled out, swerved around two courtesy trams, found the outside lane, and soon they were on Nimitz Highway heading toward Honolulu Harbor.

Paul Kalani looked about forty-five. He was tall—at least six-two—and dark-skinned. His hair was black, straight, and parted in the middle. Nowhere was there a hint of gray. A pair of reading glasses was hanging from his breast pocket. Peering between the front bucket seats, Ben noticed a slight bulge on his right hip. His aloha shirt hung loose, covering the revolver, but Ben could tell it was a .38. Tobi had told him O'ahu cops and detectives always carried weapons. The action on O'ahu was fast and heavy. It was a prime port for smuggling—drug traffic bound for the mainland, cash bound for the Far East. Hardly a week passed without a homicide, usually the bad guys icing each other. Eventually, you'd think they'd become extinct, but there'd been no such luck.

Most of the area surrounding Pearl Harbor was controlled by the Navy and Air Force. All of the major commercial shipping took place a few miles to the east, south of the downtown area and across from Sand Island.

Nimitz was congested but moving. The Waikīkī resorts were dead ahead. The skyline of Honolulu was on their left, and the Io'olau mountain range framed the tall buildings. Diamond Head crater was the backdrop for the resorts. Everywhere there were dark clouds, but none deeper than over the mountains, where streaks of deep gray fell out of the sky, warning of approaching rain. A single rainbow stretched across the sky to the southeast. And a few egg-sized drops of rain splattered on the windshield. Detective Kalani's fingers pressed the intermittent wiper button. Ben expected the wipers to be noisy. They were silent.

Ben wasn't a Honolulu fan. It was too crowded for him. Clogged with ancient tourists, too many making their first and last trips to paradise, not knowing where to go, and taking their sweet time about it. Taking pleasure in the one thing that remained in their marriages—arguing.

Subjects like where to eat, what to eat, and when to eat it. And whom to eat with, and what was good for you. And what wasn't. Ben smiled and thought about his father, sitting at breakfast quoting lines from an old radio show—the Bickersons. He would have had a field day around the Waikīkī hotels mimicking his favorite program.

Ben knew the sands of Waikīkī would be covered with bodies, even in the rain. More than eighty percent of Oʻahu's population—and an equal percentage of the tourists—jammed into the southern part of Oʻahu. It reminded him of Miami Beach.

Nimitz bent southeast. Honolulu Harbor was in sight. They passed Piers 39 and 40—the inter-Island barge operation area—where supplies left and refuse returned. Around Pier 31A Nimitz split; eastbound traffic dipped a bit south. The highway became Ala Moana Boulevard and soon all they could see were warehouses and freighters and tugs. Kalani angled right and then took another right onto an unmarked street, which dead-ended abruptly, right by Pier 2B. A green-and-white sign read—
FOREIGN TRADE ZONE.

"This is it," stated Haanio.

"Where?" asked Ben, straining his neck. The building in the photo was nowhere to be seen.

"In back."

The rain started to fall. Kalani kept the engine running, stepped up the wipers from intermittent to slow, and boosted the air conditioner to combat the condensation forming on the windows. The Honolulu detective pointed to a new steel structure. "This is an addition for storage. The reception area is in the old section."

Ben let his window down a crack. Rain came in. He rolled up the window. "Can you get closer?"

"Uh huh." They made another right into a driveway that skirted the new section and wound around to the left. Soon they were parked in front of the building in the photo. It looked remarkably unchanged, except that the stucco finish seemed lighter, even though it was wet. The sign above the side doors said—**Pacific Rim Trade Association.** Underneath were some Japanese letters. Ben assumed that they said the same thing.

"Let's have a look around."

Kalani sighed. "Fifty years is a long time."

Ben got out. He dashed through the rain and reached the front door. He heard two car doors slam, then running footsteps splashing in the puddles on the pavement. He could visualize Kalani's face. Disdain. A waste of time. And Haanio's. Smiling. Haanio's trademark.

Inside, he held the door and waited for the other detectives. They stamped their feet simultaneously. Kalani approached the receptionist.

"May I help you, sir?"

"Detective Kalani." He flipped open his wallet and snapped it shut. "These two detectives," his head moved sideways toward Ben and Haanio, "are from the Big Island. They're working on the case I talked to the guard about yesterday."

The woman was small. She looked like a mixture of several Asian backgrounds, but she spoke perfect English with no accent.

"Yes, he left me a note." She stood and extended her hand. "My name is Kim. I am pleased to meet you."

Ben shook her hand. "Ben McMillen." Haanio followed suit.

She asked, "What can I do for you, gentlemen?"

"We are trying to find out the identity of some men in a photo. It was taken just before the war, but I thought perhaps someone could check to see if you have any old records stored around here. Maybe some employment records. Maybe we could find the name of someone who left right after the war. They might be able to help us if we can locate one of them."

"That's quite a few years," she said.

"I know. What do you think?"

"There's a room in the basement . . . in the back. I know there are all sorts of old ledgers and filing cabinets in there. That is, if the rats haven't taken over."

Ben shuddered slightly. He hated rats. "Can we look?" he asked.

"I'll have to get someone in personnel to do it, or at least show me where the stuff is." Kim picked up the phone. "Let me check."

Ben paced a few steps, then turned around and paced some more. Haanio and Kalani had taken seats. Kalani had a hopeful look on his face. Ben wondered if it was real. Haanio was smiling.

After a short conversation, Kim hung up. It had been obvious from the expression on her face after she mentioned there were a few detectives standing right there that the person on the other end said he'd be right out.

In less than a minute a Japanese man came down one of the hallways. Ben noticed he had a runner's grace. The man bowed and introduced himself. His name was Peter Hirayama. He was of medium height with short-cropped gray-black hair and thin eyebrows. His face looked weary—maybe fifty—but his body was in good shape, making Ben think he might be younger. His sport jacket was beautifully tailored and his shirt looked like a custom job. A white handkerchief peeked discreetly out of his breast pocket.

"How may we help?" he asked, making sure to shake each of their hands.

Ben introduced himself and the other detectives and explained what they were looking for.

"Is someone who worked here in trouble?" he asked.

Ben took a deep breath. "Someone who worked here before the war was killed last week. We're trying to find out why and by whom. We found this picture," Ben fished a copy out of his shirt pocket and handed it to Peter Hirayama," . . . recognize the building?"

Peter nodded slowly. "This is the building." His face perked with interest. "Hasn't changed much, has it?"

Ben ignored the question. "I assume you don't recognize any of the men."

Peter shook his head. "It was long before my time . . . the war. I've been the managing director for five years. But Kim told me what you want. We'll try to track it down. We've always kept good records."

Ben said politely, "We need the information today."

"We'll assist in any way we can. I must warn you . . . a lot of things were burned or confiscated right after Pearl Harbor . . . not everything was returned."

"You still have records from back then?" asked Kalani.

"Yes. The foreign trade section of our government reacquired it, so there were no new owners to throw things away." He cleared his throat and quickly added, "However, this time there are no . . ."

"That's okay," said Ben, also thinking about the spies. "We don't mean to embarrass you."

Peter Hirayama smiled nervously.

Ben asked, "Can you spare someone to help us?"

Peter nodded. "Wait here for a few minutes. Kim, get these gentlemen tea, please." He left.

"I think we'll pass," said Ben.

Kim sat down behind her desk.

Ben faced Haanio. "What do you think, Haanio?"

"I'm game, especially if it was the same branch of their government. That's a break."

Ben looked at Kalani.

Kalani shrugged. "These records might be better than what we have downtown."

Ben wondered why Kalani seemed so reluctant. Maybe he wasn't interested. After all, it was Kona's case.

Another woman—this one wasn't Hawaiian *or* Japanese, rather she appeared to be a *haole,* pale, good posture, stuffy, probably left over from the days of the missionaries—took them down a flight of stairs and to the end of a narrow hallway that led them far into the catacombs of the basement. The farther along the hallway they walked, the stronger the smell of mildew became. Finally they reached a room at the end of the hall. Next to the door was a small sign—*Archives.* The door was locked.

The woman produced a key and inserted it, struggled with the doorknob for a few seconds, but finally it turned. A stream of dust greeted them. Ben sneezed. So did Haanio.

Once they were all inside, the woman explained how things were filed. She told them that Kim would be down to help as soon as someone was found to relieve her at the receptionist's desk. She marched out as if she had better things to do. Like the rest of her coffee break.

The room was about twenty feet square. Three sides were filled with drab olive-green file cabinets. Government issue and probably issued long ago. Heavy ones—four drawers, fireproof. They were scratched and dented, but they were solid. Stacked on top of the cabinets were giant ledgers with dark green jackets covered with dust. What space there was was decorated with rust rings that overlapped like drunken Olympic symbols. In the center of the room was a long table and three folding chairs. The table was bare. Except for more rings of rust.

The file drawer of ex-employees only went back to 1959. Ben hoped it was far enough. He'd start with that drawer. The ledgers on top of the cabinets appeared to chronicle major events. They went back before the war. Ben asked Haanio to concentrate on those, and to start his search in the late '30s, working his way toward December 1941.

Haanio took the first ledger, sneezed several more times as a new wave of dust assaulted his nose, lugged the book to the center of the room, and pulled a chair to the table. His problem was the handwriting. Although it was in English, it was small and the dampness had made the pen strokes anything but crisp.

Ben instructed Kalani to browse through the rest of the materials, looking for photos, for anything that even remotely appeared like espionage. It was lazy man's work and Ben believed Kalani was just the man for the job.

Ten minutes later, Kim entered. Ben put her to work on the ledgers, helping Haanio. He saved the piece he believed would provide results for himself. He wasn't in a trusting mood this day.

An hour passed. Glancing now and then at Haanio told him that the ledger work was slow. There were many entries. There had been no mention of Ahi Ishizu. Ben thought about that. He wondered if they should be looking for a code name. He told Haanio to pay attention to any word or phase that seemed to come up too frequently. Or that was out of context. "Maybe Ahi had a code name."

Haanio grunted.

Kalani was turning pages. Ben didn't ask of what.

His own efforts focused on reorganizing the ex-employees by the date they had left the Trade Commission. He opened each manila folder, scanned for the person's termination date, and inserted the folder in the appropriate slot in his new stack. Some of the forms in the file folders were bent and torn, and some were smeared. He made a special pile for the ones he couldn't read. He'd worry about those later. Thankfully, there weren't too many. He was surprised everything was in English. But he supposed that by 1960 that made the most sense.

Kalani asked for the photo of the four men. Ben asked if he'd found anything. Kalani answered, "Not yet."

·Ben took out the picture and handed it to the detective. Returning to his task, he caught Kim staring at him. Her face turned red when their eyes met. Ben buried his in the files.

Thirty minutes later, Ben was done. Next, he wrote down the names, telephone numbers, the last date of service, and the address at the time of separation. He only bothered with the top ten. The first went back to February 1960. It had a forwarding address. Japan. Ben sighed and frowned. The second was April of the same year. Ben opened the file. The man had left for a simple reason. He had died. The third man was an American. Ben's eyes widened. Why was an American employed by the Japanese? But his interest was held only until he read a footnote— the man had been killed on December 7. The next seven revealed nothing. His nostrils flared and he stood up, hands resting on his hips. This was a waste of time. He began pacing. How do you find a man from a half century ago?

Kalani had found a yearbook that contained pictures of each employee who had received a promotion during 1940. There were twenty men in all and two women. Kalani's page of photos had names under each picture. Ahi Ishizu was the second from the left on the second row. The other three men from the photo were there as well. Once again, Ahi was the only one who exhibited self-confidence.

Kalani let out a yelp. Haanio smiled and Ben realized Haanio had sensed his unfavorable impression of Kalani. He had also known that Ben was wrong.

Ben took the book and studied the names. Besides Ahi, there were Yasuo Sato, Niko Yamato, and Toshio Fukunaga. Ben checked them against the file folders. No matches. Kim suggested they see someone in the benefits section. Even if the men had left before 1960, there might be some record of pension or health benefits.

Upstairs, on the main floor of the warehouse, in a room filled with clerks, they found Yamato's folder. It took only minutes. He had been born in Japan, but in 1936 he had become an American citizen. He worked for the American government as a clerk. His association with Ahi Ishizu, the spy, seemed merely coincidental. He transferred to the Navy in January of 1942 and served as an administrative aide in Requisition & Supply. He went to California in December of 1943.

Ben sighed, thinking of a dreaded trip to the mainland, widening the scope of the case instead of narrowing it.

Ben read on. For a number of years his pension checks had been mailed to a holding camp. Yamato was one of the Japanese who had been confined to holding camps during the war. He thought about the camps in California during World War II. He remembered his father telling him how all the Americans of Japanese ancestry had been suspected of treason. The government assumed they would be loyal to Japan. Families were pulled out of their homes and put into holding camps. Prisoners. That wasn't the case in Hawai'i, not because the Hawaiian AJAs were considered more trustworthy—far from the truth—but the fact was there had been too many of them. There was no practical way to handle them in the confused aftermath of Pearl Harbor. So AJAs were kept under surveillance by the FBI. In fact, so many AJA young men wanted to prove their loyalty to the United States that over ten thousand enlisted. And two AJA units, the 100th Infantry Battalion, and the Regimental Combat Team, had earned special distinction.

When Yamato reached the mainland, the bureaucracy had been waiting for him. Yamato had gone to jail. Ben laughed to himself. Here was an American citizen, suspected of being a Japanese spy, in a holding camp, receiving pay checks from the United States Government. He thought $600 toilet seat covers won first prize. Not anymore.

Yamato returned to Oʻahu in 1946 and continued working for the navy. An entry in 1959—one year before the records in the basement started—showed he retired, and his checks were forwarded to an address on Kauaʻi, to the small town of Hanalei on the north shore. Ben breathed a sigh of relief. Then something made him look up. The woman who had lead them into the basement had been watching them. She abruptly turned her head and walked away when Ben noticed her. Ben watched her disappear into the LADIES ROOM. Had she seemed nervous, or had he imagined it?

He found a phone and dialed information. Niko Yamato was listed— he hadn't moved in twenty-one years. Ben dialed his number. After a half dozen rings it was answered. A soft, tired voice answered. Ben hung up. He thought about Ahi. He thought about spies. Maybe Yamato *wasn't* an innocent victim.

Better surprise him. He might have something to hide as well.

Twenty minutes later Kalani dropped them off at the airport and wished them good luck. Ben thanked him for his efforts, knowing Kalani had sensed his ambivalence. Their handshake was firm and lasting.

Given the frequency of inter-Island flights, fifteen minutes later Ben and Haanio were soaring above Pearl Harbor on an Aloha flight bound for Līhuʻe. Ben scanned the horizon and then the harbor, wondering what that fateful day must have been like.

In twenty more minutes they were back down and walking briskly to the car rental counters.

Kaua'i is shaped like a jagged ball. It is the western-most of the main Hawaiian Islands and a million years older than the Big Island. A million years greener. And the parrot fish, who for eons have nibbled on the coral, transforming the bits of crusty animal life into sand, have helped create the broadest, whitest beaches anywhere in the Islands.

Ben and Haanio headed north along the Kūhiō Highway, toward Princeville and Hanalei. Ben was driving and Haanio, his head partially out of the window, was soaking up the sun and the sweet smell of the roadside flowers.

To the right, the cobalt blue ocean was filled with whitecaps as a stiff wind raced across the water, heading directly west, toward shore. The same wind that had blown the rain onto O'ahu. Ahead, bright green fields of taro stretched for miles, broad leaves bending, tips fluttering in the breeze. And inland—*mauka,* the mountain side—the ridges that formed the foothills of the Makaleha mountain range were cloaked in an ominous darkness, as deep purple rain clouds hovered along the higher elevations. New rainbows appeared around every curve. But the dark side of things, not the brightly colored rainbows, filled Ben's thoughts.

He wondered if all four men in the photograph had been spies. He thought about what he'd read in the newspapers about foreign embassies. How many of the employees worked undercover—agents, pretending to be aides, or clerks, all the while conducting covert operations. If this were true, then maybe Yamato would be of no help. Old or not, he'd be smart enough to play dumb.

Ben wondered how he was going to get a close look at Yamato's armpit. He smiled to himself, picturing Haanio sitting on the old man's chest, while he lathered up his underarms.

Kapa'a, Anahola, and finally Princeville. Then a ninety-degree turn, a plunge deep into the Hanalei Valley, across the Hanalei River over a one-lane bridge, and then a steady climb along the riverbank to the laid-back town of Hanalei. A left off of Kūhiō Highway led them to Weke Road, which wound down toward the beach at Hanalei Bay. The records listed 3 Weke as Yamato's address.

It was the house at the end of Weke, on the water. It was freshly painted in front, but the side facing east was peeling badly. Tree ferns of various sizes clung close to the rock foundation. A few stunted palms grew in the yard of tall grass. There was no car, no carport, and for that matter, no driveway. Only a sandy path that served as a front walkway.

There was no answer to Ben's rapping on the front door and the door was unlocked but stuck, so he and Haanio walked around to the back. The backyard fronted Hanalei Bay. The public beach started at Yamato's property line, but a dozen boulders just offshore kept the beachgoers away. The backyard was small. There were a few overgrown hibiscus trees and three tall palms, their long necks arching toward the sea. Here and there plumeria bloomed. There was a small wooden bench where the grass ended and the sand began. Trampled weeds marked the path from the back door to the bench.

They both turned and faced the house. Ben's eyes darted back and forth, remembering there had been two murders. Remembering that Niko Yamato could be a spy. Carefully, he approached the back door. It wasn't locked. He motioned Haanio to follow.

The house contained five tiny rooms but no Yamato. Ben checked his watch. It was four-twenty.

"You want to search the place?" asked Ben.

"It's one thing on home ground . . . it's another when we're out of our jurisdiction," replied Haanio. "I think we should wait for him. He's an old man. If he's on the Island, he'll be home before too long."

Ben was getting impatient. "How about if you keep watch and I do a little snooping."

Haanio shrugged his shoulders. "Okay."

Ben started in the bedroom. There were a lot of photographs on a low dresser. Ben studied each one. It was impossible to discern anything from them. His eyes lingered on one—a color shot of a beautiful girl. Maybe eighteen. Twenty at most. High cheekbones, short, wavy black hair. Moist red lips. Not a blemish on her face. And something in her eyes that drew you closer to the picture. Something romantic. Something mysterious. Maybe even something slightly evil. He slid the photo out of its frame. There was no date on the back. He replaced the photo and the frame.

There was a small antique writing desk near the window. The top was cleared except for a fountain pen and an ornate glass bottle of ink. There were three horizontal drawers—all unlocked. Inside were letters, bills, the usual stuff. Then Ben found Yamato's appointment book. Every Friday was marked, as well as a few other random days, but, overall, not a busy schedule. He turned to the telephone directory and looked under *I.* Nothing for Ahi Ishizu. On an impulse, he checked *A.* Zero. Ben thumbed through the numbers. Nothing stuck out—no names he recognized.

He heard Haanio whistle. Then he heard what sounded like a cart with squeaking wheels. Quickly he went out the back door and dashed behind the thick trunk of the largest palm. None too soon. An old man came around the side of the house, pushing a wire grocery cart, oblivious to the racket the wheels made.

Ben felt something in his hands. He still held Yamato's appointment book.

Damn! We're off to a great start.

He tucked the book into his waistband and covered it with his shirt. The old man, who he assumed was Niko Yamato, disappeared inside.

Haanio tapped him on the shoulder. Ben jumped.

"Pretty menacing guy, huh?"

Ben gave him a wry look.

"Think that shopping cart turns into some kind of nuclear device?" He chuckled softly.

"Funny." Without another word, Ben stalked away, headed for the public beach. Faintly, he could hear Haanio laughing.

17

B EN SAT ON A SHADED PIECE OF DRIFTWOOD, peeling strips from a dried palm frond.

Haanio joined him shortly. "Sorry." He sat next to Ben. "He just looked so helpless." He wiped away his last tear. He cleared his throat quietly. "Whaddaya wanna do? Watch him for awhile?"

Ben glared at Haanio. Haanio swallowed his next joke. Ben looked down for a few seconds, played with the sand, then gave Haanio a sideways glance. Haanio's face sported a big grin. Ben shook his head and said, "Let's give him a few more minutes so it doesn't seem like we've been waiting for him." He poked Haanio in the stomach. They laughed.

When he had no more frond to peel, Ben stood and motioned Haanio to follow. They went to the front door, knowing it wouldn't open. Ben rapped loudly. No answer. Again, they went around to the back. Yamato was seated on the wooden bench, staring out at the water, totally absorbed, like Tobi when he was concentrating on something important.

"Mr. Yamato?" Ben waited for the old man to look up.

He did so slowly, squinting into the sun that framed Ben and Haanio. "Yes," he answered.

"I'm Detective McMillen and this is Detective Haanio. We're from Kona. We'd like to talk with you."

Yamato studied them both for a few moments. Finally, he looked straight into Ben's eyes and held his gaze for a long time. "What is it you want with me?"

"Just a few questions, sir," stated Haanio, showing as many white teeth as he could.

Though seated, Yamato bowed, but only slightly. He still seemed unsure of his visitors.

He was thin, but didn't look undernourished. His hair, what was left of it, was pure white. Long wisps started at his temples and angled back past his ears. A sparse white beard framed his mouth. Above his lips were gray and white stubbles that no longer grew. There was a pair of glasses hanging from his shirt pocket—wire frames that had yellowed with the years.

Ben cleared his throat. "Would you like to go inside?"

Yamato looked at him. "No, I like to sit out here before dinner. What is it you want?" He looked like he was about to add something, but his mouth suddenly closed and he was silent.

Ben wondered where to start. He didn't want to upset Yamato. Something told him they were on the same side, and that Ahi's death would be a terrible shock. Then again, maybe Yamato had lost touch with Ahi a long time ago. Maybe the news would just be a late confirmation.

The wind picked up a bit. Yamato brushed his hair back with the tips of his fingers. Ben noticed the brown spots on the backs of Yamato's hands.

Haanio sat on the grass, crossing his legs, placing his hands on his knees. He looked like a little boy who hoped his grandfather's story would be scary, but more important, one that he had not told before.

Ben lowered himself next to Haanio. No one spoke.

A flock of sooty terns approached from offshore. The lead tern had speared a good-sized fish. The others were in hot pursuit, trying to steal the catch. They swooped and soared and dived between the palm trees that lined the beach. All were screeching except the lead bird. He was too smart to open his mouth. An updraft caught the closest pursuer, sending it far above the others, out of contention. Then the new contender spied something moving in the water and peeled off, diving, splashing, twisting its neck, and it was airborne with a prize of its own. And before long, the first sooty was left to drift onto a rock that jutted into the ocean, where he made quick work of his catch. The other birds vanished down the coastline.

"What do you need to know?"

Ben looked at Haanio for a second. Then he turned to the old man. He felt it was best not to say anything. Let the photograph speak for itself. He took the manila envelope that had been pressed against his underarm, opened it, and dumped the contents into his lap. As he handed the picture to Yamato, he felt the old man's appointment book pressing against his back.

Yamato placed the photo next to him on the wooden bench. He slowly reached for his glasses and put them on. He was careful. The glasses seemed fragile.

Ben watched Yamato's eyes as he picked up the photograph and held it just above his lap. He saw a quick flash of shock. Then a small, almost imperceptible smile. The old man's gaze fixed itself, unblinking. Ben thought he saw two small tears in the corners of Yamato's eyes.

Finally, Yamato looked up. "Where did you get this?"

"I found it in Ahi Ishizu's house."

It was as if Ben had sucked the air out of the old man's lungs. Yamato gasped for breath. He tried to stand, but couldn't. Haanio grabbed him by the shoulders just as he was about to fall. His breathing was labored.

Ben rushed to his feet. "Are you okay?"

Yamato tried to speak. He nodded instead. After a few moments he whispered, "I am . . . all right."

Haanio eased him back onto the bench. Yamato waved him off. He raised a finger, indicating that he needed to catch his breath.

Ben was momentarily distracted by a yacht that came into view as it headed into the bay. Its billowing yellow-and-orange spinnaker flapped in the wind as the crew hauled it in and made ready to anchor. When the mainsail dropped, he focused his attention on Yamato once again.

"Have you kept in touch with each other?" he asked as gently as he could.

Yamato shook his head. Ben sensed there was a lot to tell—some things from long ago, things not thought about for many years. He wondered if Yamato would share them. Then he thought he saw Yamato's eyes glance toward his left armpit, thinking about the tattoo that linked him to Ahi. Had he imagined it? Ben narrowed his eyes.

"Is he alive?" Yamato asked, half hopeful.

Ben lowered his head and shook it slowly.

Yamato exhaled deeply. "When did he die?"

Haanio answered, "Last week. He drowned."

Reading his expression, it was clear to Ben that Yamato's feelings were not focused on his friend's death. He probably thought that Ahi had died a long time ago.

"When was the last time you saw him or heard from him?" asked Ben.

"Will you stay for dinner? I do not have much, but I would like you to stay."

"We'll stay." Haanio patted the old man's shoulder.

Ben, on the pretense of needing to use the bathroom, was able to slip Yamato's appointment book back in its place. He returned to the living room and sat with Haanio while Yamato worked in the kitchen. They didn't have much to say to each other. Not yet.

Yamato prepared a chicken, adding a black sauce that smelled like teriyaki and strong ginger. Vegetables—pea pods and carrots, and Chinese cabbage—were fried with the chicken along with some brown rice. Yamato fetched some sake and they sat on mats before a low table.

Haanio whispered to Ben, "Let him start when he's ready. You'll get much more out of him."

Ben nodded.

A full two minutes passed before Yamato spoke. "Is the food to your satisfaction?"

Both Ben and Haanio said it was.

Another minute went by. After a sip of sake, Yamato put his chop-sticks aside and began.

"Ahi was my friend. We worked for the Japanese Economic Trade Commission together. It was before the war. I had lived on O'ahu since 1926. I was a citizen of the United States by the time I met him. I was responsible for keeping statistics on things that were exported to Japan." He laughed.

Ben concentrated. The old man had been an American citizen before the attack on Pearl Harbor. He wondered if that had been a cover.

Yamato continued, his face firm once more. "Ahi was . . . Ahi was . . . he was an economist. He conducted meetings with the Americans. They were trying to increase trade between the United States and the Far East. Ahi knew much about the Japanese economy and the most expeditious way to do business. The Americans were very interested. But I'm not sure if they wanted to trade with Japan or destroy it."

Haanio shifted, then stretched his legs before crossing them again.

"Ahi was very popular with the Americans. He went to many parties. No one else at the Commission went to parties, except the big manager." He thought for a few seconds. "Tanaka was his name . . . and Ahi. They went to the parties." Yamato sucked in his breath.

Ben heard a slight rasp between Yamato's breaths. He didn't think the man smoked, he hadn't smelled any tobacco, and unlike Tobi's house, there was no scent of incense. He wondered if he was sick. Maybe asthma, or emphysema.

"He drowned?" Yamato's eyes were squarely on Haanio. "He was an expert swimmer . . . at least he was when he was younger . . . he could swim . . ." His hand made a motion meaning a long distance.

Ben interjected, wanting to speed things up. "Mr. Yamato, the truth is, we think he was taken out to sea and dumped overboard. He either drowned or bled to death because of a shark attack. I'm sorry."

Yamato's face was blank for a long time. Then he nodded. He seemed to be taking it well. He said, "For many years I thought he was dead. It is good he led a reasonably long life."

Ben stretched his back muscles. "If I may say so, you don't seem surprised to hear that he was murdered."

Yamato looked away.

"Mr. Yamato?"

He turned and faced them but didn't speak.

Ben swallowed. His throat was sore. He coughed twice. "Do you know what it means if you have a tattoo . . . a five-digit number to be exact . . . tatooed on your armpit?"

The old man's eyes widened. "So it was true."

"What was true?" asked Haanio. "Tell us."

"He was a spy."

Ben's skin tingled. He felt warm. He looked toward the bay again and watched as the crew on an anchored ketch stowed the mainsail. He licked his lips. "Mr. Yamato, we think he was murdered because he was hiding something. Do you have any idea what it might have been?"

"I knew he didn't like what he was doing, I could tell. Something was upsetting him. I think he knew about the attack. I think he wanted to stop it, but couldn't. That is why he disappeared."

"Was it information he had?" asked Haanio.

The old man shrugged, although not convincingly as far as Ben was concerned. His face seemed to take on an impish look.

Ben tried another approach. He pointed to the photo that now lay on top of the table a few feet from Yamato's plate. "Who are these other two men? What did *they* do?"

Yamato squinted. "The man on the left was Sato. I don't know what he did. Anyhow, he died during the attack. The other man was a friend of his. I don't remember him much. He drove a truck, I think. His name was . . . I can't remember." He gave another shrug.

Ben wasn't convinced. "Were they spies?"

"I don't know . . . I don't think so."

"Were you?"

Yamato raised his arms. "You may check." He laughed, but his lips remained tightly together.

"Do we have to?"

"I was not a spy. You have my word."

Ben leaned back, supporting himself with his hands, elbows locked. "May I ask you about Ahi?" Yamato's face was hopeful.

Ben said, "Go ahead."

"You said you were from Kona, was he from there?"

"He lived near a small town called Ho'omau Ranch, south of Kona, in the foothills."

"I know where it is. What happened to his wife?"

Ben tried to take the question in stride. It was possible to learn more by listening to someone's questions than by hearing answers to yours. "We have no idea."

"I know she vanished a few days before Pearl Harbor . . . just before he did."

"Maybe she went back to Japan. Maybe he sent her."

"Maybe they took her."

"They?"

"His superiors . . . if he was a spy. I told you, he was very upset about something . . . then he disappeared . . . What did he do? What did he become?"

"He was a coffee farmer," Haanio answered. "He owned a small farm in the hills."

"A coffee farmer." Yamato had a faraway look in his eyes and a smile. He was trying to picture it. "He always drank coffee. Everyone else drank tea."

Remembering Bennett's comment about Ahi's granddaughter, Ben asked about Ahi's children. Yamato said Ahi's wife had been a few months pregnant.

Ben nodded. Now he was tiring. And he believed Yamato was holding out. He stood and walked toward the rear window, which afforded a view of the entire bay. After a few moments he turned and faced the old man. "Look, Mr. Yamato, we strongly believe someone murdered him

for something he was hiding. Something tangible. I'm going to level with
you, then I expect you to do the same with me." Ben waited for a response. There was none. No commitment. Yamato didn't even bat an
eyelash. Ben continued.

"There have been two other murders . . ." Ben noticed that Yamato
stiffened for a split second. *Good.* "A young man of Japanese descent was
found murdered on a coffee farm."

"Ahi's?"

"No. But he knew Ahi. He was with him a few days before. Maybe he
was his friend. Maybe they were working on something together. Or
maybe he wasn't a friend. Maybe he killed Ahi."

Now it was Yamato's turn to rise and walk toward the window. He
kept his back to the detectives for quite a while. At last, he turned. "And
the other murder?"

"A man by the name of Jeremiah Furbee." Ben waited for a reaction.
There was none. "He worked at one of the mills . . . he was also involved
with marijuana."

Yamato's jaw dropped, but he recovered quickly, closing his mouth.
Ben hadn't missed the old man's reaction. "You know him?"

Yamato shook his head.

"You sure?"

"I never heard of him."

"You know something about the marijuana trade?"

"No!"

"He was found stuffed in a hole in Ahi's backyard. There were twenty
other holes back there. Someone was looking for something. Something
big." Ben arms went across his chest. He threw Yamato a firm, annoyed
stare. "Well?"

Yamato shuddered. His entire upper body seemed to collapse. He
shuffled to the table and sat, legs folded, his eyes holding some great
revelation. But his lips were shut.

"Well?" Ben repeated. There were goose bumps on his arms.

A shorter sigh. The sigh before you spoke the truth.

Yamato's voice was soft but there was no cracking to it. "No one ever came out and said Ahi was working for the Secret Service. But we guessed it was so. You could tell. He kept odd hours. Even when we were at the beach, his mind was working. He was calculating something. Sorting out options. His face was at the beach . . . his mind was somewhere else." Yamato stopped and took a sip of sake. "Then, in late November, he changed. Something bothered him. Something different and very important. It was like he was part of something he didn't want any part of, but he had no choice. And then a few days before the attack on Pearl Harbor, he and his wife disappeared, but not together, I don't think. There was great confusion at work. It was obvious to me that Ahi was not just an economist. The people in high positions were worried. Many men, Japanese men . . . men in dark suits, they came to work. There were meetings. I think they set up search parties for Ahi. We were asked many questions. Since I was his closest friend, they detained me for days. They came close to torturing me."

"Torturing you?" asked Haanio.

"They slapped me on the face . . ." He began to weep. "They shined thin lights in my eyes while a man pushed my eyelids up. They told me they were going to abuse my wife. But some message came. Within two hours they shut the building down. They burned some records, some they took. It was then, when they went to the vault, that everything went crazy. You say it . . . all hell broke loose." Yamato stopped to catch his breath. His eyes were wide ovals, still black, but reflective. It seemed as if he was unaware of anyone else in the room. "I heard they were coming for me. But I hid. Later, I was told that something important was missing. At the time, I thought it was documents." Now the distaste in his voice was evident on his face. "Later, when a few of us were together in one of the army camps for questioning, one of the men who worked near the vault said that there had been gold bars inside. It was part of some plan for when we," Yamato looked up, shame on his face, "I mean, when my country entered the war."

Ben leaned forward. Haanio uncrossed his legs and stood.

"Gold?" repeated Ben. "How much gold?"

"Much," answered Yamato. "If what I heard was true, more than two million dollars of gold."

Haanio let out a long smooth whistle.

"That is it. I never heard from Ahi again." Yamato closed his eyes. His lips quivered.

Ben got up and started pacing. After ten seconds he asked, "Two million dollars . . . two million back then?"

"Yes, said Yamato, eyes still shut, "back then."

"Holy shit!" Ben stood by the window.

Haanio got up and stood near Ben. "What do you think?" he asked, speaking quietly so Yamato couldn't hear.

Ben arched his eyebrows. "It would explain the holes."

"And the murders," Haanio added.

A minute passed; each man had been alone with his thoughts.

Ben cleared his throat roughly. Haanio and Yamato looked up. "Mr. Yamato? Have you ever told this to anyone else?"

"No."

Ben didn't believe him. "Never?"

"We may have discussed it among ourselves for a few days, but then we were separated. I never saw that man again . . . the one who knew about the vault. I think he went back to Japan. He was Japanese. I was the only American citizen who worked at the Commission."

"But you don't know if he told anyone else."

"I suppose he did. But let me repeat something, Detective McMillen." Yamato appeared stronger, angry. "It was a rumor. I didn't believe it . . . any of it . . . until now, until you told me about the murders and the holes in Ahi's backyard. So probably no one else believed it either. But, if it were true, then why would Ahi keep that gold for fifty years?"

That was a good question.

Ben and Haanio had much to talk about on the drive back to Līhu'e. Haanio started. "Do you think he's telling the truth?"

"What he told us, yes. But I think there's more."

"Like what?"

"Like I have no idea."

"Do you think this is really about stolen gold? I mean, maybe it *was* just a rumor."

Ben thought about that. "It's about gold all right. You're forgetting the size of the holes in Ahi's backyard. Two million in gold bars is a big haul. Damn! Two million . . . fifty years ago. I bet it's worth ten or twenty times that now."

"But why wouldn't he have done something with it in all this time?" asked Haanio.

He looked at Haanio and pursed his lips. "I don't know, Haanio. I don't know."

The cutoff to Līhu'e Airport came up, Ben signaled, waited for a few cars, and then made his left. The sky was black behind them. A rain storm was headed down from the mountains. Ben peered into the rearview mirror.

"Looks like we're in for quite a blow."

Haanio turned around and grunted.

Ben checked his watch. It was almost five. He hoped to make it to Maui by six. Lisa would be waiting. He was anxious to see her. Haanio had a different flight—direct to Kona. His flight left five minutes before Ben's.

Ben felt guilty about going to Maui, but Haanio said he'd bring Tobi up to date. Besides there wasn't much more they could do that night.

Haanio's plane departed on time. Ben's Aloha flight was delayed with mechanical problems. The posted delay was only twenty minutes. In any event, there was a Hawaiian Air flight for Kahului, Maui, that left at 6:05. Worst case he'd call Lisa and grab that one.

He decided to get a breath of fresh air instead of waiting inside the terminal. He guessed the flight wouldn't be announced for another half hour, if at all.

The rain had come in a short burst, flooding the ditches that ran along the streets. Now the air sizzled with steam, as the sun, still hot at six, evaporated the rainwater. One large rainbow framed the lush mountains to the west. It was as clear and precise a prism as Ben could remember seeing. It seemed to engulf the entire Island. People stared at it for a long time, which was unusual in a place where rainbows were a natural part of the landscape.

The smell of rain in a tropical setting was a hard scent to beat. It made you feel clean, refreshed, new. Everything looked so vibrant. And the newborn activity was breathtaking. Thousands of waterbugs dashed across puddles, making the most of the few minutes before the their swimming hole evaporated and they magically disappeared. They looked like frantic ice skaters, vying for ice time in a hockey-crazed Canadian town. Small yellow finches, flying in pairs, darted among the trees, jabbing at pieces of fruit, swallowing berries, and drinking from water-laden flower petals that had captured a tablespoonful of rain. And a noisy tour bus sped by and covered Ben's pants with reddish mud.

He stood glaring at the bus when he felt something nick at his ear. At first he thought it was an insect bite. Then he heard the *pfpt* of a second silenced bullet. Scrambling to the ground, he cat-walked behind a cement trash receptacle. A few people who were standing close to him wondered what was going on. They'd seen a man duck for cover, but their inexperienced ears never picked up the two shots. They stood gawking until he shouted for them to take cover. Some moved, others laughed, thinking it was comical.

"I'm a Kona detective. Someone's shooting. Take cover." That worked. People scattered. People screamed.

Ben didn't think the assailant would fire into a crowd. He peeked out from behind the trash container, straining his eyes, looking for some movement away from the scene, someone running for a car, someone holding a gun. He saw no one except a police officer, gun drawn, running toward him. Ben stood and flashed his badge. The policeman nodded.

"Someone took a shot at me. You check the terminal. I'll check the parking lot."

The patrolman spun around and dashed into the terminal.

Curb-side passengers were shouting. But none were pointing. Ben was sure the gunman had run for his car, not the terminal. He raced to the lot and stood behind a palm, carefully surveying the scene, looking for a car exiting a little too fast. There were only two cars moving. One had just paid the parking toll. Ben squinted. He saw a man with a little boy in the front seat. The man was tickling the boy. The boy was howling with laughter and trying to cover his midsection. The second car was approaching the toll booth. Inside was a woman. She was driving slowly. She took her time, chatted with the woman in the booth, and then drove away.

Ben dropped to all fours. When he did so, he remembered that he'd been hit, either with the bullet or a fragment of what the bullet had hit. He felt the wound—his ear was bleeding, but just a nick. He also realized it was just a few inches from the center of his brain. On his belly, he scanned underneath the parked cars, looking for a crouched pair of legs. There was no one. He got up and dashed to the other side of the lot. Back to his stomach. Tires and puddles and nothing more. As he stood, two policemen ran toward him, guns raised. The uneasy looks on their faces told Ben it was the first time the guns had been out of their holsters except for the practice range.

He was driven to the hospital and his wound was quickly patched. It was a flesh wound from a cement fragment, not a bullet. There were no powder burns. Ben knew he was lucky—it wasn't meant to be a warning shot.

It took an hour and a half to go over the incident at Līhuʻe Head-quarters. There wasn't much he could tell them. And there wasn't much else to go on. They'd recovered the bullets, both severely compressed by the impact with the cement terminal building. They could identify the caliber, but the odds were slim of matching them to the rifling of a gun barrel. Ben knew from the silenced sound that it was a handgun, but nothing more. He explained to the Captain of Detectives why he had come to Kauaʻi. The Captain knew Tobi and offered to call. Ben said he'd like to. He discovered Tobi had left headquarters and Joyce failed to raise him on the car radio, and there was no answer at home. Ben declined to leave a message other than that he'd see Tobi in the morning—first thing. No sense worrying anyone about a flesh wound.

Instead of taking a ride to the airport, Ben asked to borrow a car. He desperately wanted to talk to Yamato.

The Captain sent a detective along. They arrived in Hanalei at the house on the end of Weke Road in thirty minutes. Ben explained that the front door didn't work, so they went around to the rear. Yamato wasn't there. The back door was still unlocked. Yamato wasn't inside. They waited for an hour.

While the detective was radioing for a patrolman to watch the house through the night, Ben searched the rooms he hadn't gotten to before. He didn't find anything that seemed important. Since he hadn't spent much time in the bedroom before, it was hard to tell if Yamato had packed. Ben did notice Yamato's appointment book was gone and so was the picture of the young girl. He nodded to himself.

The patrolman showed up a few minutes later. The detective briefed him and then joined Ben.

"He'll bring him in for questioning."

Ben smirked. "He's not coming back. At least not for awhile."

They headed for the door.

The detective stepped outside first. But something made Ben stop halfway through the door frame. He stepped back inside. There was something different about the place. Something he hadn't noticed before. He stood by the door for a long time, but couldn't make it register. The longer he stood there, the more it seemed to disappear.

Ben took one more look around, shook his head, and left.

18

THE PAINKILLER HAD WORN OFF and Ben's ear burned with fire. The urge to scratch it was unbearable. He thought about pinching it to make it numb, but he had been warned about infection, so every few minutes when his hand went toward his ear, he imagined the bulbous, pus-filled pimple that would result, and quickly closed his palm and rested his hand on his chest against his heart.

After watching his chest rise and fall for a few minutes, he turned and focused on the clock radio. It was only six-fifteen. But his mind was too active and his ear too sensitive to go back to sleep.

He sat up in bed, tired. He hadn't made it home until after three in the morning, and although he was on painkiller at the time and exhausted from the long day and three plane flights, sleep had come fitfully and only after reviewing every detail of the case.

The night before, at Līhu'e Headquarters, while he waited for word that Yamato had returned home, Ben had been on the phone—first with Kalani, then with a researcher at the University, who Kalani had convinced to leave a dinner party and return to the main campus library.

There, she dug through old microfiche for a few hours and came up with a newspaper story that came close to confirming Yamato's story about Ahi Ishizu. It didn't mention him by name, but Ben had seen the fit right away. It said there was an unsubstantiated story that a man who had worked for the Trade Commission had stolen gold bars from the Commission's vault. It also said that the thief was believed to be a spy. For whose side, no one knew.

Ben had never considered that. *Which side?*

The spy's code name was *Yellowfin*. Ben had smiled to himself then. '*Ahi* was the Hawaiian word for yellowfin tuna.

The rest of the article postulated what the gold was for. What did the Japanese plan to buy?

Whose side? Double agent?

A call to Lisa. She wasn't home. Paged her at the airport. Zero.

Thinking about the spy called *Yellowfin*.

Yamato hadn't come home by midnight. Ben knew he had a better chance of running into Yamato on the Big Island, where the gold was hidden—assuming there was gold to be found.

After they gave up on Yamato, the police arranged for Ben to be flown to Keāhole in a private plane.

Ben got out of bed, worked through a series of sit-ups, deep-knee bends, and push-ups. His ear throbbed, although not as badly as he had expected. But when he was done, he felt dizzy, and he realized he hadn't eaten in almost twenty-four hours. He nearly staggered into the kitchen. Opening the refrigerator, he stood back and laughed, then squinted at the kitchen wall clock, and did a neat about-face. The refrigerator was as empty as his stomach. But it was almost seven. Time for a quick shower and Mitchell's.

As he slipped his shirt carefully over his head, there was a sharp rapping on the door. Ben saw the knob turning back and forth. Then pounding. Then, "Ben, let me in . . . are you all right?"

It was Millie. He let her in.

She immediately reached for his chin and twisted his head to one side. "That looks terrible . . . sit down in the kitchen."

"But . . ."

"Move, *keiki!*"

Just like my grandmother. 'Move, child!'

Millie held a large shopping bag and she tapped him gently with it. "I was in early. There was a message from Līhu'e about last night. I came right over."

"I appreciate it, but I'm fine . . . really. I have antibiotics."

"And I have proper medicines." They reached the kitchen. "Sit."

Ben sat.

Millie placed her shopping bag on the counter next to the sink. She extracted 'ūlei leaves, bark from the root of the 'ūlei, and a taro leaf, folded and secured with a piece of brown string. Next, out came a small wooden calabash, and piece of *koa* shaped like a drumstick. Millie shredded the leaves and placed them into the bowl. Then she stripped several slivers of the bark and added them to the leaves, then untied the taro leaf, which held sea salt, and measured a rough handful, which she threw in as well. She was smiling, pleased with herself.

After pounding the concoction for a few minutes, she pulled a clean cloth out of her bag, into which she dumped the mashed 'ūlei and salt. She made a pouch of the cloth, twisting the edges together at the top. Then she told him to place his head on the table. He joked for a second, placing his injured ear down.

"Go ahead," she mocked. "Let's see you."

His bluff rebuffed, Ben lowered his head onto the table, bad ear up. Millie leaned close and squeezed the cloth until all of the available juice had dripped into his wound. He was surprised—the burning sensation disappeared immediately. Millie dried his neck.

Ben raised his head. "Thanks. What is it?"

" *Ulei*. There's more in the shopping bag. I get it from the forest be-hind my auntie's house. Three times a day for three days. Understood?" Ben nodded. He remembered his grandmother explaining that all Ha-waiian folk medicines were prescribed in odd-numbered doses for an odd number of days.

"I'd fix you breakfast, but I have to get back."

"Does anyone else know?" he asked. Ben didn't like people making a fuss over him. Millie could. His grandmother could. But no one else.

"No. The note's on my desk. The Major might read it, but that's it. Are you sure you're all right?"

"I'm fine, now. *Mahalo*."

She gave him a kiss and said she'd see him later. Ben thanked her again and walked her to the door.

George, the burly Hawaiian cook, was at Mitchell's, but he was alone. Danny wasn't due for an hour and the first-shift waitress had called in sick, that meant, George explained, that she was hung-over or still had someone between her legs.

Ben sat at the bar and ordered everything he could think of. A three-egg omelette with Swiss, ham, mushrooms, and red pepper; two orders of wheat toast; a large guava juice; black coffee; and half a papaya. The papaya with a lime wedge came first. George retreated into the kitchen without so much as a word, so Ben sat alone, savoring the juicy fruit, tangy with lime. After he felt human again, his thoughts turned to what he had learned about the gold. But George postponed the gold rush for a few seconds when he appeared with a pot of dark Kona.

Ben grunted his thanks. His thoughts wandered back to the article that the researcher had read to him over the phone the previous night. It had appeared in the *Honolulu Advertiser*—the January 3 edition. Pearl Harbor and the War still dominated the headlines, but page two carried a story concerning the Japanese Trade and Economic Commis-sion, which had been shut down on December 8. The story had come from one of the displaced workers, a man who was being interrogated as were all Japanese-American living on Oʻahu. Once again, Ben reflected about the camps.

The article stated that the ex-employee said the Japanese Government believed the war would end quickly—that the Americans weren't ready for a war in the Pacific, especially combined with the conflict in Europe. That soon they would realize the hopelessness of their situation and come to terms. He said the gold was to be used to bribe government officials. To sway the peace negotiations even further in Japan's favor.

The person who had written the article had editorialized a little. He didn't believe the gold was for procuring political power. 'Heck,' he had said, 'If they had planned to win the war that quickly, they wouldn't have to *buy* anything—land, political influence, or power—they'd just take it. And besides, even if democracy was for sale, it would take a lot more gold than they could store in a vault.' The journalist added, 'Politicians don't come cheap.'

Ben agreed with the newspaperman—he didn't think the gold was for bribes. But as to what it *was* for—he couldn't fathom a guess.

George slapped down Ben's guava juice.
Ben grunted his thanks.
George disappeared without a word.

Ben had done the calculations based on what the researcher had told him. The gold standard had been $38 an ounce from the '30s until the '70s. The article stated that there was thought to be about two million dollars involved. At two million, the gold would weigh almost thirty-three hundred pounds. The article mentioned kilogram bars, so that meant about fifteen hundred gold bars, each weighing 2.2 pounds.

How had Ahi done it? Ben guessed by boat, and a good-sized one at that. And since he couldn't get far, especially being a Japanese in American territory, and since it was unlikely that he would want to smuggle himself back to Japan, one of the other Islands made sense. The Big Island was the farthest from Oʻahu, and it was, of course, the biggest, providing more places to hide.

George appeared with a huge omelette and toast.

Ben's mind was elsewhere and he didn't notice.

"One omelette for the V.I.P." George grinned.

He looked up and said with an inquisitive look, "I didn't think you liked V.I.P.s."

"You look more Hawaiian than *haole*."

Broad grin from Ben. "I am . . . and, I might say, I noticed the same thing about you."

George, the purebred, laughed heartily, white teeth filling his smile. Then he asked, "What happened to your ear?"

"Crazy woman."

George smiled appreciatively and then danced back into the kitchen.

Ben took a bite of the three-egg pie, burned his tongue, and gulped some juice. Moments later he was back in the maze.

For two million dollars, someone would have come looking for him. Or would they? Was there too much confusion? Did they think it was a rumor? But the top people at the Commission would have known . . . known if it were true. Maybe at the time, running for their lives was more important.

Maybe someone finally came back to find the money. But who? What is it worth now? Ten times, easy.

There's Yamato. He might be interested now, but he probably isn't connected with the murders.

Furbee was definitely involved. He's probably the one who killed the second victim and maybe he murdered Ahi, as well. Or . . . maybe the second man killed Ahi. But that doesn't matter . . . Furbee's dead and the second guy's dead . . . and besides, they were working for someone. The someone who killed Furbee. Who, dammit? Who?

The bar stool suddenly felt like his bike seat. He shifted, trying to get more comfortable. *And what about Winston Bennett?*

"You are a hard man to track down."

Ben swiveled. "Good morning, Tobi. Join me for breakfast?"

"Already eaten, but I will have a cup of coffee."

Ben got up, walked around the bar, took a clean cup from the stack, and placed it in front of Tobi. "Help yourself."

"You look pretty upbeat."

"I am. We're getting closer."

"I am all ears, but first, tell me how you burned yours."

"I'll get to that."

Tobi's eyebrows raised and his finger rested against his lips. "You mean it has something to do with the case?"

"It has something to do with getting shot at."

Ben had never seen Tobi with such a serious face.

19

AFTER THE BETTER PART OF AN HOUR and another pot of coffee, Ben had brought Tobi up to date. What he had found out at the Trade Commission. His conversation with Yamato—the revelation of the stolen gold. Then the shooting, and, finally, Yamato's disappearance. He even mentioned Millie's Hawaiian medicine, which Tobi appreciated fully. Then he followed Tobi back to headquarters.

Now they sat alone in Tobi's office. Both were anxious, now that the killer had turned and made the investigating detective his target.

"First," said Tobi, "this gold business is not to be mentioned to anyone. Who knows what havoc that will create?"

"I told Haanio the same thing."

"You can trust Haanio."

Tobi looked out of his window. He kept that pose for a full minute. Ben sat patiently, having been through this exercise many times before.

Tobi swung around and faced him. "Let us start with Ahi Ishizu." Tobi's fingertips made a flexing tent. "Ahi was a spy before the Second World War. Allegedly, he stole fifteen hundred gold bars and brought them by boat to the Big Island. He hid them and started a life as a coffee farmer, and we have no idea if he ever used any of the gold or continued spying."

Ben nodded.

"After all these years, someone found out about the gold, located Ahi, tried to find out where he had hidden it, and murdered him when he refused to tell."

"It was Furbee or the second victim," Ben added.

"I think I agree, but there are two variations. Furbee's killer could have been present as well."

Again, Ben indicated his agreement.

"And . . . the second victim could have been just that, an innocent victim . . . a friend of Ahi's."

Ben made a sour face. "That I doubt. There've been no MP reports. If someone from around here was missing, even for just a few days, we'd have heard about it by now."

"Granted. One variation, then." Tobi clasped his hands and continued. "Now, Furbee was into marijuana as well as working at one of the mills. He was part of the plan."

"Maybe not. He could have been snooping around . . . trying to find Ahi's farm. Anyone dealing with marijuana would be curious if a Kona detective came asking about one of the coffee growers. Maybe he thought there might be something going on . . . and something in it for him."

"Maybe," said Tobi. "But that does not seem as probable. I think he was part of it."

"Okay. Go on."

"All that is left is the photograph of Ahi and the other three men. You found Yamato, then he disappeared. You were shot at. Perhaps it was Yamato. Everything he said to you could have been made up to throw you off. For all we know, Yamato and Ahi were in touch, still spying."

Ben thought about that for a few seconds, then shook his head. "I don't think so. He was genuinely shocked about Ahi . . . to say nothing of his death. I think Ahi was a lot like you . . . strong principled and resourceful. Ahi took the gold to prevent something from happening, not for personal gain. I think I believe the gold story and it's basically confirmed in that newspaper article."

"What if Yamato is the one who fed that story to the newspaper?"

Ben closed an eye and raised the opposite eyebrow. He was skeptical. He shook his head. "I know what he told was the truth. But I also think there was more to tell. He's still hiding something."

"What about the marijuana connection? Are you off that? I think it was isolated to Furbee."

Ben said he was. He added a caveat—'for the time being.'

Tobi leaned forward, elbows on the desk. "It seems to me that I should take a shot at your friend Yamato . . . no pun intended."

Ben grimaced.

Tobi grinned and added, "I just had Joyce check the airlines. He flew to Honolulu yesterday."

Ben sat up. "When? What time? I should have checked that."

"He took a seven o'clock flight."

Ben's face was filled with anger. "Maybe that sunnufabitch did shoot at me! That's about when I was there . . . at the airport."

Tobi's eyes narrowed. They appeared almost closed. "I am going to find him."

"I'm going with you!"

"No, I need to talk to him . . . one old Japanese man to another. Trust me. Besides, there is someone we left out of all of this. Winston Bennett."

Ben inhaled deeply. "Well, Bennett definitely knew Ahi. But he was on O'ahu when Ahi was murdered, unless the ticket was a fake."

"The ticket was probably real, but you do not know he used it. *You know* that most Islanders walk up to the counter and pay cash. Although most give their real names, some do not. No one asks for ID. If you want to give the appearance that you went somewhere else, it is easy. Too easy. You check out Bennett. I will find Yamato. We touch base at five. I will call you here."

"Five, sure," said Ben absentmindedly. He was thinking about Winston Bennett.

———

Ben asked Joyce Ah Sing to check Winston Bennett's flights. Then Ben got on the phone, first with the *Honolulu Advertiser*. He was hooked up with the reporter who doubled as the obituary editor. Bennett had given him the first name of his sister—Alice. Ben remembered that, but he had slipped up. He hadn't asked for her full name.

Hell! I didn't even write down the first name.

He hadn't probed Bennett's alibi. There was the airline ticket. There was all the mail and the newspapers at his house. He believed that Bennett had been gone for a week, but he should have checked out Bennett's sister's death.

"Try Alice Bennett. Try the last week of July . . . wait! There can't be that many deaths, give me anyone named Alice."

"You wanna hold, or should I call you back?"

"I'll hold." Ben listened to the faint rhythmic beat of the HOLD button. Subconsciously, he tapped his fingers on his desk.

Two minutes later, the obit editor came back on. "I found an Alice Randolph."

"Good, read it to me."

When the clerk got to the surviving family members, Winston Bennett of Kēōkea was listed first.

Ben asked for the name of the funeral home, wrote it down, thanked the clerk, and hung up.

Joyce Ah Sing came into his office. Her face seem more radiant than usual. It also seemed a little red over her tan.

"What's up?"

"He was on those flights . . . at least the tickets were used, both ways."

"Thanks. Joyce, is there something else?"

She turned beet red. "Uh, no, Ben. That was it." She hurried out of his office.

Then he realized he had embarrassed her. He'd forgotten Tobi's comment that she was attracted to him. Then again, maybe Tobi was kidding. He wouldn't put it past him. He thought of Lisa. Before grabbing the phone book, he smacked his fist into his palm. *Damn! When will things get back to normal?*

He reached the funeral director at Diamond Head Mortuary right away. The mortician remembered Winston Bennett. Big man, slight Southern accent punctuated by a smattering of British expressions, abrasive at times. Red hair and a sandy complexion. Ben thanked him and hung up.

Unless Bennett could tell him more about Ahi or more about Furbee, Ben was wasting his time on the big man. He thought about what to do next. He was getting tired of driving south along Māmalahoa. But south it was going to be.

———

Bennett wasn't home. Ben checked his watch. It was Wednesday. Bag day? He hadn't spotted any coffee by the side of the road on his way down. Maybe it was too early. Maybe with Furbee dead Bennett had to work the mill. He decided to look there.

Bennett greeted him warily. Hands on hips with a frown. "I figured you'd show up sooner or later."

"Why's that?" asked Ben.

"Wondering if I killed that bastard Furbee . . . it was on the news. Well, someone just beat me to it, that's all. Given enough time, I'd be your man. Sorry to disappoint you, old boy."

Ben smiled to himself. "I don't think you killed him, but I would like to ask you some questions."

"I ain't answering questions about that weasel, period! Not unless you hand me a subpoena, and haul my ass off to jail, or . . ."

" . . . or buy you a beer?"

"Huh?"

Ben went back to the jeep and lugged out a cooler. Inside was a cold six-pack of Beck's. He held it up. "Let's sit over there in the shade and have a chat. Whaddaya say?"

Bennett licked his lips. "How'd you know I was just kiddin'?"

" 'Cause, like I said, I don't think you have anything to hide."

They picked the same spot beside the mill where Ben and Furbee had had their first and only conversation. Ben sat on one end of the log. Bennett chose to stand, resting one foot on the other end of the fallen timber, and leaning against a lone coffee tree that probably had grown from a stray bean, dropped in the rich soil long ago. Bennett's expression was sad. He took a sip of beer.

"I went up to Ahi's house," he drawled. "The police wouldn't let me get close, so I drove around by the back way. What are all those holes for?"

Now it was Ben's turn to give the wary eye as he drank.

Bennett asked, "He didn't snatch a bunch of kids and bury them, did he?" There seemed to be genuine concern in his voice.

Ben shook his head. "No. We don't know why they're there, except that Furbee was found in one of them."

"Serves the bastard right," snorted Bennett.

"Okay, let's have it . . . tell me everything you know about him. Why do you hate him so much? What'd he do to you?"

"He was selling crack."

"What! I thought he had a small marijuana farm."

Bennett took a long draw on his beer. "Used to. But he got into something more profitable. Selling crack to high school kids."

"How long's this been going on?" Ben asked.

Bennett thought for a few seconds. " 'Bout a year, I'd say. I reported him. But I don't think anybody followed up."

"Somebody must have checked it out."

"Oh, yeah! Well, you guys don't give two shits about the Kona Gold, why should a little crack make any difference." Bennett gulped some beer and walked away. Then he turned. He stood there for a long time.

Ben could see that he was flustered.

Finally Bennett spat it out, "My sister's kid OD'ed on crack six months ago. After that, she . . . she just gave up."

"The one you just buried?" asked Ben.

"Yeah, the one I just buried."

"I'm sorry." Ben let an appropriate number of seconds pass. "Remember hearing about two hikers disappearing near Ho'omau Ranch a few years ago?"

Bennett nodded.

"Think the marijuana growers might have had anything to do with it?"

"Who knows? They probably made it to the lava flows and fell into a deep fissure. That'd be the end of them." Bennett shrugged.

Ben was frustrated. Three murders—no real progress. No idea what was really going. All he had was a rumor of gold.

"Help me, Bennett. Maybe Ahi's death and this crack crap are connected."

The big man's eyebrows raised. "That bleeding son-of-a-bitch Furbee. You think so?"

Ben shrugged his shoulders. "Who'd Furbee work for?"

"Dunno."

"What *do* you know about him? Who'd he hang around with? Who were his friends?"

Bennett shrugged.

"Where's his marijuana farm?"

"In back of his house . . . way up. I think it's on someone else's property."

"Ever hear of a woman named Michiko Higa?"

"Nope."

"You sure?"

"I don't like it when people ask if I'm sure. If I wasn't, I wouldn't have said it."

"You mean you don't know anything about the drug trade around here?"

"Nope, only that it's here."

"Seems to me you're the kind of guy who'd do something about it."

Bennett fumed. "Maybe I will."

"You didn't do anything, even when you thought we hadn't followed up?"

"I threatened Furbee a time or two. He just laughed. I shoulda . . . I'm not a violent man, not any more."

"Not any more?"

Bennett was breathing hard. His chest rose and fell and Ben could hear the air escaping through his nose, like a bull ready to charge.

"I killed a man once . . . long time ago. Manslaughter. It was self-defense. I went to jail. I did my time. I promised I'd never lay a hand on anyone again." He looked down at his fist and slowly unclenched it. "If yer done, I'll be gettin' back to work. I've got bags to pick up."

Bennett spun around, almost fell, and angrily walked back to the mill.

Ben stood there for a few moments. He believed Bennett.

He left the rest of the six-pack by the log and walked back to the jeep.

As he closed the door of the jeep, he thought about Furbee. Ben had read the report detailing the search of Furbee's house. It had revealed nothing relevant. He decided it was time to check it out for himself.

Furbee had lived near a small seaside town called Ho'okena, about five miles south of the mill. His house was a mile inland. Dense foliage covered the sides and the back. Behind that there was a clearing.

As Ben pulled up in front of the small one-story ranch house, he noticed tire marks everywhere. If the number of vehicles was any indication of the number of cops and technicians that had been there, the place had been given a thorough going-over. He hopped out and walked toward the front door. Before he'd taken two steps, the intoxicating smell of marijuana assaulted him. Ben decided to have a look around outside and circled the house. The yard was overgrown with weeds and tall grass, all matted down from many footsteps. There were some scrub trees in the back, but mostly there was lava covered with brown grass. Ben could see the ocean a few hundred yards away to the west. And one other house was in view about the same distance north. He walked a bit deeper into the forest. The smell of marijuana was much stronger and his eyes watered. Then he came to a smoky clearing. Usually, the crop was cut down and kept for evidence. But the Eradication Team had burned it to the ground. Maybe they had enough evidence.

Ben felt a little light-headed, glanced around quickly, and headed back toward the house, thinking—no need for evidence when the suspect was dead.

Inside, the place was a mess. Apparently, the team that had searched it had no respect for the dead. But maybe they found it in such disarray that they felt it wasn't worth being neat and careful. Their impatience wouldn't make his job any easier. There'd be no logical order to where he found things—sometimes that was important. He couldn't be sure if he found something that was broken, whether it had happened before or after the search. He made a mental note to report this to the Lieutenant in charge of the search team.

An hour and twenty minutes later, Ben had come up with nothing except a mild backache from bending and lifting, and a headache from inhaling what was left of Furbee's crop.

He sat on the couch, between two springs that were about to give, and thought about what he was looking for. Furbee's banking records might help. He was sure Tobi had had those impounded and he could go through them at Headquarters. But marijuana was a cash business, and although he thought Furbee had been an asshole, he didn't think he was stupid. The financial trail wouldn't be easy to follow. An appointment book might reveal something—a telephone number, a meeting place, something. But he hadn't found one. He wondered if the search team had. Ben shifted and stretched his body carefully as he felt his muscles tighten. The couch wasn't a good place for his back, so slowly he forced his way to his feet, stood, and stretched some more. Standing felt better.

Leaning on the Suzuki jeep, arching his back, something nagged his brain. Something he had put off to the side before. He needed Furbee's connection up the chain. He thought he knew where the chain ended. Michiko Higa. He wondered if Tobi had talked to her since Furbee's death. *What did Tobi say when we were in Serrao's office? He said he'd checked a source. Like it was simple to get hold of her. Shit! Maybe she's listed.*

On impulse, he raced back inside, ignoring the shooting pain in his lower back. He remembered seeing the phone book on the floor near Furbee's wicker night table. He opened it, thumbed to the *H*s and then followed his finger down the middle column. There it was—

Higa Michiko Kohala Ranch 889–4503

He picked up Furbee's phone. It was dead.

———

Millie greeted him in the hallway. She herded him toward an empty desk and made him sit as she examined his ear.

"Looks good, but keep using the *'ūlei* for two more days."

He promised.

She had a message from Tobi. He had arrived on O'ahu. Yamato had been to the Trade Commission and asked a few questions. Tobi had lost his trail after that, but one of Yamato's questions had been about relatives of the man in the photograph who had died during the attack on Pearl Harbor. His widow lived on the North Shore. That's where Tobi was headed.

Ben thanked Millie and rushed to his office, closed the door, and reached for the phone. He dialed Michiko's number, which he'd memorized. While it rang, he thought about where she lived. Kohala Ranch. A wealthy community on the western edge of Parker Ranch. It was for the rich and their horses. Miles of trails and grassland, the distinctive smell of eucalyptus, a beautiful view of the ocean in front, and a backdrop of clouds swirling around the slopes of Mauna Kea.

Near the ranch. Cowboy boots and tobacco chewing. He wondered if Furbee had once worked there. *Maybe that's where they met.*

Fifth ring.

Tobi lived nearby. Maybe ten miles.

Seventh ring.

Would there be bodyguards?

Ninth. He hung up and sat down, rubbing his back with both sets of fingers, stretching his shoulders until his spine groaned and cracked. It seemed strange to him that she didn't have an answering machine. Someone like her must live off messages. Maybe it was disconnected. Maybe on purpose. He went to find Joyce.

She was in the Squad Room sitting by the window, sipping coffee.

"Any idea where Cooper is?"

Joyce gave him an accommodating smile. "He said he was going to the Ishizu place to pick up someone. Said he'd be back at one."

"Pick up someone?"

"That's all he said."

"When you're done, radio him, and tell him I need to see him right away."

"Sure thing, Ben."

"Thanks." As he left the Squad Room, he checked his watch. It was one-fifteen.

Back at his desk he sat thinking about the chewing tobacco and boots and marijuana, and cowboys rolling their own cigarettes. Ten minutes passed.

Jack Cooper came through the entrance to Criminal Investigation and announced his arrival with a quick, shrill whistle. Ben looked up. With Cooper was a beautiful Japanese woman. She just about took Ben's breath away. He stood, eyes transfixed. She had softly curled black hair with a satin-like sheen. Dark oval eyes, and deep red lips. The deepest red lips he'd ever seen. Her skirt was bright yellow, her beige blouse tight-fitting.

But what he noticed next was that the whites of her eyes were red and her nose looked raw, and her mascara needed touching up. Why had she been crying? She bowed her head slightly. Her face looked like it hadn't smiled in a long time.

Jack cleared his throat to get Ben's attention. Ben's eyes shifted in his direction. Jack seemed nervous. His jaw was firmly set, puffing out his cheeks.

"This is Ishizu's granddaughter," he announced.

20

B EN CAME AROUND HIS DESK. The woman seemed a bit old to be Ahi's granddaughter. This woman looked thirty-five, or forty, but Ben had never been good at guessing a woman's age.

He extended his hand. "I'm sorry." It was all he could muster. Over the last week, he'd felt an attachment to Ahi, spy or not. Long ago, in a history class in high school that had been discussing World War II resistance groups and espionage, Ben had decided that if he were asked to spy for his country he'd do it. No question about it. He believed Ahi's past had simply caught up with him. Even so, Ahi had been somehow different. Ben firmly believed he had been trying to prevent a war, not start one.

"Thank you," she said. She sniffled and blinked out a single tear.

"Have a seat . . ."

She smiled weakly. "My name is Sachi Kamimura."

Ben remembered the name from when Tobi translated Ahi's letters.

Jack excused himself and headed for his desk. Passing close to Ben he whispered, restricting the movement of his lips, "I checked her passport . . . it's fine. Even her picture's good." He winked.

Sachi sat and crossed her legs. Although she was careful to pull her skirt lower, the deep slit up the left side showed plenty of thigh.

Jack sat and scooted closer. Then he looked at Ben. "Your lead."

Ben's face was grim. He wasn't sure where to start or what to say. He tried to look comforting. "Can I get you anything? Water?"

"No, no thank you."

"How did you find out? We had trouble reaching you. In fact, I didn't know we had."

"I was on a school trip. Sometimes when we are between semesters we take the children to see other places in our country. We were on a geology expedition on one of the remote islands. We were out of communication for a few days. When I returned to my apartment, my landlord handed me a message from the police. I came immediately."

Her English was nearly perfect, hardly an accent, and no hint that she hadn't been born and raised in America. Tobi had said she taught English. That explained her speech, but it didn't explain the class trip. "I thought you taught English . . . not science."

"I volunteered for the trip. I love the children and even we teachers need to broaden our education. You agree?"

Ben smiled demurely for a second. Then he became serious again. "You understand we believe your grandfather was murdered?"

Sachi nodded and folded her hands into her lap. "Yes."

"So we can't release the . . . you can't make funeral arrangements yet."

"I understand. I went to his farm first. I didn't know where else to go. The policemen there called detective Cooper. I would like to go back and go over his things when I can. Some have been in the family for many generations. But first, I must see him."

"Of course, but I must tell you . . ."

She inhaled, filling her lungs. "Detective Cooper told me how you found him and of the sharks. But I must see him." She started to cry. "I must," she sobbed.

Ben got up. "We'll go right away, then out to the farm. Jack, let Tobi know where I am. He's checking in at five."

Jack nodded and stood.

Sachi's eyes closed for a few seconds and her lips moved. She appeared to be praying.

They were at Kona Hospital for a short time. Ben watched Sachi as she viewed her grandfather. She stared at his face for a long time. Then, finally, she closed her eyes. She bit her lip, hard. It bled. Ben watched as she tasted the blood, like she was sharing some part of her grandfather's death. After awhile she opened her eyes, brushed away the tears on her cheeks, and said that they could go. She refused Ben's handkerchief.

On the way to the farm Ben carefully asked his questions. He wanted to see if she knew about the gold. But he had to build up to it.

"How many children did your grandparents have?"

"Just one . . . my father."

"Was he born here?"

"No, my mother returned to Japan just before the war. She was a few months pregnant, I think."

"When was the last time you saw him? . . . Your grandfather, that is."

Sachi was staring out of the window. Her thoughts seemed divided between the past and his question. "I visit twice each year," she answered plainly. "I was here four months ago."

"Did your grandfather act like anything was bothering him?" he asked.

Sachi shook her head idly. "No. He seemed fine."

Ben pressed on. "This is a tough question, but what did you know of your grandfather's activities around the time of the Second World War?"

Her voice was angry and loud. "What do you mean by that!"

He realized he'd been impatient, interrogating her as if she was a suspect. "Ms. Kamimura, believe me, I didn't mean anything personal. I . . ."

Sachi interrupted. "Personal! He was my grandfather. He was Japanese. What could be more personal than a question like that?"

"I wasn't trying to condemn the Japanese. We have reason to believe your grandfather's murder has to do with something he was hiding, either a secret, or something of value. During the autopsy, we discovered a small tattoo on his armpit. Members of the Japanese Secret Service were tattooed like that. We've talked to people who believe he was a spy. But . . ."

"You . . ."

Ben raised his voice. "Let me finish. I believe that when he found out what was going on . . . about Pearl Harbor, I mean . . . he left. He disappeared. He didn't approve and wanted no part of it. I need your help. I'm trying to find out who murdered him, and two other men for that matter. I need you to tell me what you know about his past." He gave her a long look, then concentrated on the road once more, keeping her face in his peripheral vision.

Sachi stared at him for a few seconds before it appeared to register. She slumped in her seat. "Two other men have died?"

Ben set his jaw and nodded. He could feel her eyes.

Just then they came to a sharp curve. The jeep's tires squealed. Ben tapped the brakes a few times until the highway straightened. Then he downshifted into third.

"Were they friends of my grandfather?" she asked.

"I hardly think so. In fact, one might have been your grandfather's killer."

Sachi seemed calmer. She cleared her throat quietly. "I see." She turned halfway toward Ben. "I don't know much about his life. When I was little my father told me that his mother had to return to Japan in a hurry. It was a few weeks before Pearl Harbor. I knew nothing of my grandfather until I was six. That's when my father died and my mother brought me to Hawai'i for the first time. He lived in the same house as now. He built it himself."

Ben stole a glance at her. Her eyes were glazed. "When was that?"

She hesitated. "A long time ago. Thirty years to be precise."

"Nineteen sixty?"

She nodded. "Yes."

"Where is your mother now?"

"She is in a government hospital . . . she has not been well for a long time."

"I'm sorry," said Ben.

"My grandfather was not a spy," she said firmly.

"How can you be sure?"

Sachi had no answer for that.

They drove the next few miles in silence. Ben thought about the woman next to him. He figured her for one of the new breed of Japanese women. Not timid. Not condescending, but independent, strong. Although it was nice to see the respect for her elders. That was one thing that set the Japanese—and Hawaiians—apart from many other nationalities, especially his generation of Americans.

He hardly knew anything about his father's parents. They had died before he was born. It had been different on his mother's side, but not by much. He had met his Hawaiian grandfather once. It was difficult now to visualize his face. He had passed away just before his Hawaiian grandmother had come to live with them. Ben thought about how much he missed her, his *kupuna wahine*. He remembered many of the things she had told him. But he had tuned out on much more. Sports were more important to him then. It seemed tragic that he'd only spent a few years around her, instead of a lifetime. Now he realized, as he sat next to Ahi's granddaughter, exactly how much his Hawaiian heritage meant to him.

He had little to pass along to his children. Suddenly, Ben felt like an old man. Right now, he had little prospect of even having children.

As they passed Captain Cook, his thoughts turned to Lisa. He pictured her eating lunch with a mainland business man. A forty-year-old, manicured executive outfitted by Ralph Lauren or Pierre Cardin. Handsome, staring into her eyes, making his hand available if she wanted to touch it. He had two homes, not a borrowed apartment. Prospects, not suspects. He was successful, financially independent, and the only shots fired at him were political volleys that he deftly returned with topspin for winners.

And then there was Sachi sitting a bucket seat away. Out of the corner of his eye he studied her profile. He could see the outline of her breasts against the thin fabric of her blouse. He shifted uncomfortably and wet his lips as his eyes wandered lower, following the curve of her hips and her long legs. He let out a deep breath and made a soft noise with his cheeks.

She's grieving and I'm leering. He shook his head and tried to concentrate on driving. Then again, he was sure he felt *her* eyes on *him.* Thinking. Sizing him up.

"What do you think he was hiding?" she asked.

Her question startled him a bit. They had been riding in silence for ten minutes.

"You mean you think he may have been a spy?" he asked.

"I'm not conceding that, but if someone killed him . . . and those other two men . . . then maybe there was something he was hiding."

Ben didn't like the idea of answering questions instead of asking them. "I have no idea. I thought that's where you could help. If you knew about his being a spy, then maybe you knew about something he was hiding. Something he had held onto for all these years. Something that would implicate someone."

"What would anyone have to fear from an old man who held onto a secret for fifty years?"

"The longer you hide something, the more valuable it becomes." Ben smiled to himself. He was beginning to sound like Tobi.

Sachi turned her head in his direction, parted her lips, but then held onto what she had planned to say.

Here goes. "What about something of value then?"

Sachi laughed. "You've been reading too many detective stories. You've been inside his house. Your people searched it thoroughly. What did you find of value?"

Ben's narrowed his eyes. "What about those paintings?"

Sachi grinned. "He would be pleased you said that. They are valuable to me because he painted them, but hardly valuable art."

"When did he take up painting?"

Sachi thought for a few seconds, shifted in her seat, and faced Ben more directly. "Maybe five or six years ago. Why?"

"I just wondered."

"You find me attractive, don't you?"

Ben widened his eyes. "Ahhh . . ."

A short laughing sound came from deep inside her throat. "Sorry. I shouldn't have said that."

"Why did you then?"

"Because I speak my mind. Because you have been sneaking looks at me. And because I have been sneaking looks at you."

Grieving?

"You look a little disappointed. If you think I should be upset . . . I'm more angry than upset. My grandfather was my last relative. My mother . . . she . . . she cannot recognize me. My visits here were the only family things I could look forward to. Now I'm all alone." Her voice got defiant. "Don't flatter yourself, maybe I just need someone to help me through this . . . maybe anyone will do!"

Downshifting, ramming the gearshift into second, Ben turned left, gave the jeep some gas, and they lurched up the rough drive to Ahi's house. He slowed after the jolt of the first large rut.

Jesus!

21

THE YELLOW PLASTIC POLICE LINE BAND was gone. It had been taken down to encourage Furbee's killer to resume his search of Ahi's property.

The farmhouse, cast in the shadows of the surrounding trees, looked peaceful, like nothing had happened. All the tire marks from official vehicles had been swept away. Only the killer and the police, and Ahi's two neighbors—who promised cooperation—knew that Ahi wasn't inside preparing a meal, or in the back, picking coffee berries. If there was that much gold, then the killer would return. Maybe a week, maybe a month, but he'd be back.

It was a simple trap, but sometimes those were the ones that worked. Two uniform patrol were hidden in the forest—one guarding the front entrance, the other the back. The man in the front had been the one who'd intercepted Ahi's granddaughter earlier.

Ben knew where to look and subtly nodded in the direction of the man guarding the front of the farmhouse. Ben watched Sachi out of the corners of his eyes. She was scanning the trees. It didn't appear that she'd located the patrolman, but Ben could tell she knew he was still out there.

They mounted the front steps and Ben gave the doorknob a quick twist. Ahi's neighbors had said that he never locked it, so it had been left unlocked. Ben stepped to one side, motioned Sachi inside, and followed, closing the door behind them.

Sachi's eyes misted. She stopped for a second and her knees buckled slightly. She put her hand on Ben's shoulder and buried her face into the crook of his arm. Ben could hear her small sobs, feel her warm breath, and her wet eyes. And he picked up the faint scent of her perfume, which he inhaled deeply. She remained near him for a few seconds, then straightened and wiped her eyes with the tip of her finger.

"I'm okay."

Ben bit his lip and nodded.

The air smelled musty and felt heavy. Ben thought about how the Hawaiians watched over the dead before the death feast and burial ceremony. The corpse would be face up on the floor, feet pointing toward the front entrance. The close relatives would sit behind the remains, the next of kin near the head. As a relative was seen approaching the house, someone from within would cry out in grief. The forthcoming mourner would wail out a prayer for the dead called a *ue helu,* and then join those inside. Ben wondered what the Japanese did. He was not about to inquire.

Sachi asked if she could open a few windows. Ben took the one in the bedroom, Sachi opened its opposite in the kitchen. A fresh breeze rushed in.

"The smell of death?" she asked.

Ben didn't know what to say.

Sachi didn't seem to be looking for an answer and walked directly into her grandfather's bedroom to his desk. Pulling out the chair, she sat down, then slumped a bit before she regained control.

Ben stood behind her, watching carefully, hoping that something she lingered over might provide a clue.

The first thing she picked up was her picture. She held the frame, caressing the wood, feeling more than the smooth finish. Feeling her grandfather holding it, seeing his reflection in the glass as he gazed at her. She replaced it carefully. Then she opened the top desk drawer. Quickly she spun around.

"Where are my letters?"

"We have them at headquarters. You can have them back soon."

Sachi gave him a doubting look and turned. The second drawer was where Ahi had kept the few financial records he had. She went through the papers quickly, only pausing to ask Ben if there were any bills she should pay. He thought it was a strange question, but realized people say and ask silly things when confronted with a traumatic experience, especially the murder of a loved one. He said he didn't know, but not to worry about it. The third drawer, Ben knew, was empty. Apparently, Sachi did, too.

She stood, looked down at Ahi's sleeping mattress, let out her breath, and walked to the closet. She opened the door and moaned softly. Carefully, she extracted her grandfather's ceremonial robe and turned to face Ben. "It's beautiful, isn't it?" Her eyes were wide and bright now.

"Yes, it is. I admired it . . . before." He winced slightly, but Sachi didn't seem to notice his embarrassment.

"It has been in the family for many generations. It gets passed from grandfather to grandson, skipping a generation each time." She closed her eyes. Two tears squeezed out and dropped to her cheeks. "Only now, there is no grandfather. And there is no grandson. I was his only hope." She carried the robe to Ahi's sleeping mat and kneeling, laid it out, stroking the silk as she pushed away the wrinkles and folds. Then she stood back and admired it again. "I will take it with me, if that is okay?"

"That's fine." Ben waited a few seconds, then spoke. "Sachi, is there anything missing?"

"I don't think so, but I don't know. This robe was the most valuable thing he owned. I guess the *only* valuable thing."

"To him. But maybe there was something else that would be of more value to someone who didn't understand the tradition of the robe."

She looked around quickly. "Not in here. Everything seems fine . . . at least this is how I remember it from my last visit."

"Before . . . we found some money. Not much. It was hidden behind a painting."

"I remember that. Now that you say it. He told me it wasn't much."

"I don't think that's what the . . . person was looking for."

Sachi seemed uninterested in the money. She bent and started folding the robe. After handing it to Ben to carry, she returned to the main living area. Other than some pottery and some books, the room was spartan. Ben had gone through the books before, page by page. There were no hidden sheets of paper. No inscriptions or secret messages. He realized then that he hadn't looked inside the two vases that sat on the bookshelf. Maybe there was a key. Maybe a piece of notepaper. He didn't want to look while she was watching, so he waited. His moment came soon, for Sachi became absorbed in one of Ahi's paintings. He placed the robe on a squat, lacquered table.

First vase. Empty. Second one. Empty again. A deep frown crossed his face. He didn't know why, but he had really expected to find something. He joined Sachi, who was observing the artwork. He watched the corners of her eyes as they traced her grandfather's brush strokes, but mainly he was staring at her head. Glossy black hair, a few loose strands resting on her fragile-looking neck. As his eyes moved down the length of her body, Ben thought about how beautiful she was and wished that they'd met some other time.

"He painted well," Ben said.

"He could have made a living at it." She pointed. "This one is special. This one is about me."

Ben viewed the painting. Dark green mountains, a valley, surging water coming from the ocean, rushing inland. *Tsunami.* A tidal wave caused by an earthquake somewhere in the Pacific.

"When I was six there was a great *tsunami.* I was here with my mother, visiting grandfather. It was the first time . . . after my father died. Hilo Harbor was devastated. Many people drowned. I was in the fish market with my mother. While she shopped for dinner, I wandered toward the docks to watch the fishermen. I remember it so clearly. As if by magic, the entire harbor emptied. The water simply receded . . . far past low tide. It seemed to disappear. Everything was still for a few seconds. People stopped talking. The water birds became still. Even the palm leaves on the trees stopped chattering. That never happens . . . there is always creaking and swaying and the fronds rustling in the wind. Some people ran out into the bay to gather up fish that had become stranded. Then there was a terrific noise . . . like . . . like many stampeding horses and water buffalo. I remember looking up, toward the sea, and seeing a great wall of water rushing toward shore. People started screaming and running. Carts overturned. Animals got loose and trampled everything, crashing through the market trying to escape the great wave." A long, hard shudder came from her body. She blinked a few times before continuing. "I stood paralyzed. I couldn't move. When you are six, you understand danger, but not death. You don't realize that you can die. Only old people die, and even then you do not fully understand it. After old ones die, young ones still ask when they are going to come back. You cannot comprehend that they are never coming back. It may be a long time, but you believe they will come back.

"The wave was only a few hundred feet away when a pair of hands grabbed me by the shoulders and lifted me. It was a man. He ran and for the first few steps I didn't know who it was. I was more afraid of the man than of the great wave. But soon I managed to twist around and face him." She sucked in her breath slowly. Almost painfully, she exhaled. "It was him. It was grandfather. I could feel his heart pounding, the strain in his breathing. He managed to tell me not to worry. We would be safe. People were screaming. I will never forget the looks on their faces. Since then I have seen many pictures of people running from the cloud of fire and smoke from the bombs that ended the war. The expressions of these people running from the *tsunami* were the same. Utter fear. Very little hope. Praying for a miracle."

Ben was mesmerized.

"He carried me over his shoulder. I could see it, water fifty feet high. Finally, the wave crashed behind us. Everything in its path was destroyed. I could hear palm trees snapping, people screaming . . . then disappearing in the white surf, only to reemerge, their arms and legs twisted into horrible positions, lifeless. Animals were squealing, too. Everything joined the wall of water. Then grandfather couldn't run any more. He was out of breath and we were on a small mound of earth . . . maybe ten feet high. I was scared. He kept going, walking, stumbling, then running for a few more paces. I could feel his body tighten with cramps. Then we fell. He yelled for me to crawl. We crawled together. The water came closer, racing inland. I remember looking back. The water in the harbor seemed fifty feet higher. Bodies of people and dogs and cats were floating and drifting out to sea. I clawed at the ground. I couldn't go on. Suddenly, I felt his hand grab my wrist. I looked up. He looked terrible. His face was white. His eyes bulged. But he was standing. He pulled as hard as he could and dragged me with him. Then he collapsed next to a tall palm. We wrapped our arms around it. He shielded my body with his. He told me to close my eyes and think of flying my kite. I had a beautiful dragon kite he made for me. We would go down to the meadow near Kealakekua Bay and fly it for hours. I closed my eyes and imagined it. The kite flew proudly. I heard him yell for me to hold my breath. He barely got the words out when the water rolled over on us. I held my breath. My head pounded. Then, suddenly, it was gone. As quickly as it had come . . . it was gone. We coughed, but soon we were smiling at each other. Then we both cried. He stroked my head. I have never felt closer to anyone in my life. I don't expect I ever will."

Ben's heart was racing. He was perspiring. He swallowed.

"The funny thing is, he hadn't come with us to the market. He stayed here. He didn't like to shop. That was women's work. But a half hour after we left for Hilo, he followed. He had never done that before, my mother said. Never once had he been to the market.

"Later, when I was older, I asked him what had made him come that day. I remember his eyes brimmed with tears. He said he could feel that something was wrong . . . that I would need him."

"And your mother . . . ?"

"She made it up the hillside safely. She was farther away from the water to begin with. She was lucky."

"So were you."

"So was I."

Sachi caved in. All her anger let loose. "Why did they kill him? Why?" She crumpled into Ben's arms sobbing. Her sobs soon turned to tears. It was a long time before she let go.

As Sachi calmed down, Ben remembered reading that Hilo had been hit by two major *tsunami* in the last century. One in 1946 and another in 1960. He looked at the painting. He felt like he had known her much longer than a few hours.

He felt he was going to know her much better before long.

They spent the next hour gathering a few more things. Mainly utensils, or other odds and ends that Ahi had hand-carved. Before they left, Sachi returned to the paintings. She said she'd come back for them with special shipping containers. Then she paused for a few seconds, standing in front of the painting that had caught his attention when he and Tobi had searched Ahi's house. She seemed to be thinking, trying to make out what the painting represented.

"What about this one?" he asked. "Is there a story?"

"This one is new. He must have done it after my last visit."

"What do you think it means?"

She didn't answer right away. She seemed to be in a trance. "Pardon?"

"Do you know what it's about?"

"I guess he visited the volcano and he wanted to paint it."

"That steam looks like how you described the surf of the *tsunami*."

She smiled but her thoughts were far away. Maybe back in 1960. Then she turned toward Ben. "I'm sure he could have saved me from that. Lava doesn't move so fast."

"No. But after it covers you, it doesn't recede."

"What a horrible thing to say!"

"I'm sorry. I guess your story just got me carried away." Ben stared at the picture. He was thinking. Something was nagging at him, tearing at the edge of his thoughts. He turned and faced Sachi. Her eyes were like two black mirrors. He saw his reflection. His look of concentrated wonder. The look when you first recognize a strong attraction to someone and you desperately want to know how they feel about you. But the darkness in Sachi's eyes sheltered any message she might have been sending. Although she was thinking—he could sense that. About him? About her grandfather? About the gold . . .

———————

It was near five by the time they left the coffee farm. Sachi looked hungry and tired. Ben suggested they get something to eat.

"Do you want something fancy or simple?"

"Simple."

"Need to go to your hotel and change?" he asked.

Sachi had been staring out of the jeep's window. She shifted and faced Ben. "I left in a hurry. It was hard enough to obtain a flight. I don't have a hotel reservation."

"We can take care of that after we eat. There's a place up the road. Good food. I know the owner. And it'll be quiet until eight or so."

"That sounds fine," she replied.

Ben changed the subject. "What's it like teaching English?"

She smiled. "Easier than teaching Japanese."

Ben grinned. He relaxed his grip on the steering wheel. "How old are your students?"

"I teach an accelerated class. There are fourth, fifth, and sixth grades." Her face slipped away and she was soon staring out of the window once more.

Ben remained silent, focused on driving, waiting for her to say something. He wanted her to ask a few questions about him. Nothing came.

"What are you thinking about?" Ben asked.

Sachi didn't answer at first. Then she wet her lips, leaving her tongue pressed between them for a long time. Her mouth opened slowly. "That outside of a few aunts and uncles who live far away, I have no one. Grandfather was far, but at the same time he was close. You develop a special bond with someone when they save your life. Especially if it was someone you loved before. Whenever you start to get annoyed or even angry with them, you stop and think that you wouldn't be here if it wasn't for their courage and love. It makes you realize the bigger picture. It takes the edge off of your anger. I think it must last forever."

Ben thought about that. He'd saved Lisa's life. Where was the special bond? Maybe that was it. Maybe she felt it and he didn't. Maybe the problem was that he didn't understand what he really meant to her. Suddenly, he felt guilty about his feeling toward Sachi.

"Is something wrong?" asked Sachi, sliding a little bit closer to the edge of her bucket seat.

"Nothing."

"There's something? What?"

He glanced at her before focusing on the road. "I saved someone's life. Just last year. You made me think about that special bond."

"Is it someone close to you?"

"Was. Is . . . I guess."

"Who?"

"A woman."

"A woman you love?"

"A woman who confuses the hell out of me. But maybe I confuse the hell out her, too."

Sachi reached over toward the steering wheel and placed her hand over his. "It will work out. It seems to me . . ." Almost inaudibly she cleared her throat. "It seems to me that she's lucky to have you."

Ben felt a flush cover his face. He wanted to be alone. He wanted to walk along a deserted beach and think. A long walk—miles. He decided that right after dinner he'd drop Sachi off at the Hilton—he assumed he could get her a room there—head back to the apartment and go for a long walk. No bike ride. No swim. No training. Just thinking.

Keauhou.

"Here we are."

Dinner was good. Swordfish steaks with mango butter. A bottle of white zin. Danny Mitchell asked him where he found her. Ben just gave him a quiet snort.

The Hilton was booked. So was the King Kamehameha. So was the Kona Surf. The only thing available was Keliʻi's couch. Ben offered her the bed in exchange for the couch. She thanked him and prepared for a bath. Ben said he'd be back in an hour.

He hopped onto his bike, even though he had promised himself a long quiet walk. There was something about neglecting his training that always made him feel guilty, even though he probably trained more than most men in his age group.

The ride was terrible. He couldn't concentrate on anything. Not Lisa. Not Sachi. Not the case. Not even riding the bike—they were enemies again. His calves burned, the wine blocked what his brain was trying to sort out. He had eaten too much and his stomach cramped. And the bike seat felt like an unlubricated proctologist's fist.

He lasted twenty minutes.

Sachi was sitting in the living room, drying her hair with a towel when he returned. She was wrapped in a white terry-cloth bathrobe with light-blue piping that ended a good six inches above her knees. She smiled at him.

"I feel much better. How was your ride? I thought you'd be gone longer."

"My mind wasn't on it."

"I'm sorry." She stopped rubbing.

"Not your fault. Is there still hot water? It doesn't last long."

"I think so."

"I'll be right out." He marched into the bedroom. After he found a pair of cotton shorts and a T-shirt and was heading into the bathroom he shouted, "There are some coffee beans if you want to make some."

"In a few minutes . . . after I finish with my hair."

Ben blew across the top of his steaming mug and then took a sip. It was good. Sachi put milk and sugar in her coffee and then held the mug in her hands and smiled, as if the warmth of the mug spreading across her palms soothed her pain. She was seated across from him, legs tucked under her. The robe was closed tightly around her body, held in place by a light-blue terry-cloth belt knotted to one side.

Ben sat, forearms resting on the arms of a deep, square chair, coffee in one hand, flexing his free wrist, observing his tan that appeared darker than usual against the white fabric of his T-shirt.

"What is this Ironman you have on your shirt?"

"It's a triathlon they hold here in Kona."

"I've heard of triathlons . . . is the Ironman special?" Sachi arched her back after the question. The outline of her breasts was more evident.

"It's the most grueling one. Most triathlons are a mile swim, a forty- to sixty-mile bike ride and a fifteen-k."

"Fifteen-k?"

"Fifteen kilometers." Ben was about to translate it into miles, but realized it was unnecessary. Americans were about the only ones who hadn't converted to metric.

Sachi nodded, grinning, but appearing a little nervous.

Ben tried to swallow the small lump he felt in his throat. It wouldn't budge. He cleared his throat. "The Ironman is 2.4 miles in Kailua Bay, 112 miles along the Queen K . . . that's Highway 19 across the lava beds . . . and some of it along 270 to Hāwī at the northern tip of the Island, and then a marathon . . . again over the Queen K. It's usually hot . . . ninety degrees and it feels like a hundred and twenty."

"And you compete?"

"I have twice." He thought about last year's interruption and this year's promise. *Shit, it's only two months away. What'll get in the way this time? If I'm still working on this case, I'll . . .*

Much later, near midnight, as he lay on the couch unable to sleep, he heard the bedroom door open and saw a faint light and then a shadow on the living room wall. As Sachi came closer, the shadow on the wall became smaller. He closed his eyes, but not completely. She passed him and went to the kitchen. He expected her to open the refrigerator, but she didn't. Instead, she opened the sliding door and carefully, quietly, pushed it closed after she stepped onto the *lānai*. He opened his eyes. She stood there for a long time. Ben could see that she was mesmerized by the quarter moon shining brightly in the night sky. There was no wind, at least not much. The silver path that the moon laid down over the water hardly moved. He heard her sigh. In the moonlight he could see that she was naked. He felt strange. Before—before he had met Lisa— he would have gotten up and joined her. But now, he just lay there watching, feeling somewhat aroused, but there was no real urge, no yearning. He thought about the things she had said that afternoon. The story of the *tsunami* was amazing. He thought about the things she had lingered over. The robe, the paintings. Just then a breeze came up. His skin tingled. Goose bumps stood up on his arms and legs. He thought of her skin. Her goose bumps. Small beads of perspiration formed on his brow and his neck.

The sliding door opened. Sachi stepped back inside. Then she walked toward the living room. Toward the couch.

Ben tensed. Then slowly, muscle by muscle, he made himself relax and partially closed his eyes.

Sachi was standing over him now. He could hear her breathing, smell her perfume. It was faint, but it was hard to forget. She bent over and rested her knee on the couch. Closer. Ben kept his eyes open just a crack. She leaned forward and kissed him lightly on the forehead. And then she held a few strands of his hair, rubbing them lightly between her finger tips. She kissed him again—this time a little harder. Then Ben felt the cushioned seat rise, free of her knee.

Ben opened his eyes. He saw her standing, facing the water.

And then she returned to the bedroom and closed the door.

22

TOBI AWAKENED EARLY, DRESSED QUICKLY, grabbed a large beach towel, and went outside. The sun was already above the horizon. He was late and was shaking his head. He found it hard to believe that he had slept so well in an unfamiliar bed. After finding a flat patch of grass, Tobi spread out the towel, dropped gracefully to his knees, and lowered his head. Later, when his prayers and chants were completed, he sat, legs crossed beneath him, reflecting on the previous day.

He had arrived in Honolulu at twelve-thirty and met with Detective Kalani for an hour. Then they went to the warehouse at Pier 2B. The receptionist, Kim, greeted them. She had seemed nervous and had stuttered a bit, but finally told them that a man fitting Yamato's description had been there the day before. Tobi had asked questions about the men in the photograph. Kim said that since Mr. Yamato had worked there previously, he had been given an address on the North Shore for the widow of one of the men in the photo. They took that information and hurried away. The address led them to a sister of the man who had been killed during the Japanese attack. But the sister, who lived alone, hadn't been home the day before when Yamato had been looking for her. She said no one had left her a message. She didn't know who Niko Yamato was. Dead end.

Meanwhile, three Honolulu patrolmen were stationed at the inter-Island terminal, each holding sketches of Yamato, each with orders to detain anyone who even slightly resembled the drawing. And all three inter-Island carriers had been notified to report if Niko Yamato made a reservation. Tobi talked to dozens of cabbies and bus drivers. No one remembered the old man.

But Tobi didn't think Yamato was trying to hide. Just that he had things to do, now that he knew of Ahi's death.

Tobi had taken the last flight to Kaua'i the previous night. Checked Yamato's house. It was unlocked, dark, and empty. He searched briefly, using a small flashlight, but he didn't believe the house held any secrets—only Yamato did. Then he checked into the Hanalei Resort. The owner was a friend of Tobi's counterpart in Honolulu. He had provided Tobi with a small room that faced east.

A pair of squabbling Zebra doves broke his concentration. He turned off yesterday and thought about what today might bring. He believed he'd find Yamato. He hoped he would tell him the truth. Tobi stood and faced east, staring in the direction of Yamato's house, a few miles away. He walked back to his first-floor room.

He had a quick breakfast in a restaurant a short distance down the road—one frequented by locals. He had smoked salmon, a dry, black currant scone cut in half, half a papaya, and herb tea with lemon and honey. And then a short ride in his rented jeep. A short ride to Weke Street.

He hadn't notified the Līhu'e police that he was coming. It was late when he arrived. And he knew, if he had, that they would have insisted on coming along. He counted on Yamato's cooperation, but only if he came alone. One Japanese man to another.

Weke Street was just waking up. There was a round woman walking a dog. A pickup truck, driven by an older Hawaiian man, passed him with what appeared to be the man's two teen-aged sons riding in back. They were sitting on the bed surrounded by gardening tools, laughing. He heard an off-key rooster sounding a bit bored with his routine. He heard distant doves. He smelled bacon. And, as he neared the public beach, he saw a light on in Number 3 Weke.

He pulled over, killed the engine, and waited. He would be cautious. Ben had been shot at, after all. Although he hadn't met Yamato, Tobi had a strong feeling that Yamato had not been the one who fired at Ben. And the light didn't necessarily mean that it was Yamato who was inside. It could be someone else, maybe the person who took a shot at Ben, maybe the person who killed Jeremiah Furbee, or severed the neck of the second mystery man. Or even the person who dumped Ahi Ishizu at sea. After all, they had only guessed that the second man killed Ahi, and that Furbee had killed *him*.

And they had no idea who the third person was, the person who finished off Furbee, the runty man with small boots.

Tobi got out and walked in the shadows as he approached the house, taking the route around by the beach, then along the shore, and toward the back of Yamato's house. It was quiet except for the fishing waterfowl and the waves that gently lapped the shore as the tide began to turn from high to low. He paused for a second to watch a pair of blue herons in flight, awkward when their skeleton-like wings were moving, graceful when they glided.

The light went out. Tobi hustled to the side of the house and pressed his body against the wall. The window next to him was open and he could hear clearly the sounds from inside.

A yawn. A quilt being removed. Sandals flopped onto the floor. The quilt again, he guessed, covering a sleepy old man. It could only be Yamato. Where had he gone? Why had he been out all day and night? What was so important that he had left Kaua'i—which from Ben's description of him seemed highly unlikely—and flown to Honolulu and back? What had he done there? Whom had he talked with? What did he get? Why hadn't he gone to the Big Island? To Ahi's farm.

The sun freed itself from the shadow of Anahola Mountain to the east, casting its brilliance over Hanalei Valley. The entire right side of the house sparkled and made Tobi blink several times. Then he sensed that something was wrong. He was a bit late with his discovery.

"Who are you?" asked Niko, standing by the window, his hand outstretched, holding onto the window shade's pull-string.

Tobi cleared his throat softly. All he could see was what was near the screen—Yamato's hand on the shade. Tobi hoped his other hand wasn't holding a gun. "My name is Tobi Otaki. I am the Captain of Detectives in Kona. Detective McMillen . . . the man who was here two days ago, and Detective Haanio . . . they are both my men. I would like to talk with you." Tobi had turned and faced the window so that Yamato could see him. He tried to look friendly and innocent.

"You could have knocked on the front door."

"There have been three murders and Detective McMillen has been shot at. I could not be sure who was inside your house. I came to wait for you. I saw a light. When I saw it go off, I came closer to investigate."

"Is Detective McMillen all right?" asked the old man behind the screen.

Tobi's eyes had adjusted and he could Yamato's face and other hand. No gun. "He is. Just a nick." Tobi concentrated on Yamato's expression. "He was shot at the Līhu'e Airport, right after he left you. Around six. Nearly the same time as your flight." Tobi drew in his breath.

The old man's shoulders slumped. He wet his lips. "Come to the back door. I will let you in."

Tobi stopped thinking of the man as Yamato. He was Niko now.

Both men squatted before the low, lacquered dining table, and simultaneously each crossed his legs as he sat. Niko offered tea. Tobi accepted. They sipped. They stared at each other. Niko put his porcelain cup on the table. Tobi took another sip, then did the same.

The room darkened as the sun went behind a bank of clouds. Tobi could feel his heart going at a slightly faster pace than usual. Looking around, he realized how similar Niko's house was to Ahi's, and although Ahi's was more rustic, the furnishings were comparable. For that matter, both Niko's and Ahi's homes weren't much different from his own.

"We are both honorable men," he stated.

Niko hesitated, then nodded.

Tobi wondered which one of them Niko had doubts about. "But I think you held back something from my detectives. Not that you did not tell the truth . . . I just think there is more to tell."

"And you thought that if someone of Japanese heritage came to talk to me, I would divulge everything."

Tobi did not hesitate. "That was my belief, yes."

Niko's firm expression changed into a wide grin. "I appreciate that you gave me an honest answer." He looked toward his bedroom and stared for a few moments as if his secret was hidden behind the paper screen. "Now it is my turn." He shifted and then clasped his hands and rested them on the table.

Tobi clasped his but kept them in his lap.

"The story of the gold is true. But why the people in the Economic Trade Association had it . . . that reason I mislead your detectives about . . ." His sigh was sharp and somewhat pained. "It was for something terrible. Something I have trouble believing to this day. I promised Ahi I would never talk to anyone about it. But now, I think I must."

Tobi waited as the old man uncrossed his legs, stretched, and re-crossed them.

After a quick glance upward, Niko was ready. "A few days before the attack, Ahi took me to dinner. I could tell he carried a burden. He looked tired, beaten. The sparkle in his eyes was gone. He had not been the same person for several weeks. After we ate, while we were drinking tea . . ." A small smile slipped from Niko's mouth. "*He* was drinking coffee . . . I was drinking tea."

Tobi nodded politely.

"He told me of the Japanese plan to strike. I was stunned. I did not know what to say. I was of Japanese birth. I loved my country. But I was an American citizen by then. And American or not, the government of Japan did not have the right to attack Pearl Harbor. The only person who felt more strongly about that than me was Ahi. When he saw I was completely with him he told me of another plan. It was much worse than the first. Much worse. You have heard of the Manhattan Project?"

Tobi eyes widened. "Of course," he answered warily.

"There was a man . . . I do not know his identity, neither did Ahi, or surely he would have killed him." Niko paused, appearing to be visualizing his friend as a murderer. "This man had the plans for the atomic bomb. He was an American, but he hated the United States. Ahi said that the man had been kicked out of the project. Ahi wasn't sure why. All he knew was that the man wanted revenge. He offered the plans to Japan. That was what the gold was for . . . to buy the plans." Niko's head bowed.

The entire room seemed void of air. Tobi had trouble breathing. The concept of Japan having the A-bomb was so overwhelming that Tobi had to brace himself with his arms. He was shaking. "You mean both sides would have had the bomb."

"Worse, the Japanese government would have also given the plans to the Germans."

Tobi got up. His breathing was still shallow. "And they would have perfected it and used it long before the United States did. We would have lost the war. But even that would have been secondary. For soon afterwards, I am sure, the Emperor and Hitler would have destroyed the world while seeking to destroy each other."

There was total silence. Seconds seemed like minutes.

Tobi's face was sporting a strange smile. "But it didn't happen. Ahi stole the gold—history's greatest hero, except the world never knew."

"It is better left unknown. This knowledge would change how people feel about each other. The Americans, what would they think? What would they do? Old feelings . . . bad feelings . . . the fires might be rekindled."

Not until the sun broke free of the clouds and illuminated the house did Tobi speak again. "Why did you go to Honolulu yesterday?"

"A woman there, a sister of one of my old friends . . . I thought she might know where the others are. They should know about Ahi. The real Ahi. She wasn't home."

Tobi nodded. "So what do these murders mean? Was someone trying to unearth these secrets?"

"It is far simpler than that, I think." Niko's head fell to his chest. "It is only about the gold. And what is worse . . . I am the one who killed Ahi."

Tobi was confused. "You are not Ahi's murderer. I know you had nothing to do with it."

"Maybe I was not there," said Niko, his head still down, "but had I not told my daughter about the gold . . ."

Tobi was speechless. "Who? When?"

"My daughter."

Tobi was thinking. He could feel the pieces of the puzzle gathering in his head. The problem was that they wouldn't stop swirling. "What did she do . . . what did she say when you told her?"

"I thought she was just listening, but I think she was planning. I trusted her. Now, I find out she cannot be trusted." Niko shook his head.

Tobi asked her name. Niko stared at him for a long time. Then after what appeared to be a lot of soul-searching, he went into his bedroom and returned in a few moments, holding a framed photograph tightly in front of him. Tobi understood—Niko had vowed never to utter his daughter's name again. She had disgraced him. Tobi could sense the dreadful feeling that consumed the old man. Slowly, Niko held out the frame. Tobi reached for it and grasped it. Not until their eyes met did Niko finally let go.

Tobi looked. His jaw dropped. Astonishment slapped him in the face. Tobi swallowed.

Niko's eyes widened with amazement. "You know my daughter?"

"When did you say you last saw her?"

"A month ago."

"Here?"

"Yes. Right here. She came for dinner. She comes every month." Looking down, now, Niko's lips quivered. "But, no more." He stood and appeared to be collecting himself. When he spoke again, his voice was louder, firmer. "How do you know her?"

Tobi's head pounded. He hadn't heard the question. Turning slowly, he faced Niko and focused on the old man's eyes. "Did she ask you about the gold, or did you decide to tell her."

"I told her a long time ago. Maybe ten years."

"But this time you mentioned Ahi."

Niko sat. "His code name. Yellowfin. Who is on guard with their daughter?" After a few moments when the old man seemed suspended in time, his shoulders slumped, and his eyes filled with tears. "She betrayed me and so I have killed my friend. I murdered the world's greatest hero." His head hung as though it would never again find a reason to rise.

Tobi didn't try to console him. Niko remained seated, head bowed. Tobi knew the feeling. Maybe not on the same scale, but he knew what being ashamed felt like. He let Niko be.

Tobi went to the window and thought about his casual approach to the marijuana trade. He saw no harm in growing a few plants for personal consumption. Many Kona families did it. Did you arrest all of them for growing a few plants by the side of their homes? He knew the big growers were in Puna—out of his district. Much closer to Hilo.

The Big Island's Eradication Program had many boosters, but he hadn't been committed enough to add one more voice. He had always believed the problem would take care of itself—that if the industry grew, the budget for the Eradication Program would be approved. If it didn't grow, then what was the harm?

And if guilt showed itself by making you hot and cold at the same time, then Tobi's icy palms and burning chest were sure signs of blame.

He thought of Ben. He'd let Ben down. It was as simple as that.

Tobi took a deep breath, filling his lungs. He let it out ever so slowly. He had to ask Niko a question.

"Do you know what your daughter does for a living?" Tobi asked it softly, so as not to cause Niko any more pain.

Niko bowed his head deeper into his lap. That was his answer.

Tobi stood and leaned against the counter, thinking, putting the final pieces together. At last he said, "Come with me, Niko. It's time to solve this thing."

"Where are we going, Tobi?"

"Ahi's."

"Do I have to face my daughter?"

"I think you must."

23

B EN'S HEAD JERKED AND HE WOKE to the uneven roar of the jeep's engine. He dashed to the front door and pushed opened the screen just in time to see a faint cloud of red dust at the top of hill by the main entrance. He ran back to the couch, scrambled into his pants, stopped, ripped them off, and headed for the bedroom. In seconds he was in a pair of Spandex racing shorts and a tight-fitting tank top. His handcuffs were still on the dresser. He tucked them into his waistband, in back. Then he was struggling with his cycling shoes. As he quickly laced them, his eyes darted around the room, looking for anything that the woman had left behind as a clue. Not to where she was headed—he knew that— but to who she was, because she surely wasn't Ahi's granddaughter. He spotted nothing, except her suitcase, which was void of any identification.

He reached for the phone to call headquarters. It was dead. He noticed the modular cord was missing. Without hesitation, Ben bolted for the door, grabbing his helmet from the top of the dresser as he passed.

His legs burned almost immediately from the lack of a warm-up, but this was no training ride. He had little time to catch her. He wondered if she'd figured out where the gold was. If she had, then she might not be headed to Ahi's farm. Ben didn't believe the gold was there. But if she was headed there, how did she expect to get by the policemen guarding the farmhouse? Did she have a gun?

"Shit." He realized they'd recognize her from the day before. He'd introduced her as Ahi's granddaughter. He'd told them they'd be back. She had his jeep. All she had to do was to tell them that he had had something else to work on, and that she wanted to go through her grand-father's things privately, so he'd loaned her his jeep. "Damn!" Besides, uniforms were suckers for pretty women. Just like detectives.

A quick check of his watch told him it was just past six. She'd waited until it was a little past first light so she wouldn't arouse suspicion. It was natural that she'd want to get back there early, but not when it was dark. That's why she'd gone back into her room after she'd come in from the *lānai* and kissed him. When he saw her go back to bed, he had relaxed and fallen asleep, not suspecting anything. It gave her the opportunity to take his keys and sneak out.

Calculating that it was twenty miles to the coffee farm, Ben thought he could make it in slightly under an hour, maybe even forty-five min-utes, since much of the road past Kēōkea was downhill—a steady grade of about five degrees. Given the curves in the road and the high center of gravity in the jeep, he didn't think she could average more than forty without risking an accident. That would give her about a fifteen- or twenty-minute head start. He believed that she'd spend at least that much time at the farmhouse. He could catch her. But only if he and his Trek were friends.

Of course, he didn't want to chance missing her, so he planned to stop the first car and take it. But unfortunately, this far south in the Kona district, near dawn, there was no traffic. Tourists slept late. Local coffee and mac nut workers would already be in the fields. Even the swampers wouldn't show up until much later.

Maintaining a speed of thirty was easy after he hit the downgrade. The burning sensation in his calves was gone, but it was replaced by a dull headache. Probably the wine and the fact he hadn't slept well, dreaming about Ahi. He had had many short dreams about the coffee farmer, many of them ending with Ben trying to save the older man, failing each time. One had Ben riding his 'aumakua across the waves, trying to reach Ahi before a posse of sharks ripped him to threads. But the spinner dolphin suddenly disappeared from beneath him, and he floundered in the swells, unable to swim a stroke.

He was hungry; he was used to eating breakfast. Something, so he wouldn't feel light-headed. And sometime during the night, he'd rolled over onto his side and torn off the scab that was forming on his ear. Now the wound rubbed constantly against the inside of his helmet and he could feel it bleeding once again. He hadn't had time to apply Millie's medicine. But he put all that in the back of his mind. It was time to think. To figure this out.

If this woman isn't Ahi's granddaughter, then who is she? Is she one of the killers?

What was it he had noticed about her that rang a bell? Something had given him the feeling they'd met before, although he knew she had a face he couldn't have forgotten.

Is it her voice? Have I talked to her before? Maybe on the phone? What women have I talked to on the phone? Joyce and Millie, and that one call to Lisa.

There was none that he could think of. *Wait! The researcher at the University. She knows the police are interested in a story about gold. She has all the material at her fingertips . . ."* no, her voice was much higher, almost whining.

He spent the next ten minutes putting the series of murders in perspective.

The second man, whoever he was, killed Ahi. Tried to get him to tell where the gold was hidden . . ." then knocked him out, took him out to sea off Kealakekua, and threw him overboard. Then Furbee killed the second man.

Why? Were they working together? Maybe that's it. They were working together and they argued, or maybe Furbee planned to double-cross him all along. But then who killed Furbee? This woman? Why do I think she's a killer?

The sun rose above the mountains. Filtered beams angled across the road and disappeared into the foliage on the *makai* side. Swirls of mist, broken by the wind of Ben's bike, rejoined the pattern after he passed.

Then his pace got the better of him. There was no salvation for his calves. His left leg cramped so badly that he had to stop peddling and begin coasting as best he could. He bent and massaged his calf, kneading the muscle, hoping to loosen the fiber and tissue that felt like it was being twisted in a ringer.

Thankfully, it was downhill the rest of the way. The rest gave his legs new life. Soon he could peddle slowly. He passed the turnoff to ʻŌhiʻa Mill. Hoʻomau Ranch—the location of Ahi's coffee farm—was only a few more miles.

The woman. There was still something else that bothered him. But once again, he couldn't extract it from his brain. Couldn't connect the two pieces of information—the two events that floated around inside his head and somehow fit together. Ben concentrated on the bike ride, hoping to clear his mind.

He came to the dirt road that led to Ahi's farm, took a sharp left, bounced off the edge of a partially buried boulder, and made it a few hundred feet more before the grade and the ruts made it impossible to ride. He flicked one foot out of its binding, then the other, and hopped off the bike. Wheeling the bike up the incline, running, breathing hard, he noticed two sets of fresh tire marks on the road, crisply carved into the red earth that had been washed clean as a slate from the heavy rain during the night. The woman had been there and gone. He dropped his bike and ran, shouting for the men who were hiding in the forest. He spotted them both standing in front of the farmhouse, hands on their holsters until they recognized him. They relaxed and started walking toward him.

"How'd you get here?" asked the shorter of the patrolmen. "On foot?"

"That woman is not Ahi's granddaughter."

The two patrolmen exchanged glances.

"She took my jeep. I biked it here. How long ago did she leave?"

The same officer who had spoke before said, "About ten minutes ago. She left without saying anything."

"Did she take anything?"

"Just a painting . . ." rolled up."

Ben dashed inside. He knew which painting would be missing, but he wanted to be sure.

He was right. It wasn't the tsunami scene, it was the one of lava pouring into a steaming sea.

Outside, he asked to borrow a car. The other patrolman pointed toward the back, saying they had parked them at one of the other farms bordering Ahi's property. Ben told them to radio Tobi. "Joyce or Millie can track him down. Get him back here right away. Have him follow me."

He told them where he was headed. Both patrolmen gave him odd looks. Ben snapped at them, "Just tell Tobi where I'm going!"

They nodded quickly, respectfully.

He left, running at full speed, dodging the holes in the backyard like a tailback, knifing through the trees, angling left toward the other farm. He heard one of the officers trailing him, racing for the radio in the other car, his slower footsteps becoming fainter and fainter as the forest engulfed them both.

Twenty feet from the Ford Explorer he felt a slight tearing in his calf muscle. He walked gingerly the rest of the way.

The painting was the only one of a Hawaiian landscape. A scene of volcanic lava pouring from Kīlauea, carving a path to the sea, and ending with a huge spray of steam at the expanding shoreline. If Ahi was true to form, if he took the gold to prevent a terrible disaster, then it seemed only fitting that he buried it in a place where it could never be recovered, under the molten rock of the newest spot on earth. Ben marveled at Ahi's scheme. He didn't know the melting point of gold, but a rich lava flow surely wouldn't leave it looking the same. And after the ground cooled, the gold would be buried under tons of frozen magma. Probably forever.

The borrowed Ford Explorer handled nicely and Ben raced south, then east, to a spot southeast of Volcanoes National Park that had once been the town of Kalapana. Now it was a riverbed of lava, some of it frozen and black. Some still moving like a molten glacial river, destroying homes, incinerating palms, creating a gray forest of ash, not unlike the nuclear winterscape Ahi had prevented. It would be another hour before he got there. Maybe he could intercept her, this mystery woman. Maybe . . . if she didn't think she was being followed, but Ben doubted that. She had fooled him with her impersonation of Ahi's granddaughter—tears, grief, compassion. And that incredible *tsunami* story. She had figured out where the gold was. She wouldn't be careless. She'd assume someone was coming after her. In fact, Ben guessed, she probably knew it would be him.

The tsunami *story . . . something wrong there.*

He came to the downward side of Kīlauea's lava flows, on the Chain of Craters Road, a narrow road that connected seven moonlike mini-craters and then wound down toward the ocean. It was an eerie sight. Orange, shades of black and deep gray, and rich brown. Low-hanging mist and the smell of sulfur becoming more noticeable mile by mile. Seven hollowed cones, the ashen buildup of the sequence of seven craters formed many years ago. And in the soft red earth that made up the shoulder of the road—fresh tire marks from his jeep cutting corners around the curves.

At the sea, the road flattened out and turned eastward. He knew from what he had read about the eruptions of Kīlauea, that the road ended a few miles ahead where the lava flows, as recently as three weeks ago, had severed the roadbed and torched the majestic palms that lined the black-sand beach at Kalapana. In the distance he could see steam billowing from the water. At first it looked like the morning mist. But as he drove closer, he could see the remaining glow of molten rock that had been heated above 2000° F. And he could see utility poles that had snapped under the surging pressure of the flow and burned. The only remnant of the huge masts were the ends that had been pushed to the side, out of the path of the stream of lava.

His jeep was parked on the black sand, near where the road ended, in a small grove of palms that had been spared Madam Pele's wrath, safely away from the smoldering black rubble. Closer, the smell of burning rubber became intense. A huge pile of old tires was smoking in a quagmire of cooling magma. The smoke irritated his eyes. It reminded him of his surf shop. He rubbed at the soreness in his calf.

Ben turned off the Explorer's engine and coasted toward his jeep, and then braked. He got out and left the door open. His leg was worse than he thought. The calf knotted, shooting searing pain through his left leg. He stumbled. The sand was soft and it muffled his sound. As he sat, gingerly rubbing his muscle, he scanned the horizon for the woman. She was nowhere in sight. He guessed she might be armed—in fact, she might even have his gun—so after a few minutes, he limped over to his jeep and checked the glove compartment. It was locked. He walked, favoring his left leg, to the Explorer, and opened the glove compartment. The patrolman's weapon wasn't there. He leaned against the fender, waiting for the cramping to disappear.

The water was calm, giving no evidence that only a hundred feet away new land was being created. The billowing clouds of steam rose in slow motion, lazily creeping higher into the sky, floating out to sea to join the early morning cloud bank that hovered a few hundred yards offshore. The wind picked up and blew the ground-level cloud cover inland, exposing her silhouette. Suddenly, the floating pieces of the puzzle began to fall into place. He'd seen her profile before. With lips pursed tightly together and a brow furrowed with concentration, he focused on the woman standing on the beach. It was the profile of the woman driving toward the toll booth at Līhu'e airport after he'd been shot at. There had been a man and a small boy in another car. And this woman in the second vehicle. Then he remembered going back to Yamato's house and sensing something that soon disappeared. It had been a smell. A mixture of lavender and something bitter and sharp, something acrid-smelling. He righted himself. His calf was not much better, but the wrenching pain was completely out of his mind. There was no room for the gripping spasm. Lavender and the faint smell of marijuana. And that's what he'd smelled each time he got close to her. That renewed scent of lavender and marijuana that disappeared in a few moments, after his nose became accustomed to it.

This *was* the person who had shot at him before!

There was something else. He racked his brain, forcing out the last clue. 'I was his only hope,' she had said. The robe passed on from grandfather to grandson. If she was the only hope to have someone's grandson, then she was a daughter, not a granddaughter!

She's Yamato's daughter and—he squeezed it out of his brain—*Yamato told her about Ahi and his gold!*

He walked stiffly but briskly along the back row of trees toward her. As he walked he reached behind his back, feeling for the cold steel hoops, one in his waistband, the other hanging out. He was within fifty feet and she hadn't turned. She seemed trancelike, staring down, as if she realized that Ahi had done well. There was no way to know where to dig. There was no chance to recover the gold. Her head turned—not toward Ben— but in the direction of the recent flow, still steaming, small fires at its leading edges. Mesmerized. Knowing that Ahi had watched this same flow. Knowing that he buried the gold one night right where the lava was sure to reach. How long ago? It didn't really matter. Even if it was just a few weeks before, it was too late. The gold was gone.

Her hands were by her side. Ben could see no weapon. He approached carefully, his footsteps completely silenced by the soft sand. And then, without warning, she spun around and faced him. He expected her to run. He expected a chase. Or maybe a concealed weapon. But no, she was beaten. Her face was blank. Lost. It was then that Ben realized that she must have been on this quest for a long time. For her it wasn't fresh. She looked exhausted. She slumped and fell to her knees. Her face took on a childlike expression.

One last shred of the past crept into his mind then. It was something from three years ago. He wasn't sure why, or how, but he remembered being in the Keauhou Shopping Village, at Drysdale's, sharing a pitcher of beer with Jack and Harry and Tobi. Tobi's chair was turned away from them. He was watching the news on one of the TV monitors, looking detached. Ben and the other two detectives were arranging the next day's fishing sojourn. Eventually, Ben's attention had shifted to Tobi as Tobi watched the screen. Connie Chung, sad-faced, was describing a disaster. Tobi wasn't listening. He wasn't tuned into the tragedy. He was relating to something that bothered him. His gaze was on the newscaster. Her eyes. Her mouth as it moved. It reminded him of someone. Someone he missed. Someone he lost. Lavender and marijuana.

Ben looked at her now. Her eyes had never left him. He cleared his throat and spoke softly. "You're Michiko Higa, aren't you?"

Her astonishment was impossible to hide. "How . . . ?"

"And Niko Yamato is your father."

She was blinking rapidly, mouth gaping.

"You had me for awhile. I don't know if it was your beauty, or your acting, or the story of the *tsunami* . . . but you had me." Just then, something else occurred to Ben, more evidence that he needed to share, as if the more he figured out now, the more he could diminish the degree of his culpability. "And another thing . . . you never asked me about my ear. At first, I thought you were being polite. But you already knew all about it."

Michiko composed herself. She folded her hands into her lap and took a deep breath. The final piece clicked in Ben's brain. "The *tsunami*. The one in '60 hit at one in the morning. A little late for a little girl to be shopping with her mother."

Michiko hung her head for a few moments and then looked up and continued. "You are clever. Tobi used to speak much of you. How someday you would head the department. Maybe he is right."

"Should I fill in the rest?" Ben asked.

"No . . . let me say it. I need to say it myself."

And so she told him her story.

"My father told me about Ahi and his gold a long time ago. I thought about it often. As you saw from my father's house, we never had much, just his pension. But I was able to go to school. And like Ahi's real granddaughter, I was a teacher. History. But I wanted more. When he told me how much gold was stolen . . . I knew it was worth ten times that. It took me a long time to track Ahi down. My grandfather never told me his name. He wouldn't. A month ago he told me his code name."

"Yellowfin."

"Yes. Yellowfin. Anyway, long ago, he told me that he thought Yellowfin . . . I mean Ahi . . . He told me he didn't think Ahi had gotten too far with all that gold. He guessed Maui or here. I spent a year working on Maui before I gave up. I came here nine years ago, partly to work . . . I was offered a teaching position in Hilo . . . and partly to look for the gold." A painful sigh. "And then I got hooked up with a few marijuana growers . . ."

Ben raised his hand to stop her.

Michiko shook her head. "I saw that they needed organization. I think at first they liked having a . . ." she smiled ruefully, " . . . a beautiful woman around. But I had a knack for organization, and soon they were making a lot of money. The police stayed away because we kept a low profile. Besides, I made sure we exported everything. Everything. The police were only going to get serious about us if the community wanted us stopped. And the only way that ever happens is if we're selling it to their children."

"Furbee sold crack to children."

"That is one of the reasons he died." Michiko raised her hand again, holding him off. They were going to do this at her pace—it was her story. "Keep Tobi out of this. We fell in love. He didn't know what I did for a living in the beginning. And to his credit, when he did find out, he ended it. I don't know how he feels today, but I still love him." Tears welled in her eyes and she blinked them out onto the black sand. And then the wind picked up, and in the distance whitecaps appeared, and large waves crashed against the new lava rock. "Then there's poor Ahi."

Ben felt a tingling sensation along his spine.

"One day last month I went fishing. I caught a tuna. A yellowfin. It took an hour to land him. Almost two hundred pounds, but I did it myself. Anyway, afterwards, this Hawaiian boy on the crew, every few minutes he would pump his fist and chant in a deep voice—' 'Ahi, 'Ahi.'

He was celebrating. After awhile it sunk in. *Ahi.* Yellowfin. It was worth a try. I had some of my organization ask around. Two weeks later Furbee came up with Ahi Ishizu the coffee farmer. The rest you know."

"That simple?"

"Yes, that simple."

"Did Furbee kill Ahi?"

Michiko shook her head. "No, I sent someone I thought had a little more tact than Furbee."

"That wouldn't be too hard."

Michiko gave him a weak smile. But immediately, she was serious again. "I wanted the gold. I didn't want Ahi to die."

A helicopter passed overhead and continued toward the chain of craters.

They both looked up for a second.

"The man you found at that other coffee farm killed Ahi. His name was Masami Ogata. Furbee killed him." She stated it plainly, without remorse. "Masami had ideas of his own. That's something I cannot tolerate in my position."

"You had Furbee kill him."

Michiko didn't answer.

"And *you* . . . you killed Furbee?"

"Does it matter?"

"Of course it matters."

Just then the ground shook. Ben stood and looked toward the north where he thought he heard a rumbling sound. Madam Pele was awake. A few miles back Kīlauea was coughing ash thousands of feet into the air. Lava started flowing once more from a southern vent, and soon, in the distance, the crackling of burning brush could be heard, and the fiery lava river started to move toward the sea. When Ben turned his attention back to Michiko, she was holding a small pistol aimed at his head.

"You are too trusting, Ben McMillen. Tobi would have searched me first. *Then* he would have sat in the sand and talked."

Ben's heart pounded. He knew one thing. You had a chance to talk someone out of shooting you, but only if they had never killed before. Once they had passed that first barrier, other killings didn't matter. What he needed was time.

Michiko got up. "Walk with me. This way." She flicked the small gun in the direction of the lava flow.

At the shoreline the lava was still moving a few inches each minute. They walked slowly, Ben a few paces in front. He had visions of burning beneath the lava. She'd probably shoot him, drag his body right in the lava's path, and wait for it to cover him. If she laid him crossways in front of the molten rock, it would only take an hour before he was completely enveloped and all traces of his body gone.

The ground shook once more hard enough to create a sizable fissure a few miles inland. The flow of lava would increase. Maybe a foot every few minutes. He'd be gone in less than fifteen minutes. It was only eight-thirty. No one, no tourists, would make it down the Chain of Craters Road before ten. If the mob only knew. This beat cement shoes by a long shot.

He thought about his grandmother then. About her stories of Pele, the fire goddess. In every story some malicious deed, usually disrespect for nature, had been the preamble to Pele's anger. It was then that she destroyed the land and those who betrayed its sacred resources. Then why was he to die? He was a good guy.

A black shape appeared in his peripheral vision. Ben heard a thud and a gasp, and he whirled around to see the pistol flying toward the water and Tobi landing softly in the sand. His mentor had tears in his eyes as he looked down at Michiko who'd fallen from the force of the leg kick. Tears in her eyes, too. For her defeat. For the man she loved. For the realization that there would be no talking herself out of this.

Then running footsteps. It was Niko Yamato coming toward them. He was breathing hard. His face was contorted with pain. But not from the exercise—from the shame. He stopped a few yards from them and stared at his daughter, and when she looked away, he fell to his knees and put his face in the sand.

24

THREE DAYS LATER, AN ASSEMBLY OF PEOPLE, most of whom were strangers to each other, stood on the black sand beach where Ahi Ishizu had buried his gold. That window of time between dusk and darkness was upon them. That time when the birds were quiet, and the tide started to recede, and the sun's last rays looked like tiny yellow points piercing the horizon, just before the purples and salmons painted the clouds. And the time when the trades died to a whisper.

The latest eruption of Kīlauea had fed more lava down its slope and across the smooth, undulating surface of recent flows, and then into the ocean. Clouds of steam like night ghosts rose eerily into the darkening sky, blocking out the wakening stars for a short time. Then evaporated into the warm air. Embers glowed in the dark and small fires burned randomly along the leading edge of the black river.

Tobi was there, standing next to Ben.

Winston Bennett was close by, holding a broad-brimmed hat across his stomach. Reverent for one of the few times in his life.

Haanio was by himself, off to the left, perched on a rock that jutted close to the lava flow. His eyes were closed. His face unlined, relaxed.

Tobi noticed Ben's gaze and whispered, "He's praying to Kāne to take care of Ahi."

They had located and contacted Ahi's real granddaughter. She'd made it to the Big Island earlier that afternoon, a few hours before the memorial service. Now she was leaning against the wiry frame of Niko Yamato, her eyes brimming with tears that spilled over and ran down her cheeks. Niko was biting his lip, trying to hold back his own tears, but soon, he too, was crying.

And behind them were hundreds of people of all ages—the coffee farmers of Kona and their families. They were huddled in mass near the remaining palms, unmoving, each with their private thoughts, and prayers for Ahi Ishizu. Their long shadows folded into the approaching darkness.

Finally, the sun disappeared completely although its light still reflected along the cloud bank that had hovered over the Pacific all day. These streaks of sunlight made the sunset one of the most beautiful Ben could remember. The lower layer was yellow and white. Higher up, the layers were fiery red and orange with salmon-colored tips. And above that, the upper stratum formed a long, deep purple brush stroke that filled the entire horizon, finally disappearing into the farthest edges of the western sky.

In the background the earth rumbled and shook. Madam Pele had joined the procession, in her own way, chanting for a hero.

Only four present—Ben, Tobi, Haanio, and Niko—knew the story of the gold. They had agreed that it was best left untold.

Ben shuffled his bare feet in the rich sand, feeling the cool grains between his toes, thinking about the man he had never met. Maybe the bravest man there would ever be. Had he not given up his wife and unborn child, his friends, his country, the Second World War might have had a catastrophic ending. For back then, no one had considered a nuclear winter. No one had truly understood the devastation of nuclear warfare. If the Japanese had been successful in purchasing the plans to the atomic bomb in the winter of 1941, then . . .

Ben shuddered. He didn't want to think about it any more. Yet to think that this decision, this act of courage, had come from a man of only twenty-five was amazing in itself. Ben thought back, to when he was twenty-five. He never would have been up to the task.

Here's to you, Ahi Ishizu. God bless you!

Ben bowed his head. Tobi slipped his arm around Ben's shoulder.

And yet, in a way, it was ironic. This magnificent act of bravery would have passed through time unknown had it not been for the greed of one woman. Ben turned and looked at Niko and Ahi's granddaughter. All this for an innocent story he had told his daughter. Ben hoped the old man would not blame himself for too long. But with a friend dead and a daughter headed for prison, Ben knew he wouldn't find his way alone. He hoped Ahi's granddaughter would help him through it.

He turned back toward the sea and Lisa's face appeared as an image on a darkening cloud. She looked tired. Alone. Her expression was questioning. And her questions echoed his own. What would become of their relationship? Did she miss him?

I miss you.

He couldn't hear her answer.

Another rumble from Kīlauea. Madame Pele was restless.

Many of the farmers now lit torches, dipping tree limbs wrapped in dried taro leaves into the lava. It was time to carry out the words in Ahi's last poem.

Tobi stepped forward carrying the small urn that contained Ahi's ashes. He held the urn high into the night sky. Then he took a few more paces until he reached the water's edge. Kneeling, he closed his eyes, and chanted.

Ben heard—

. . . i ka makani kuehu lepo . . .
—knowing it meant 'in the dust-scattering wind.'

Tobi continued, but the wind drowned most of his words. Then he slowly stood and lifted the cover of the vessel and carefully tilted it, sprinkling half of Ahi's ashes onto the new lava flow, and then leaning forward slightly, he dusted the water with the rest of the coffee farmer's remains.

Farther out, the ocean churned and transformed into an energetic silver ribbon. Suddenly, the sparkling band moved closer and a large school of yellowfin appeared extraordinarily close to land. It was over in seconds. They zipped by, angled away from shore, and then raced out into deeper water and vanished. Their wake sent Ahi Ishizu on his journey.

And Ben thought to himself . . . *That's the way I want it to be for me . . . some to remain here . . . for this Island has become part of my soul . . . and what's left into the ocean . . . because I'd like to spend the rest of my time on this earth traveling the high seas.*
Like Yellowfin . . .
Like Ahi Ishizu . . .